THE DARK
IN-BETWEEN

THE

DARK

IN

BETWEEN

ELIZABETH HRIB

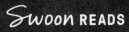

NEW YORK

A Swoon Reads Book
An imprint of Feiwel and Friends and Macmillan Publishing Group, LLC
120 Broadway, New York, NY 10271

Our books may be purchased in bulk for promotional, educational, or business use.
Please contact your local bookseller or the Macmillan Corporate and Premium Sales
Department at (800) 221-7945 ext. 5442 or by email at MacmillanSpecialMarkets@
macmillan.com.

Library of Congress Cataloging-in-Publication Data is available.
ISBN 978-1-250-24274-7 (hardcover) / ISBN 978-1-250-24276-1 (ebook)

Book design by Cindy De la Cruz
First edition, 2020

10 9 8 7 6 5 4 3 2 1

swoonreads.com

To Ashley,
the first to hear this story.
And to Mikey,
for talking plot points.
#SiblingGoals

PROLOGUE

Twenty-eight . . . twenty-nine . . . thirty. Two breaths.

THE BOAT IS beautiful, covered in a pearly blue sheen that sparkles with bits of glitter under the sun. It speeds through the harbor, sending waves flying as Liddy cuts hard to the side, spraying a group of seniors in a paddleboat.

Casey topples back into her seat with a giddy grin and catches her ball cap as it tries to fly off her head. "I can't believe that woman rented you a boat."

"The keys were sort of sitting on the counter when I went in to inquire. So . . . let's call this more of a test drive."

"What?!"

"It's okay!" Liddy throws her head back and laughs at the look on Casey's face. "Live a little."

"How about we just take it back to shore now?"

"C'mon," Liddy says. "Exams are finished. School's out in a few days. This is a party! Have some fun, would you?" She puckers her lips, blowing Casey a kiss. "Call Evan and tell him what he's missing. Maybe he can ditch his parents."

Casey rolls her eyes, tugging on the straps of her life jacket. It's a little too big, coming loose in places. "He probably doesn't want to add 'boat thief' to his résumé before senior year starts."

"We're only borrowing it. We'll put it back before anyone notices it's gone. Besides, you know what I always say—"

"'If you're not living, you're dying.' Yeah, I know. So where does prison fit into your grand scheme?"

Liddy flattens her lips into something resembling a duck bill and Casey fights a smile. "Five more minutes," she says with a wicked look in her eye. "Then we'll take it back."

We are *already on the water*, Casey reasons, her resolve crumbling. She jumps from her seat to stand beside Liddy, whose life jacket flies open behind her like a pair of orange wings. "Does it go any faster?"

Twenty-eight . . . twenty-nine . . . thirty. Two breaths.

NIGHT DESCENDS AROUND them; bonfires on the beach turn the top of the water into glassy, liquid fire. Flickers of orange stain the surface, throwing up splashes that look like flame as Liddy cuts around the island in the middle of the harbor.

Casey laughs, holding on tighter and urging Liddy to go even faster as they stretch that five minutes into something closer to an hour.

They hit the waves they've created, the boat bouncing over them, each crash drowning out the sound of their giggles.

Then Casey suddenly sees the rocks rise out of the water, drawing toward them like two fists poised for impact.

A wave roars over the top of the rocks and both girls are launched from the boat, sinking beneath the strangling surf.

Casey thrashes in the water, lost in the darkness as her life jacket comes loose again, ripped away by the current that lives below the algae-covered coast. She finds Liddy by feel, a mess of hair and floating fabric. Her hand is like silk in the water, smooth and slippery. Their fingers tangle and tug, the ocean trying to rip them apart.

Another wave rolls into them, the current tugging until Casey thinks the pressure might tear her skin from her bones.

Liddy holds on.

But everything hurts in the dark and Casey can't bear it.

She lets go.

Twenty-eight ... twenty-nine ... thirty. Two breaths.

SHE HEARS HER ribs crack before she feels it. They creak inside her body, echoing all the way up to her ears and playing on repeat inside her head. Like the hinge of a door that's come loose, rubbing where it shouldn't. Rib against sternum.

Creak. Scratch. *Snap.*

A mask smothers her, pushing air in, forcing it to the very bottom of her lungs, fighting against the water already taking up

3

space there. The pressure is unbearable and she thinks she might burst open.

"Breathe!" someone says as sand molds against her shoulders and ankles, the depression sinking with every thump of hands against her chest. "Come on, kid! Stay with me."

Where's Liddy? she wonders, reaching out into the black void. Pressure mounts behind her eyes. *Squeezing.*

"I've got a pulse."

Red and blue lights peek in through the slits in her eyelids, blinding and blurring. The colors bleed together, separated only by spots of inky darkness and shifting shadow as sirens scream above her: a banshee song that drags her into a dream.

And when she wakes to the din of machines, tied down by tubing to a hospital bed, the dream shatters.

Liddy is dead.

ONE

IT TAKES ABOUT six weeks for her fractured ribs to heal. And all that time, it hurts to cry.

Specifically, ugly crying hurts—the kind with gasping sobs and hiccups. The kind of crying that happens when someone dies.

She can't even mourn her best friend properly because the paramedics who saved her life had to break her bones to do it. They probably weren't thinking about that while trying to restart her heart.

Funnily enough, it's all Casey can think about. Especially today.

Smoothing wrinkles from her black dress, she hurries down the porch steps of the town house and jogs across the dandelion-spotted lawn to her car. Plucked from the very back of her closet, the dress smells like stale detergent, and there's a tiny grease spot on the skirt that didn't come out at the dry cleaners. Casey scrubs at it with her thumb.

The last time she wore an outfit like this was when she buried her parents. She was nine, and the church smelled like barbecue coals.

Casey gives up on the spot, figuring she's already made the appropriate kind of effort for this afternoon: nylons without runs, black flats, and a hair clip to contain the flyaways. Her aunt Karen would be proud.

She's even put on mascara and a little bit of blush, so *Liddy* would be proud. A dull ache swells in her chest as she yanks on the car door; Casey takes a few gulping breaths to try to push it away. Her ribs still twinge a bit when the air fills the very bottom of her lungs. Karen says that ache will fade soon. And she'd probably say that it's good for her to get out of the house, even if it's just to attend Liddy's memorial service. Truthfully, she'd be glad Casey was leaving her bedroom.

On the driver's seat sits a bunch of wispy white feathers, maybe blown in through an open window, though Casey can't remember the last time she's taken a drive. Definitely before the accident.

She brushes the feathers off her seat, watching as they spiral toward the ground like autumn leaves. As if foretelling the end of one season and the beginning of another.

Is this what an existential crisis feels like? she wonders. Or maybe this is just how death operates—leaving her looking for meaning in every little thing.

Without another thought, Casey stomps on them and climbs into her car. After leaving her neighborhood, she drives down a straight stretch of road overflowing with shops. She passes Lynn's

6

Bakery with homemade bagels on display first; then the post office, which doubles as the pharmacy, already flashing a CLOSED sign in the window; and finally the art gallery, which boasts its new metal ocean exhibit—ironwork sea creatures twirling from strings hung along the storefront.

She turns after the hockey arena, which hosts more bingo nights than hockey games, onto the cul-de-sac where Evan lives. His truck is in the driveway when she pulls up, and the nerves in her gut calm to a gentle flutter. She does everything with Evan. She has since they were babies. Memorials for their best friend would be no different.

Being stuck in the hospital after the accident meant that she couldn't attend Liddy's funeral. Despite his grief, Evan had done his best to give her a play-by-play of the ceremony when he came to visit her later that day, but it hadn't been the same as saying goodbye herself. She couldn't get closure by association.

She beeps her horn twice, as is their tradition. Evan swings the front door open, standing there in khaki shorts and a snowy gray T-shirt. His hair is swept to the side, held expertly in place with a precise amount of gel that he's perfected over the course of their high school careers.

Seeing him eases something in her and Casey gets out of the car, crossing the lawn and climbing the porch steps to meet him.

"Hey," he says.

"Hi."

Evan hangs by the door, arms propped against the frame, highlighting the fine definition of muscle he's developed from landing all those jump serves for Westwood's senior volleyball

7

team. He's already got a watch tan, and she taps his wrist teasingly when she gets close enough.

"Been spending a lot of time outside. Gardening." He sticks out his tongue. "My mom said being outdoors is good for me. I thought she meant like the beach, but she actually just meant chores. It's a raw deal."

Casey holds up her phone, where the memorial is listed in the online version of the town paper, *Coastal News*. "You didn't tell me this was today."

Evan blinks at the screen, then crosses his arms. "Well, you haven't exactly been taking my calls most days."

"I answered your texts."

"With emojis," he argues, like the little symbols have personally offended him. "What does a thumbs-up and a crescent moon even mean?"

"That I was free to hang out tonight." She wants to tell him to get with it, but maybe having entire conversations with just emojis and the excessive use of exclamation points was a skill shared only by her and Liddy. "Were you going to go?"

"I hadn't decided yet." He looks her up and down as if noticing her outfit for the first time.

She ignores the way his roaming eyes make her feel—he's just taking in all the black, she tells herself—and nudges him inside. After all these years, his house feels nearly as familiar as her own.

"Well, go get dressed," she tells him. "I want to go, and you have to come with me."

"You said you wanted to go for burgers."

"And now I want to go to the memorial."

"So . . . burgers is a no-go, then?" he teases, probably trying to get her to smile. He throws his hands up as the look on her face only darkens. "All right, look, my idea of a fun time isn't hanging out with a bunch of old people who think they knew Liddy better than us. But you're right, we should probably both be there." He hesitates at the bottom of the stairs. "But burgers after, right? And before you say anything, grief makes me hungry. It's a perfectly normal reaction, look it up."

He climbs the stairs two at a time, and Casey follows him.

It occurs to her that he looks different somehow. She hasn't seen much of him since his hospital visits, which is practically a lifetime for them. It's not for lack of Evan trying though, she's just been busy with . . . well, grieving really ate into most of her free time. Now that she's here, it's less of a struggle and she finds herself drawn to his steady presence. That grounding force in the midst of the chaos.

"Did you cut your hair?" she asks.

"My mom wouldn't let me leave the house looking like I 'just crawled in off the street.' Her words, minus a few more colorful descriptions that I'll save your ears from."

She can tell he's hoping for a laugh, so she gives him one. "It must be mom-approved if she let you out of the house again."

He stops at the top of the stairs and twists on his socked feet to see her. "She said it was tolerable. But I used a lot of product to tame it, so she thinks it's shorter than it really is."

Casey reaches out to touch the gelled tousles of brown hair. They fold in easy waves, his natural curls held close to his head. "I think it suits you. You've outgrown the beach-town-local look. It was cute when you were fourteen. Now it would just impede your vision."

Evan makes a *pfft* sound. "What's there to see here that we haven't seen a thousand times before?" He makes a left into his room and Casey follows, slumping down on his bed. "Any suggestions on attire?"

"Something simple. And preferably clean."

Evan picks up a pair of shorts.

"Not those," she says immediately.

He chucks them back where they came from and dives into his closet, practically bodysurfing his way to the back, fighting to free a garment bag from the temperamental hangers.

Casey gets up. "I'll let you change."

He lets the garment bag flop onto his bed where she sat and kicks the door closed, muttering something about just wearing jeans under his breath.

Casey paces the length of the hall, studying the pictures on the floating mantels on the wall. Most of them are of Evan. There's some of her too, standing with a younger Evan, their faces wind-kissed, freckled, and crazy-eyed due to copious amounts of sun and sugar.

Casey touches the photo. Her parents had still been alive then.

She follows the tarnished silver frames through a scrapbook of her youth. There's her and Evan as babies, sharing teething rings. As toddlers, sharing chicken pox. As cubby neighbors in elementary school when they swapped lunches almost every day. Liddy had moved to town in the third grade, got assigned the coat hook directly between her and Evan, and the three of them had been inseparable ever since.

Until now.

The door pops open and Evan kneels, lacing up a shiny black shoe. When he straightens up, she gets a proper look at him. He's wearing a black dress shirt tucked into gray pants. There's no tie but he looks . . . *good*. All sleek lines and sharp points and soft blue eyes.

"You can say it," Evan says.

She snaps back to reality. "Say what?"

"That I clean up nice." He tugs on his pant leg. "Even my socks match."

Casey huffs and turns away as warmth floods her cheeks. She's been flirting with this line for a while now. These feelings. That space between friendship and *more than*. It's not the right time to cross it. She *knows* that. Not while they're both missing Liddy. Honestly, she's not really sure if there ever will be a right time. Maybe the history between them is better left this way.

"You look nice, too," he offers. "I meant to say it before."

Then he goes and says things like that, and Casey's unsure of everything all over again.

"These are my funeral clothes," she says, trying to dismiss his comment. She picks at the hem of her dress, crumpling it in her fist and then pressing it back into smooth lines against her thighs.

Evan sighs, hands in his pockets as he sways into the hall. "You can still look nice."

"Come on," she says, turning down the stairs. "You're making us late."

He follows her to the car and climbs into the passenger seat.

Beside him, she fumbles with her buckle, the nerves starting to return. It feels weird being in the car without Liddy calling dibs on control over the radio.

If I have to hear any more of Evan's easy country listening, she'd say. *I'm gonna lose it. He's like a little old man in the body of a teenager.*

The memory almost makes her laugh, but she catches herself. Casey stares at the radio, then looks away, struggling under the weight of such heavy silence.

Evan reaches over, his hand nudging her shoulder. When he pulls away, he twirls a feather between his fingers and flicks it out the window.

"You ready?" he asks, tapping his hands against his knees in a drumbeat. Maybe he's as nervous as she is.

"Ready as I'll ever be."

Evan rests his polished shoe on the dash, and they drive just beyond the edge of town, closer to the harbor. Here the houses rise up between stately trees, each one a looming mountain built behind giant iron gates. The road curves gently and the houses grow taller and older, towering so high they cloak the entire manicured street in shadow.

Casey pulls over against the curb where men and women clad in suits and frilly, buttoned blouses have congregated. She sucks in a breath.

"It's okay," Evan says reassuringly. "You got this. *We* got this."

Casey nods repeatedly, like she might be able to convince herself that she really wants to be here. She *needs* to be here.

"You know, maybe we should get away for a while after this. Take that road trip my parents keep promising for our senior year," Evan says. "I'd like to drive down the coast and be real tourists for once. We could rent a nice car, swim at all the beaches along the way. I'll probably get a bad sunburn, but you love when that happens. Don't think I've gone a summer without being photographed looking like a lobster."

"Yeah, all right," she mumbles.

Evan pokes her in the arm and she touches the spot automatically, turning to glare at him. "What was that for?"

"You're not even listening."

"I was. You said road trip."

"But you weren't really considering it."

Casey shakes her head, wondering if she'll make it inside before the overwhelming urge to throw up consumes her. "Sorry. I can't focus on anything else right now."

Evan puts his back to the window, blocking her view of the front door. "Are you okay?"

"No..." she begins, hugging the steering wheel tightly. "I... don't know."

"Talk to me."

She drops her hands and wrings them in her lap. "People finally stopped staring at me. Now it'll start all over again." She lowers her voice, imitating. "'Oh, look, there's the one that survived! From the accident at the harbor, did you see? How tragic. How sad.'" Her hands go still in her lap, defeated. "I'm tired of being the local celebrity—especially for this."

"Someone will catch a giant fish soon, break some world records, and then you'll be old news. I promise." Evan places his hand on top of hers and squeezes. Once. Twice. "It'll get easier."

"Is that what your mom says?"

"And my stepdad and my therapist and . . . Ray Larkin from fifth period English class." Evan looks confused about that last one. "I bumped into him the other day at the grocery store. He was surprisingly insightful for a guy who only attends two classes a week."

"Yeah," Casey says. "Karen told me the same thing. It gets easier. Wait it out." But things only seemed to be getting harder the longer they went on.

"All these people can't be wrong," Evan says, taking a long look up the landscaped path to the house. "Based on probability, I mean. Reality is a different story."

"Then let's hope probability wins out," she says, finally getting out of the car. The stifling summer air squeezes her lungs as she inhales. "Maybe I should have stayed home."

"Is that what you want?" he asks. "If it is, we'll go back right now. We don't have to talk about it."

"Think I'll regret it?"

Evan closes his door. "I think you'll wonder about it until you do."

She wraps her hands around her elbows, coming to stand by him. "Is this how you felt at the funeral? All panicky and sick-like?"

"Pretty much. Rotated between nausea and crying and bouts of unexplained laughter." She glances up when he shrugs. "Liddy probably would have thought it was hilarious."

Casey averts her eyes as an older couple passes them on their way to the house, ogling and whispering. "At least at home, I wouldn't have to deal with things like that."

Evan stuffs his hands in his pockets as they wander up the pressed-stone walkway. It's cooler in the shadow of the house and Casey shivers, tucking her arms closer to her chest.

"Doesn't it seem a little early for a memorial service anyway?" Evan says as they draw toward the stairs. "I mean, she's barely been in the ground a month."

"Evan!" Casey hisses, looking over her shoulder for anyone who might have overheard. Thankfully for the moment, they're alone. "Seriously?"

"Oh, you know what I mean. Liddy does, too." He kisses his hand and points up to the sky. "And let's be real, she'd be mortified knowing that her parents were doing this all over again."

If they weren't, Casey thinks, she might never have another chance to say goodbye. After the funeral service, Liddy's body had been driven across state lines to the town where her father had grown up, to be buried with all the other Courtlands in the family cemetery. So there isn't even a grave to visit here.

They stop at the front door, greeted by a brushed-gold knocker shaped like a lion's head. The house towers above them, taller than it is wide, with steepled windows and latticework balconies.

"There's still time to bail," Evan whispers. "Liddy won't mind. And no one will even notice if we're here anyway."

Casey eyes a few of their classmates coming down the

sidewalk. "They might not notice if we're here," she says, "but they'll sure notice if we're not."

Evan sighs but reaches out and pushes the door open.

INSIDE THE MAIN foyer, people chat softly in clusters. Some of the kids from school look their way, giving polite waves or nods or tight smiles. A few of the guys from Evan's volleyball team come up and clap him on the back. Benny Fergus, the team's setter, whispers something that makes Evan smile, and then pats Casey's head like she's a small child.

Man, death makes people weird.

Other kids avoid them entirely. But mostly, they just avoid looking at her or making eye contact. Probably afraid that she'll lash out or contaminate them with her death cooties.

The murmurs pick up as Casey cuts through the parlor, and she pretends they're not about her. The one who lived. When she reaches the main sitting room, those worries dissolve instantly as she works to catch her breath, clutching at the tight stitch in her chest.

A photo of Liddy is staged there, blown up to staggering proportions, its bright smile shocking in its likeness. It's only a photo, of course. But it's candid, catching Liddy in a moment of unfettered joy. That's the real Liddy—a measure of happiness that could never be contained.

Lidia Elisabeth Alexandra Courtland is written in black calligraphy along the bottom of the portrait. Beside it sits a round table, upon which guests are signing a memory book dedicated to Liddy. Casey thinks of the stories she could fill that book with. She doesn't even think there are enough pages to capture what she'd say if she started writing.

"She hated when people used her full name." Evan wanders toward the table with an ease Casey can't seem to master. She feels nothing but out of sorts here. He picks up one of the printed memorial cards, waiting in line to sign the book. From his spot, he flashes the card toward her. A short prayer and another picture of Liddy covers the front. He snorts. "Remember this photo?"

"She hated it. I can hear her little squeak of disgust in my head." Despite her best efforts, Casey grins. "She'd totally do that frustrated hair-flip thing."

Evan laughs, the sound warm, but it lasts only a moment before he clears his throat and averts his eyes, running his hand over the back of his neck.

In response, goose bumps spread down the length of Casey's arms, and she turns to look over her shoulder, peering through her hair.

Mr. and Mrs. Courtland—Liddy's parents—stand across the room, noses turned up in that snobby, standoffish way of theirs. Not for the first time Casey wonders how the two of them ended up with Liddy as a daughter. They turn away quickly, pretending they haven't seen her, sipping expensive bubbly and making pointless chitchat with friends and relatives. There's a lot of emotion there, lingering between them: hurt, confusion, blame. It's exactly what Casey's feared every time she meets eyes with a stranger on the street. And again, it's like every eye in the room is suddenly trained on her, wondering how she'll cope with the pressure.

"Hey," Evan whispers, stepping closer to her. "Ignore them."

"I can't," she says under her breath. "Help me find a piece of furniture to hide behind."

He takes her arm and leads her toward the refreshment table, which is piled with silver trays, expensive lace doilies, and multi-colored pastries; it looks like an experiment in pastels. "You know how Liddy felt about all this fanfare."

"That's not why they're looking at me like that," Casey mumbles. Liddy's parents had always been somewhat distant with her friends. But now, it isn't aloof disinterest Casey feels when she's near them; it's a sharp stab of blame, and it's worked its way somewhere between her ribs, nudging at her heart.

She winces, hand held against her chest like she might be able to patch the wound that's been festering since the morning she awoke in the hospital, very much alive, without Liddy.

"Don't do this, Casey." Evan's thumb brushes her elbow, trying to pull her back from the swell of darkness in her mind, but his fingers are a warmth she can't appreciate right now.

"It makes sense," she says, pulling away from him. "I'm a walking reminder that the paramedics only saved one of us that night."

Just knowing that Liddy's body had lain in the hospital at the same time as hers, pasty and stiff on the frigid morgue table, lungs filled with fluid, still drowning even in death ... it makes her sick. Casey brings the back of her hand to her mouth, resisting the urge to retch.

Evan picks a lemon square off one of the tallest platters and takes a neat little bite. After rolling the taste around on his tongue, he discreetly spits the crumbs into the overgrown spider plant that hangs by his head.

"None of this is your fault." He wipes his mouth with his shirtsleeve. "That tasted like soap."

Casey keeps her eyes firmly on Evan. Behind his head, the shapes of Liddy's parents take form again and she feels that invisible wound in her chest split a little wider. "Try telling them that."

Evan sighs. "Look, today it's you. Tomorrow it'll be the woman at the boat rental shack. Next week it'll be the paramedics that couldn't restart her heart in time. Then it'll be me for bailing on you guys to go to that stupid family luncheon with my parents. That's what people do when they're grieving, they find other things to blame. Other *people*."

Casey swallows hard, forcing down the sick feeling. Maybe they're right, though, to blame her.

I never should have let go.

In her head, that day is still a blur of shrieking metal and blinding ocean spray. One moment she'd been searching the coming twilight for the first wink of stars and the next . . .

She didn't remember in pictures exactly, because the images were blue and purple and black, like the bottom of the harbor. But she could remember the jump of her heart as the boat capsized against the rocks and the crush of surf that had rolled her over and over.

The tide had caught her limbs, surging up and down as it pushed the breath from her lungs. And against her hands, she could remember the rough scratch of underwater rock and the slick feel of algae as she tried to protect her head. There was something else, too. The silk of skin against hers. Liddy's fingers tangled with her own, and then nothing but the frantic thought that raged against her temple. *Get to the surface.*

Had Liddy had that same terrifying thought? Had she had the same realization that she couldn't tell up from down in the dark?

"It was an accident," Evan says simply. "Nothing you did or didn't do would change that outcome."

"You weren't there," she says. "You don't know that."

"You guys wore life jackets. Liddy was just dragged under when the boat tipped. You know this."

But did she? Casey can't remember breaking the surface. She can't remember the first rush of oxygen into her lungs. So, at what point had she been saved and Liddy lost?

Other flashes of that day rush back—Liddy's easy grin, the excitement that bled into her laugh, the rev of the boat's engine— and with it a wave of nausea.

"I have to use the bathroom," Casey says, turning on her heel and rushing toward the back of the house. She takes the main set of stairs. They curve sharply, and she races onto the landing, past the photos of Liddy at equestrian training, vocal recitals, and family vacations. The entire house is a testament to the wonderful person Liddy had been and now serves as a stark reminder of everything her parents had lost—everything Casey had lost in a best friend.

Hands grappling for the right door, she takes refuge in the bathroom, only to find a framed photo of Liddy staring back at her from the shelf mounted beside the sink. It seems that with her passing, more and more pictures had appeared in the house.

And she was always wearing that impossibly bright smile.

Casey tips the photo facedown and barricades herself behind the bathroom door, pressing the lock with her thumb and running her hand up the wall for the light switch. There's a fuzzy edge to the silence in the dark. Almost like watching a snowy television screen. The sound of nothingness, of that blurry noiseless whisper, grows into a pulse she can feel beat beneath her skin as she slides down against the door.

If she squeezes her eyes tight enough, all she can see is black.

Shapes grow out of the darkness in her mind. *Tall reaching tree limbs. A black wood, shrouded in shadow and stone, covered in mounds of turned earth.*

Casey tries to blink the images away. It's not the first time this has happened, these grief-induced daymares.

... Casey?

She freezes. The voice is new.

"Liddy?" she whispers, lifting her head in answer like she's just been called from the other room. It's so real that a desperately foolish thread of hope blooms in her chest before reality crushes it.

She closes her eyes again, hands shaking against her knees.

The trees whip by her, snaggled branches pawing like hooked claws. Someone gasps.

The hair on her arms stands tall and Casey scrambles to her feet, stumbling toward the sink. In the mirror, her face is the same pale shade as the porcelain, and there's something terrifying about the wide set of her eyes. She groans and splashes water on her face, rubbing her cheeks to get the color back.

Casey!

She turns, grabbing the sink for support, and glances around the bathroom—from the marble-tiled shower to the claw-foot tub to the pressed beige towels stacked neatly in the linen basket by the door. She's alone. Alone with an overactive, grief-stricken imagination.

That's what her aunt would tell her. This is to be expected after a traumatic event. Grief does funny things to a person. This is *normal*.

After all, she's been through this process before. When her parents died, she stood in front of their matching coffins, memorizing their faces—the funny curve of her dad's nose and the long lashes that framed her mother's pretty brown eyes—holding those images for all the years that she would have to spend without them.

People had thought she was strange then. A little girl, standing and staring.

So this is okay. Grief is normal. Grief is . . . strange visions and Liddy's voice inside her head?

A hard knock raps against the door.

She jumps, almost whacking her head on the edge of the framed mirror.

"Casey? You okay in there?"

Casey flings herself across the room and opens the door with shaking fingers to find Evan standing there with a sheepish grin on his face.

One shoulder turns up in a shrug. "Wanted to make sure you hadn't flushed yourself down the toilet. Trust me, I want to make an escape as bad as you do, but there are probably better ways."

"Yeah, sorry," she gasps, fleeing the bathroom. "I'm fine."

"Good." Then, looking out over the gathering from the top of the stairs, he says, "What do you say we get out of here soon? Maybe grab that burger. I think there's a marathon at the drive-in tonight."

"I don't know," she says. She's not sure dinner and a movie is exactly an appropriate post-memorial activity.

He nudges her with the back of his hand. "I know I'm bad at this death stuff. Insensitive or whatever. And I make things awkward." He tugs on the collar of his shirt. "But that's because all this is for show. None of it's really Liddy."

"Not really," she agrees.

"Exactly. So let's go to that movie. We can have our own little send-off for her."

"Our own little memorial," Casey says, reconsidering the idea. Truthfully, Liddy would have loved it. She had lived for long summer nights spent under the stars, for bonfires, midnight swims, and movie marathons with endless tubs of popcorn. "All right."

"You're in? For real?"

"Yeah, let's do it." Who says she needed a formal invitation to say goodbye to Liddy? This place was making her paranoid anyway.

"Great!" Evan exclaims.

"Let's go downstairs and sign that book first." She wants it known that she was here, to leave a record of the fact that she showed up. For someday when she's no longer on display, and just a girl allowed to miss her best friend.

TWO

EVAN CATCHES HER arm as they head for the stairs. He slides his hand from her elbow to her wrist and squeezes. Once. Twice. For a few moments, she forgets about everything else.

The crowd at the bottom of the stairs has dispersed; more people have moved to the little balcony area to enjoy the late afternoon and reminisce.

"Evan!" someone calls and he lifts his hand in greeting.

"I'm just gonna—" he begins.

"Go," Casey insists. "I'll be over there." She nods to the table with the memory book.

"I'll catch up in a minute," he promises.

She watches him slide easily through the crowd. No one stares. No one gawks.

Ignoring the jealousy stirring in her stomach, Casey makes

her way over to the memorial table. A couple of girls stand there. Casey recognizes them as members of the school dance team Liddy was on. Amanda Norberry, a statuesque girl with a passion for hip-hop, reads through pages of the memory book *ooh*ing and *ahh*ing at the stories. The girl beside her is Sophie Cavanaugh. She's petite with wavy blond ringlets, and is snapping photos like she's entered a contest for most consecutive selfies taken.

"It's just so sad," Amanda says to Sophie, waving her hand in front of her face to preserve her mascara. "And right before senior year, too. Like, what a time to go."

"I know, right? I can't believe this kind of thing actually happens." They snap a picture together in front of the memorial photo. "It really makes you think." Sophie fiddles with her phone. "So, hashtag 'RIP' or, like, 'Miss you, babe,' plus ten thousand heart emojis . . . What do you think?"

"There's the face with that little halo," Amanda points out. "Aw, it's an angel. Too cute."

Casey's heart lobs painfully against her chest. "Are you kidding me?"

The words come out as a hiss, something dark and jagged.

"Oh, hey, Casey!" Amanda says, a shy smile curving her lips. "It's really good to see you out."

Sophie hastily stuffs her phone in her pocket, then tips her head and bats her eyelashes in a bad porcelain doll impression. Casey figures she's trying to evoke innocence. An *oops, my bad* kind of situation. It doesn't work.

"Did you actually just take a photo?" Casey's teeth grind together. "Who does that?"

"We didn't mean anything by it," Amanda explains. "We loved Liddy like a sister. The whole team did."

"Like a sister," Casey repeats. "Yeah, apparently you love her so much you have to post pictures of yourself at her memorial service online, follow it up with a witty bunch of hashtags and see what your followers think."

It's like some sick, twisted social event. Is that what the rest of them are here for? To snap some classy photos on the balcony, throw up a peace sign and a duck-face or two and see how many new followers they can drum up with washed-out filters and sympathy?

"Why stop at the angel?" Casey continues coldly. "Couldn't find a little tombstone emoji?"

Amanda's jaw drops, her face flushed with embarrassment. Her eyes cast around at the crowd that's gathered, a murmur of nosy intrigue bubbling up around them.

Good, Casey thinks. *Be mortified.*

"*Look*," Sophie says, tossing her blond hair and lowering her voice. "If you want me to delete it, I will. Okay? No big deal." She pulls out her phone and swipes her finger over the screen. "Here. It's gone. Can you stop acting so shocked? As if fifty other people haven't already posted photos."

Sophie shoves the phone in Casey's face and she sees a rolling screen ranging from somber, heartfelt send-offs to goofy selfies, all taken inside Liddy's house.

Casey doesn't have the words. Is she appalled? No. Furious? Maybe . . . Devastated? That's the one. They were treating Liddy like some trending fad and hopping on before her fifteen minutes of fame are up.

Casey tries to catch her breath as she backs away from the girls. She feels like she's pinwheeling through the crowd, falling and fleeing all at once.

She has to get away from here. From them. From everyone acting like it's okay that Liddy's gone.

"Casey?" someone calls after her.

It sounds like Evan. It's probably him. She doesn't know who else would care enough to call through the crowd. But she's already running, pulling the keys from her pocket. She doesn't stop until she reaches the car.

"Casey, wait!" Evan says. He catches up to her on the sidewalk.

"I can't, Evan." She pulls the door open, sighing shakily as she tries to get control of herself. "I have to go."

"I'll go with you."

Her fist balls around the doorframe. "I just . . . need some time, okay? Can you get a ride?"

"I . . . Yeah, sure." His hand feathers through his hair. "I'll ask one of the guys, I guess."

Casey nods and gets in the car. She doesn't look back as she speeds away from the pretty seaside manors. Her fingertips blanch around the wheel as she tries to keep from bursting into tears.

As she nears downtown, traffic is bad. Being a coastal town with the perfect ratio of quaint shopping ventures to mom-and-pop dining establishments means the streets are flooded with an obnoxious number of beachgoers and vacation club members from May to September. Even now, as the sun sits low in the sky, Main Street is packed with families making their ways to and from the water, carrying an assortment of beach umbrellas, coolers, and screaming toddlers.

She idles at the same light for seven minutes, waiting for tourists to read their GPS instructions. She watches green come and go three times.

While Casey waits, she studies the line of cars and the people sitting inside those cars. It begins as a calming exercise, a way to dull her mind to the scene at the memorial. By the time she's done, she's memorized every color combination of baseball cap, sun hat, and Hawaiian shirt. It's like her own personal game of Guess Who? She even studies what's left of the clouds, sparse and puffy, dotting the sky in between the orange fade-out that begins as the sun touches the horizon.

A feather blows across the windshield, white and silky looking. It gets stuck, suctioned to the glass right in her sight line. Casey sighs, blasting the windshield with washer fluid before turning on the wipers, swiping the feather away.

The longer she sits there, the more she thinks about Liddy's memorial. She can't help it. The thought is obsessive, knocking at her temple until she gives into it, recalling the look on Sophie's face as they struck a pose and snapped the photo. The tittering laughter. The hushed giggles.

A sick, tight feeling spreads across her chest.

Sophie and Amanda didn't really know Liddy. Not in the same way Casey did. *None* of those people did. Who were they to trivialize her memorial into a few hastily snapped selfies and stupid hashtags?

She squeezes the wheel as a flash of fiery anger grabs her. It fades as her phone rings on the passenger seat.

Casey glances at it and sees Evan's face light up the screen.

She feels bad about leaving him, but the pressure against her chest only tightens, and she ignores the phone call, letting it go to voicemail.

She just wants to get home.

Giving up on Main Street, Casey cuts left into the Stop-n-Shop parking lot. A horn blares, and she throws her hand up in an apologetic wave before driving around the gas station and through the gravel lot at the back of the building. The last time she did this she ended up with a nail in her tire, and she and Evan and Liddy had spent forty minutes working out how to put the spare on.

If Liddy in a sundress and ballerina flats wielding a lug wrench doesn't perfectly capture her personality, Casey doesn't know what does. Liddy was good at proving people wrong, at showing up when they underestimated her.

Casey bumps along the gravel, avoiding potholes and biting her lip until she reaches a flat stretch of road.

The nice thing about the tourists is that they don't really deviate from the giant green signs that point the way to the water, so while they all sit in traffic on Main Street, Casey can turn onto the back road that curves behind the Stop-n-Shop.

It's a longer route, but there isn't another car in sight, not even a pair of floating headlights in the rearview. Casey settles back into her seat, fingers drumming the wheel as she fiddles with the radio. She's flipping through a few stations, back and forth, trying to skip the commercials, when she first sees it.

A dark shape appears between the orange-tinted clouds, hurtling toward the ground. For a moment she thinks it might be one of the giant birds that flood town during the summer to hunt along the beach and steal snacks from tourists, but before she can discern the shape, it's swallowed up by another patch of clouds.

Casey glances at the road. Trees rise up on either side, curving at the tips to create the impression of a tunnel as she pulls up to a four-way stop. Looking left and right once, she turns back to the radio, flicking the dial to the last station, hoping the commercial for lawn care and pest control is over.

Then, on the road ahead, a shadow appears from that dark shape above, spreading against the pavement like spilled paint. The shadow shifts, drawing closer and closer to the front end of her car.

Casey leans over the steering wheel for a better view and looks up. The hard rubber presses into the bottom of her throat as her jaw drops.

This is no bird. Whatever it is, it's far too big and falling far too fast.

Distinct shapes take form—arms, legs—spinning wildly through the air.

Casey gasps as it hurtles directly toward her car.

"Holy—" Casey throws the car into reverse and guns it. She swerves to the side in her haste, accidentally blasting the horn as she crashes back into her seat.

Heavily, it hits the ground in front of her car, throwing up pieces of gravel that ricochet off the hood and windshield, leaving small fissures in their place. A tremor runs beneath the car and the entire thing seems to sway like a boat over a wave.

Casey watches it all in silent horror, unable to move, gripping the steering wheel and gearshift and breathing like a runner after a marathon.

She reaches for the keys bobbing near her knee with a shaking hand and turns off the engine. Then her hand falls to the door handle, and she rolls out of the car, failing at anything resembling coordination. Hot dust-filled air sweeps around her as she uses the door as both a ladder and a shield, climbing it like a monkey. She rests her chin on the curved edge of the frame.

And then she sees it. *Him*.

The pavement is caved in around the body, thick chunks turned up around the edge of the crater. In the middle of it all lies a boy, flat on his back, limbs splayed wide.

Casey turns to look up and down the road. She's alone. They're *alone*, she realizes with a jolt of panic. They. Them. The body and her. One girl and one dead guy who fell out of the sky and almost totaled her car.

She leans over and clutches her knees as her body begins to shake. Her brows furrow together. Help. That's what she needs: to call for help.

Coming to her senses, Casey grabs her phone off the passenger seat and then inches closer to the crater, trying to get a better look. There's still a lot of dust in the way; it rises up in clouds around her as she takes a tentative step toward the body, using one hand on her car to steady herself. The air feels sooty and thick. When she cuts her hand through it, she feels tiny grains and feathers. Soft puffs of white swirl around her feet as the scene settles.

Weird. Her heart jumps as she sees the full reception symbol light up in the corner of her screen. She dials and presses it to her ear. As she waits for the call to connect, she moves toward the deepest part of the crater and shouts, "Hello?"

There's no response.

"Of course not," she whispers.

She shuffles closer to the body, every cell inside her recoiling. Her heart thuds so fast she feels like it's about to burst from the effort.

"911," the operator says. "What is your emergency?"

"I—" What is she supposed to say exactly?

Then the boy coughs, and she sees his eyes snap open, concrete dust fluttering from his lashes.

Casey screams in shock, scrambling back on her hands and feet, dropping her phone somewhere in the rubble. She reaches for it blindly. "What the hell is happening?"

The boy clenches his teeth and groans, sitting up on his elbows. "Don't," he mumbles. He begins to move, shifting and tensing.

Casey feels her fingers wrap around her phone. Then, with surprising agility, the boy reaches out toward her. "Stop."

Where she's expected blood and gore—broken bones at the very least—is a pair of wide eyes, staring at her, glazed and white, almost like some sort of ghostly mirror.

He mutters something that sounds like *Gabriel* and she shudders, trying to shake off the fuzzy, muted ring echoing in her ears. It makes her dizzy and her thumb, as if with a mind of its own, hits the red END CALL button.

A feather sweeps by her hand, this one larger than all the others, and the boy tracks it with his eyes. Suddenly, he's on his feet, tipsy at first until he finds his balance. He starts chasing the feathers around the crater, scooping them up and stuffing them in his pockets.

He's a lot taller now that he's standing. And not so much of a boy. Lean but toned. Face smooth but with a shadow along his cheeks and chin. His white shirt is torn near the ribs and at the collar. His jeans fared better on impact, but look washed-out under a layer of dust. Oddly, he's not wearing any shoes.

He catches a few more stray feathers and tosses them into her lap. "Hold on to these."

Another breeze whispers through the crater and he goes chasing a feather onto the road.

Casey lies there, half on her back, clutching the feathers and her phone, disoriented and still dizzy. *This can't be happening.* Her heart gives a great lurch in response. *It's impossible.*

It's insane! her inner Liddy screams.

She crawls to her feet and hurries to the top of the crater, the climb awkward with full hands.

Feather-boy stands farther down the road, studying the length of a feather against the sunset. Maybe it's the shadow he casts upon the ground. Or the way his silhouette glows with the sun behind him, but fear prickles at the base of her spine.

She lifts her phone to her ear again, hitting the power button, and his head snaps toward her. He closes the distance so quickly Casey trips into her car, thumping against the passenger door.

"Don't touch me," she says, shrugging away from him.

His eyes are a pale blue now, like his faded jeans, but they begin to swirl, ghostly and white. The dizziness fills her and she clutches the car with one hand as she looks him over: cheeks ruddy with life, dark hair pulled into a knot at the back of his head, and a fistful of feathers.

"How about we don't make any other calls right now, okay?" With gentle but insistent pressure, he tugs the phone away from her ear. "It'll only complicate things."

He raises a brow, almost in question, but she finds herself nodding. Why is she nodding?

"I'll take these," he says, relieving her of the feathers she's gripping like a lifeline. He studies these too and, after a moment of deliberation, he sets a few of the smaller ones free. As soon as he looks away, the dizzy pressure in her head fades.

"There's not a scratch on you," she whispers. Her brows draw together in confusion. Something like fear still hammers against her rib cage, but curiosity swells and shoves it to the background. "How is that possible? You fell."

"Yeah, and let me tell you. It hurt. A lot. But I'm fine."

"You can't be fine," she retorts. She looks to the sky and waits to see something, anything to explain what or where he fell from. Only there's nothing. Nothing but sky. "How are you just *fine*?"

"We should get going." He ignores her question and looks

over his shoulder at the empty road. "Or else we'll have a lot of awkward questions to answer."

"Questions," Casey repeats. Then a spell seems to break and she pushes off the door. "What the hell—"

"You really need to stop saying that, Casey."

"How do you know my name?"

"I know a lot of things. All of which are better explained away from here."

"I don't think so." Casey crosses her arms, fear becoming defiance. He walks around the car to the driver's side, and she marches after him. "What are you doing?"

"I already told you. We need to leave." He pulls the door open and she pushes it shut again.

"That's not how this works."

He looks over his shoulder, squinting into the distance. "We won't be alone for long. The authorities will come to investigate your call."

"Good. *Great!* Then maybe you can explain to them this giant hole in the road and how exactly you came hurtling out of the sky."

"Is that what happened?" he asks, and there's something akin to amusement in his voice.

"That's exactly what happened," Casey says. "I know what I saw."

"I never said you didn't. The police on the other hand—" He lets her weigh the meaning of his words for a minute. He's so tall he has to tip his head to look down at her. "So, what'll it be? A nice chat with the police or . . . ?"

"Tell me what's going on," she insists. "Then I'll decide whether or not we hang around for the cops."

His eyes narrow, like he's testing her resolve. When she doesn't budge, he sticks out his hand toward her. "Fine. My name's Red. Nice to meet you."

Casey looks at it for a moment, then frowns. "Red what?"

"Red. Full stop. Now can we get out of here?"

"Definitely not. I'm not in the habit of picking up hitchhikers on back roads. Especially when they fall out of the sky. Which is still my biggest question here, and I think you're kind of glossing over that whole point by telling me your name and thinking that it's enough."

His eyes begin to swirl again and she snaps hers closed, turning her head away. "Stop that. What are you doing?"

He sighs. "Please just get in the car."

"No."

"I forgot how stubborn humans could be."

"Humans?" Her stomach dips and lurches, her breath coming a little shallower. After a moment, she cracks one eye open to see him with his hand pressed to his stomach. Her mind automatically jumps to images of punctured organs and internal bleeding thanks to all the *Grey's Anatomy* marathons she and Liddy watch.

No, wait. *Used* to watch.

"Are you okay?" she asks quietly.

"I forgot what hunger feels like." He shakes his head, almost fondly, and her moment of sympathy dissolves. "Anywhere good to eat around here? I'm starving. And if we're gonna talk about what's been going on with you, I need a burger or something."

"A burger—" Casey rubs her fingers against her eyelids, massaging away the ache that's formed there. "First you tell me how you just appeared out of the sky. You literally fell from the clouds, got up, and chased a bunch of feathers around. Now you want a burger. I mean . . ." She laughs humorlessly. "You know how ridiculous that sounds, right? And what was that thing?"

"What thing?"

Casey rolls her eyes, getting annoyed at having to repeat herself, at him dodging questions faster than she can come up with them. "With the eyes and the dizziness," she says.

"It's called a veil."

"A what?"

"I'll explain later."

"Not later. Right now," Casey insists.

"Fine, we'll talk while we drive, but tell me something first." He looks at her with an intensity that makes her drift back into the car door. "What do you remember about the night you died?"

THREE

"WHAT ARE YOU?" Casey asks, trying to keep her voice from quivering as she hugs the steering wheel so tight, her limbs begin to feel like lead weights.

"Red," he says simply.

Her hands slip from ten and two. She wipes her sweaty palms on the bottom edge of her dress, but it doesn't help. "I didn't say 'who,'" she says. "I said '*what*.'"

Red waves off her question. "We've been called many things across the centuries. Messengers. Guardians. Deliverance. Angels."

At that she laughs. It happens suddenly, the disbelief shooting out of her. "Give me a break."

"Turn here," he says, gesturing to a side road.

Casey glances at him questioningly, but turns, some part of her working on automatic as she tries to process the last twenty minutes. Then she hears the sirens. Of course he wanted off the main road, with its unexplainable, gaping hole, while he's still inconveniently caked in concrete dust in her passenger seat.

Red turns his neck from side to side as he settles into the seat. A terrible cracking noise sounds, but his sigh is one of relief.

Casey can't help but worry. On the outside, he appears fine, but that doesn't mean his insides aren't damaged, his organs floating in a stew of blood and broken bones. "Do you need a ride to the hospital or something?"

"I'll be fine in a while," he says. "Always takes a bit to work out the kinks."

Casey pulls into the small parking lot behind JoJo's, one of the oldest diners in town. *Bad idea,* she thinks. *This is a bad idea.* She can't be feeding strange boys that fell out of the clouds. What is wrong with her? What if someone she knows sees her? Oh, God, what if it's Evan and the guys, getting that burger he was craving so badly earlier? How the hell is she supposed to explain this?

Red studies the building and the customers inside the diner through the window. The booths are packed. They always are. "It's probably better that we don't talk inside."

She notes his clothes again—thin, ratty, and covered in bits of gravel. "Right," she says, taking her keys and wallet from the center console. "You stay here. Don't go anywhere. Don't talk to anyone. Don't even look at anyone. Understand? I'll be right back."

Casey looks back twice—once as she steps out of the car and again from the sidewalk—just to be certain she hasn't imagined the whole thing. "There's a boy sitting in my car," she mutters to herself. "He fell out of the sky."

She blows out a rough breath as she opens the door to the diner, which is famous for its all-day breakfast and burgers. Inside, a scrawny kid with bony arms and floppy hair stands behind the counter in a green apron. He greets her with a wave, showing off his braces as she hurries past cherry-red booths packed with families. A pair of condiment-wielding children rush past her, brandishing ketchup and vinegar bottles like toy swords.

"Can I help you?" the kid yells over the noise when she reaches the counter.

She looks up at the menu in a daze, then back to the car outside. "Uh, yeah, can I get combo one, please."

"All right. Would you like fries or onion rings? For a dollar more you can also upgrade to—Miss?"

She looks back at the car again, leaning around an elderly couple standing in her way. Red's still seated in the passenger seat, looking dutifully out the window.

"Miss?"

"Uh, one of each. Whatever. It's fine." She shakes her head and fishes in her wallet for a twenty-dollar bill. She tries to smooth it out as she places it beside the cash register. "Also, that's to go, please."

The couple behind her gawks as she cranes her neck to check on the car one last time. She plays it off like a stretch.

A few minutes later, the boy places an oily, brown paper bag on the counter. It smells heavenly. She grabs it and bolts for the door.

"Miss, you forgot your change!"

"Keep it," she calls over her shoulder. A weird sense of relief envelops her when she sees Red in the car, still waiting. It confirms she's not dreaming.

She pops open the door and climbs back inside.

"You look worried," he says.

"I'm—" Casey frowns at him. "Honestly, I thought you might have tried to steal my car or something."

Red grins. "I'm hungry, not a car thief."

"Right." Casey drops the greasy paper bag in his lap. "Enjoy, I guess."

"This smells amazing." He opens the bag and hunts around inside, popping a couple of fries into his mouth. "I'd forgotten."

"So . . . what do we do now?" she says.

He turns to her, cheeks stuffed, and states, "Now I help you."

Casey wants to laugh again—not just at the comical contrast of his chipmunk cheeks and serious eyes, but also at the absurdity of the statement. What could he possibly do to help her? Unless he turned out to be a certified grief counselor as well as whatever else he believed he was, Casey didn't figure very much.

Red swallows and swipes his arm across his mouth. "You've been different since that night, Casey. I know you've sensed it."

She goes cold, her body responding to his observation, and she doesn't know what to say. What night was he talking about exactly? The accident? But he couldn't know about that. And what did he mean by 'different'? A flash of the vision in the bathroom catches her off guard and she has to work to push it away. She has to push them all away. All the strange dark pictures that

41

unfurl like movies in her mind. The ones that started after the accident.

"This is ridiculous," she says out loud. She needs him to hear it. *She* needs to hear it.

Red nods in agreement, but doesn't try to explain away anything. Instead he says, "I can help you." He pops another fry into his mouth. "If you'll let me."

"If I'll let you," she repeats.

"I know what's been happening. The odd, flashing visions. The voice that echoes in your head, too real to be memory."

She tips her head back against the seat, trying desperately to ignore how closely his words resonate, feeling like an idiot for even entertaining him. But . . . a small *What if?* circulates her thoughts. Because how could he know what the darkest parts of her grief looked and sounded like? How was he even alive after a fall like that?

People don't fall out of the sky. It's not possible. Except . . . he'd called himself an angel.

Casey rubs the heels of her palms against her eyes. "All right, then," she says, swallowing down a lump of emotion before giving him her full attention. "Let's say you can help me. Spill. Start with the weird, flashy visions. What am I seeing? And why can I hear the voice in my head?"

She doesn't say that it's Liddy's voice because there's a small part of her that isn't ready to accept the implications of that.

"Because you died," Red tells her, as if it was the simplest answer in the world.

"I didn't die," she says, jaw clenched. "In case you haven't noticed, I'm sitting right here." She waves her hands over herself dramatically. "Very much alive as far as I can tell."

"You did," Red argues gently. "That day, beneath the water."

Casey bristles, her entire body flushed. "Excuse me?"

"The accident killed you."

"That makes no sense."

"Your heart stopped, Casey."

"They got it beating again," she insists.

"In the moments between, when it lay still, you were dead."

She shakes her head, starts the car for lack of anything better to do, and tries not to stare at him.

"Where are we going?" he asks, grabbing the roof handle to steady himself as she zips out of the parking lot.

"I'm going home. And you're going to be quiet for a minute. I need to think."

This is a lot to process—*Red*'s too much to process, spouting weird things every other second and badgering her about the accident.

. . . And did he really come plummeting out of the sky? That definitely happened, right?

She stops at the next intersection as the light turns from yellow to red, her brain stuck on an endless loop of *What if?* . . . *What if?* . . . *What if?*

"It's called a Limbo-walker," Red says casually.

"A what? What is?"

"It's what you are now. Someone who can navigate Limbo, the space that exists between the living and the dead."

"Because I . . . died?"

"And then came back," Red says, "on your own. That's the important bit. It wasn't the paramedics on that beach that brought you back to this world. It was *you*."

"Why can I ... Can others ... ?" She shakes her head as the light turns green.

"Because for a time, you were one of them, Casey."

"One of what?"

"A lost soul." Red gestures with a fry. "When a person dies, sometimes their soul doesn't move on right away. Sometimes it gets trapped in Limbo. After a time, that soul finds its way out—to the light or the dark. But there are rare instances when a soul doesn't move on, but instead finds its way back to the physical plane of its own accord. This is what happened to you."

"That sounds impossible."

"As impossible as people falling out of the sky?" he asks. "You saw that with your own eyes."

Six minutes later, Casey pulls into her driveway. She's been watching the dashboard clock with more attention than she's been giving the rest of the road, half expecting Red to disappear each time the numbers change.

He doesn't, though. He simply sits next to her, watching each pass of her hands over the wheel, each flick of the turn signal, like they're in a silent standoff. Each of them waiting to see who caves first, who laughs and yells *Just kidding!*

She fiddles with her phone in her pocket, wondering what Evan would think of all this. Would he even believe her?

Who am I kidding? I don't even believe this.

Casey looks from Red to the front door, and without

speaking, he seems to understand, following her up the porch steps and into the house.

Inside, he looks around with a curious eye, some kind of vague familiarity softening his features. His hand trails over furniture as they walk: tables and chairs, sofa cushions, even the delicate lampshades that warm the living room with hues of lilac.

Casey heads for her room, hearing Red keep pace behind her. He pauses in the doorway, doing a generous sweep with his eyes. Casey regards her strange guest, masking the paranoia and nerves in the hard clench of her fists.

Red takes a few tentative steps inside her room, perusing the assortment of trinkets and keepsakes that have amassed on her shelves over the years. He pauses by her desk, placing the bag from the diner carefully on the edge. "Who lives here?"

"Me and my aunt."

"Your aunt?"

Casey nods. "I've been with her since I was nine. Since my parents passed away, I guess."

"And this is Liddy?" He points to the corkboard above her desk. It's jammed with pictures of her and Liddy and Evan. Their burgundy school uniforms are featured in some. But mostly it's a collection from their summers spent at the beach.

Casey takes a photo off the board and studies it. Liddy's very blond hair and bright smile are gleaming, her eyes squinting against the sun. It's a candid shot, but utterly perfect.

Casey lifts her head. "How did you know about her?"

"You weren't the only one who died that night."

"Do you know—" Something beeps in the house and Casey

recognizes it as the sound of her aunt's car locking up. "Oh, crap!" She lurches forward and takes Red by the shoulders. "You can't be here."

She hears the garage door open and Aunt Karen drop her bag on the kitchen table.

"What?" Red asks.

She shoves him toward the closet, pushing on his chest until he thumps against the wall. "Stay here and keep quiet. No talking. No moving. No . . . anything. Okay?"

"But, what if—"

"I mean it," Casey warns. Red presses his lips together and she rolls the door closed.

"Case?"

She looks over her shoulder just as Karen's head pops around the door. She's dressed in blue hospital scrubs, her stethoscope strung around her neck. The ID badge pinned to her top reads N.R.T. *Nursing Resource Team.* Beneath that it says KAREN, RN. *Auntie K,* Casey used to call her, back when her parents were still alive. She's too old for that now.

Karen sits on the chair by Casey's bed, running a hand through her hair. It's the same dark brown Casey's mom's had been, with the same freckled cheekbones and dark lashes. Only their eyes are different. Her mom's had been warm and rich, like heated honey, but Karen's are light and piercing, the same blue as the sky after a summer rain. Her eyes are so like Evan's, calculating and curious.

Casey wonders if everyone looks at her like that now, like she's a problem that needs a solution. The closet door starts to slide open and Casey jams it closed again, hand clamped around the jiggling knob.

"That door giving you trouble again?"

"No. It's fine." She raps on it hard with her fist and growls at the flecked white paint, "It's *fine!*"

"Are you okay?"

"Yeah, good. Fine," Casey babbles, somewhat breathless. "Today's been . . . fine."

Karen frowns. "You sure?"

Her aunt's curious eyes move from the doorknob to her face, and Casey knows she's staring down years of stealthy prying and chronic need-to-know disease. If she's ever going to become adept at lying, now is the time.

"Everything good with you and Evan?" Karen asks with a measure of practiced disinterest.

"Yeah. Why?"

"He called and told me that you ran out on the memorial service tonight." She waits, letting Casey absorb that. "He said he couldn't get ahold of you after. That you wouldn't answer your phone. He was worried. It made me worried. You see how these things go."

As Karen gets up from the chair and draws closer, Casey's entire body stills, praying that Red doesn't make a sound. Karen presses a hand to her cheek. "I didn't know you'd decided to go."

"I . . . wasn't as ready as I thought, I guess." She decides that in this instance, a dose of the truth is the fastest way to ease Karen's concern. "I heard some of the girls from school talking and taking photos like it was junior prom and not Liddy's memorial. I couldn't handle it anymore and I just left."

"It's normal to miss her, Casey. No one can fault you for that. Or for needing some time to get your head straight."

"I know. People keep telling me that. I get it. I'm allowed to miss her. I'm allowed to cry and be angry and punch my pillow or whatever works."

"And you're allowed to go out into the world again." Karen drops her hand and instead wraps her arm around Casey's shoulders, drawing her away from the closet. "It's not up to you to fix other people or make excuses for Liddy's death. But if you want to talk to someone else, I can make that happen."

Casey shakes her head. "I did counseling after Mom and Dad died. I don't think it helped."

"Okay. Just . . . keep it in mind."

"I will," she lies.

Karen kisses the side of her head and leaves. Casey closes the door after her.

Behind her, the closet door peels open very slowly, the metal tracks creaking; Casey resists the urge to turn around and kick it closed again.

Red's head pops out of the dark space between the edge of the door and the frame. "Is the coast clear?" he whispers.

"Barely," Casey hisses. "You're like the annoying brother I was fortunate enough to never have."

"I came from a large human family. Four brothers between us. Trust me, I'm not that bad." He rolls the door open farther and steps out of the closet. Casey tenses, listening for the telltale squeak of the hardwood in the hallway to signal Karen's coming back. She draws closer to the door until her ear is pressed against it.

Downstairs, the water in the kitchen turns on, and Casey sighs.

"What are you doing?"

Casey spins around. Red's leaning so close they almost knock heads. "Don't do that!" she hisses through her teeth.

"I'm sorry." His mouth pulls into a tight line. "I'll remember all these things soon. Just give me some time."

"What things?"

"*Human* things."

Casey gives one slow nod. She's been trying really hard not to freak out. Granted, there's a lot to freak out about when a boy falls from the sky claiming he's an angel.

Red kneels, snatching up one of the feathers that have fallen from his pocket.

White feathers, Casey thinks, remembering the feathers in her car earlier that day and the one Evan had plucked from her clothes.

Red glances at her. "The heavens didn't leave me much to work with."

The heavens?

Casey pushes that thought away. "What's the deal with the feathers?"

"How else am I meant to protect you?"

"Right," she mutters. *What a weirdo*, inner Liddy says. She hears Karen move downstairs and Casey presses her finger along her mouth, hushing Red.

"We have more to discuss," he whispers. "There are some things you need to understand."

Casey crosses her arms. "Then talk. Tell me why exactly I'm hiding an angel in my bedroom. Why are you here besides to tell me I was dead and now I'm not? Because that part I probably could have lived without knowing to be honest."

"I'm here to make sure you don't make a mess of things. Especially things you don't understand yet. And—"

The floor creaks on the stairs, then retreats, like Karen had changed her mind about coming up.

"So, you're what?" Casey says. "The angelic janitorial squad?"

"No, more like your divine babysitter. They have enough to do upstairs. We don't need to be running around after a power-tripping Limbo-walker. But if you must know—"

"I must."

His brows lift at her interruption. "I'm here because of Liddy."

It feels like a punch to the gut, and Casey wants to double over. Before, when it had just been about her, she could wave away the ridiculousness of it all. But now Liddy's part of it, too? "What about her?"

"Specifically, because of your connection to her." He holds up two fingers. "When two people die together—same time, same place—it creates a commonality between them as their souls occupy the same bit of Limbo. A link forms between them. Like a thread. Usually this isn't a problem. The souls cross, going on their way. But your case is special. You *didn't* cross over. You came back."

"And . . . ?" Casey says quietly, feeling a bead of guilt leak down her spine.

50

"And Liddy didn't," Red explains. "That thread connecting you is stretched now, from Limbo to this world. It's why you can hear the whispers of the dead. It's Liddy's voice cutting through. It's also why you see flashes of her."

"The visions? Those are real?"

"Daydreams. Nightmares. Visions. Whatever you want to call them. It's Liddy reaching out. Trying to bridge the gap between you."

"She's trying to contact me?"

He nods. "You have to help her cross over and sever the link between you."

"Cross over from Limbo," she says, trying to wrap her head around it. "What if I can't?"

"That's not on the list of options."

"Why not?"

"Because this link between you has created a tiny fissure in Limbo. And if Liddy can reach you, other things can, too. Dark things."

Before she can open her mouth to press Red for more information, the doorbell rings. Then the alarm system beeps as the front door opens.

"Casey?" a voice calls.

It's Evan.

"Hey, you!" she hears Karen call from the kitchen.

"See anything gross and disgusting today?" he asks her.

"Do you count?"

Evan laughs so loud, Casey's heart jumps. "I walked right into that one, didn't I?"

"You make it easy, kid."

They share other words that are suddenly too low for Casey to hear. It's clear they're talking about her. She's always the cause of the murmurs and whispers and haunted, pitying looks now.

Then she hears Evan's feet on the stairs.

"Hide!" she says to Red.

"What?"

"You heard me!" She shoves at him, but he doesn't budge this time. "Get back in the closet before he sees you!"

"You should talk to him."

"Oh, yeah, and tell him what exactly? That I picked up some angel-baby—"

"Angel-baby?" Red says with surprise.

"That's what you're acting like right now." Casey uses her shoulder to press against his chest and he finally relents, moving toward the closet. "There's no good way to say I found you in a crater on the side of the road. It just doesn't work."

Evan's shadow moves beneath the door, and she races to cut him off.

"Hey," he says when she pulls the door open. "The Stop-n-Shop was having a sale on those chips you like, so I picked some up for tonight." He tosses the bag at her and she catches it. "Also, thanks for ditching me at the memorial, by the way. It wasn't awkward at all."

"Look, Evan, about tonight—"

"Aw, don't tell me you're bailing. I'm sorry. You know I didn't mean it. The thing about you ditching me. I get it." He takes a breath. "You're okay, right?" She can hear how hard he's trying, how much this means to him. She also knows she isn't the only one mourning Liddy's loss. Evan had been her friend, too.

She hears a noise in her room and Casey turns her head sharply.

"Is everything okay?" Evan asks. He touches her arm to get her attention. "Casey?"

"I just . . . Stay here, okay?"

She leaves him in the hall as she slips back into her room. She doesn't know how to explain Red—or any of it—to him yet, but she knows they certainly can't meet here.

Turning, she half expects to find Red snooping through her drawers. Instead, he's gone.

"Red," she whispers. She whips around. The bag from JoJo's Diner is gone, too. "Red?"

She throws open her closet door, diving right through the clothes, feeling from corner to corner in the darkness. Then she rushes across the room to her bed, throwing herself down on her knees and looking under it.

"Lost something?" Evan asks, pushing the door open.

"I—No. I haven't."

"Then what are you looking for?"

She sits on the floor. *Where is he?* "Nothing." Has she completely lost her mind?

Evan holds out his hand and she grabs it, letting him pull her to her feet. He doesn't let go when she's up, but tugs gently, until they're close enough for her to feel the heat of his skin and the soft cotton of his shirt brush against her arms.

"C'mon," Evan says quietly. "Forget about today. Forget

about Amanda and Sophie and Liddy's parents and everyone else. We don't need any of that pomp or decoration or even those terrible-tasting pastries. You know Liddy wouldn't have wanted it."

"It's not that easy to just forget it all." She looks away from him for a moment. "Not when you're the one everyone is staring at."

His forehead wrinkles. "I know, but—" Casey shakes her head, but he pushes on. "People shouldn't make you feel like you have to grieve one way or another. And you don't have to feel bad for living your life."

"Can you stop with the therapy talk, please? Between you and Karen, I can't take it anymore. I know these things. Been there, done that. Remember?"

"Right, yeah." His face folds in an awkward apology, remembering her parents. "It's just . . . Liddy's gone, and now there's these moments when I feel like there's this space between us. I know you need time, we all need time. I just don't want that space to get any bigger."

"Me neither," she says honestly.

"Then let's go do it right. Remember Liddy by doing something that made us all happy. She'd want you to be happy."

"Evan—"

"She'd want you to keep living, Casey. Wherever she is, she'd want you to move on."

Casey's free hand falls against her thigh. Liddy isn't just anywhere, though. According to Red, she's trapped in this Limbo place. But where is Red now? Gone. Disappeared. Is he coming back? Is she even certain the last few hours happened?

She wants to tell Evan about Red. She really does. But where's her proof?

"I got orange soda in the truck." He gestures with his thumb.

She deflates a little at the look on his face. He's trying so hard to honor Liddy, and to make her feel better. To be present. To be that person who shows up when everything else is falling apart. Despite his own grief, Evan's the one trying to hold everything together.

"That was her favorite," Casey says.

"I thought we could toast her or something." His shoulder lifts shyly. "It's dumb."

"It's not dumb."

"Yeah?"

Casey gives Evan a nudge toward the door. "Go tell Karen we're going out."

Evan puts his hands in his pockets, backing out of the room slowly. His eyes linger on her, a triumphant kind of grin on his face. "Well, okay, then."

When he's gone, she gathers her things, eyes lingering on the places Red had stood, replaying the strange things he told her.

Find Liddy. Cross over. Sever the link.

What does that even mean? Thinking about it makes her head ache, the pressure swelling against her skull. She rubs at the space between her eyes, grabs a sweatshirt from her closet, then joins Evan in the front hall.

Karen stands with him, yawning. When Casey gets to the bottom of the stairs, Karen reaches over to kiss the side of her head. "All right, have fun. But not the kind of fun that I have to get involved in, please."

Casey rolls her eyes. "I won't."

"I know."

Casey wonders if Karen's remembering the phone call from the police after she and Liddy had been pulled from the water. After she'd lain on the beach, some stranger pounding on her chest. After she'd been strapped to a stretcher and rushed to the hospital.

If she does, Karen doesn't say anything. She just squeezes Casey's arm once before shuffling her way down the hall.

"Ready?" Evan says cheerily. He pulls the door open for her.

She glances at him and the urge to tell him everything about Red and Liddy and Limbo overwhelms her. But Red's not here to help her explain. All she has are a roomful of feathers, a missing crater-boy, and a swirling pit of worry in her stomach.

FOUR

A BAG OF snack food is packed on the seat between them. Casey picks it up and puts it on the floor by her feet, preparing to slide over closer to Evan, making space for Liddy on her other side. Then she realizes that space will always be empty now, and everything inside her crashes together. She grabs the door handle to keep from toppling over.

Evan doesn't notice, just throws his arm over the seat as he turns around to reverse his truck onto the street. "You know, Amanda felt really bad after you left. She came to find me to apologize. She wants you to know that she's sorry and that she didn't mean to disrespect Liddy's memory."

Casey purses her lips. "And Sophie?"

"I couldn't tell, she always has that sort of vaguely annoyed look going on."

"Okay, well, what do you want me to say?"

Evan clicks his tongue. "Nothing. Just thought you should know."

"I didn't overreact," she huffs.

"I never said you did. Honestly, I probably would have done the same thing."

"Would you have? Because I'm pretty sure the guys from your team were taking photos."

"I would've stopped it if I'd seen it," Evan insists.

Casey stares at her reflection in the glass. "I know. I'm sorry. Displacing my anger."

"Displace away," Evan says.

She knows he means it, and that's not fair to him. She turns her head to tell him she's sorry again, but he's not paying attention.

"What's going on up there?" Evan says a moment later.

Casey glances out the windshield. There's yellow caution tape strung along the side of the road, blocking off something surrounded by traffic cones. A police cruiser is parked on the shoulder, lights flashing, and a deputy sheriff directs traffic around the cones.

Casey fidgets in her seat, knowing this is where she picked up Red.

"Think it was an accident?" Evan slows down, jaw dropping as he sees the crater. He rolls down his window. "Hey, Joe!" he shouts, waving to get his attention. "Joe!"

The deputy looks over, unimpressed.

"Just kidding, Deputy Brown."

"Move along, Evan."

"What happened?"

The deputy waves them on. "Keep driving. You're holding up traffic."

Evan reluctantly obeys, and the flashing lights begin to drop away behind them. "That hole was freaking *huge*!"

"Maybe something fell out of the sky," Casey mutters drily.

Evan snorts. "Like what, a meteor?" He slows to a stop at a traffic light. "You think it was an alien spacecraft and the government rolled up and took the evidence?"

"Do *you*?"

"I don't know, but this is the most interesting thing that's happened since the seniors put all of the shopping carts on the roof of the Food Surplus as their class prank." He turns, following the line of the coast toward the drive-in. "What happened to your car, by the way?"

"What do you mean?"

"Saw your windshield had a crack when I pulled into the driveway. Did that happen today?"

"Oh. Yeah." She shrugs, her heart beating a little faster. "A rock flew out behind a truck downtown. Nicked the glass."

"I hate it when that happens."

He bought the lie so easily, she feels a twinge of guilt in her gut.

"Me too," she murmurs.

THE DRIVE-IN IS packed to bursting with cars. To find parking, Evan has to wedge his truck between a pair of campers; children spill out around them in a never-ending wave, screaming as they're set free. A few of them press their faces to the windows of his truck and blow raspberries, leaving greasy smudges against the glass.

"Ugh, why are you like this!" Evan yells after them. "I was *never* like this as a child."

Casey grins at the sheer look of disgust on his face as he rolls the window down. "Oh, yes, because we were so well behaved."

"I was a model child, thank you very much."

"You used to stomp on my Lego houses when I wouldn't let you help me."

"I was giving you the chance to experience creative freedom," Evan says diplomatically. "Popcorn?"

"Is that even a question?"

He ducks out of the truck, pointing an accusing finger at the window-defacing culprits, before weaving his way through the lot. His head bobs between vehicles, his face shifting from neutral to a hearty smile as he runs into some kids from school. Casey squints, recognizing them as Rob MacKee and his girlfriend, Kirsten; they'd all had the same Spanish class last year.

Evan exchanges one of those weird boyish handshakes with Rob and chats for a minute. Then Evan points toward her suddenly, motioning to the truck. Casey feels like a deer in headlights as Kirsten looks over, her lips stretching into something that almost resembles a smile. Clearly she wouldn't know what to say because she can't even get her face to decide on an emotion.

Rob lifts his hand in greeting; less weird, just as awkward. Casey waves back, debating about diving onto the floor for cover.

Evan leaves Rob and Kirsten and joins the line for popcorn,

basked in the too-bright light of the concession stand. It paints him in a glow, the light turning yellow around his silhouette.

Casey leans her head out the open window. The day had been a wild ride from start to finish. The memorial . . . Amanda and Sophie . . .

Red.

Part of her is still worrying over Red's disappearance from her bedroom. For a moment, though, another part of her relishes how good it feels to be out with Evan just doing something normal. How nice it is to pretend, even for a little while, that this is any other summer.

That Liddy isn't dead.

Evan hurries back to the truck and hands her a bag brimming with popcorn through the window.

"I put extra butter on. I know our cholesterol levels will suck when we're fifty, but that's a tomorrow problem, right?"

"Right," Casey agrees, her stomach already growling at the smell.

She pops a couple of pieces into her mouth, grinning eagerly when Evan climbs back inside the truck, and then reaches over to dump a bunch of M&M's over the top of her popcorn. He smiles at her with the corner of his mouth.

"So, what's on the agenda?" she asks.

"Double feature that starts with *The Mummy*."

"Nice."

"I thought you'd like that."

"How can anyone not? Ancient Egypt, the undead, a hilarious sidekick, a librarian who kicks ass . . ."

"Is this movie why you wanted to be a librarian when you were ten?"

Casey glares at him. "Maybe. I also wanted to be able to summon the dead after watching it all summer, so there's that."

Evan chuckles. "You should put that on your résumé after high school. 'Career aspirations: Raising the Dead.'"

He glances at her before he even finishes speaking, eyes wide with apology.

Every conversation inevitably goes this way now. There's no way to keep Liddy out of it.

"If you could bring your dad back, would you?" she asks quietly. She tucks her legs up onto the seat and throws a piece of popcorn at him.

He bats it away. "I don't even know if he's alive or dead," Evan says. "Mom never talks about it, and I never ask. Guess I always thought he was dead because that's easier than accepting he was a loser who walked out when I was a baby."

"Think you'll ever ask her?"

"No."

"Why not? Don't you want to know?"

Evan's face wrinkles in thought. "I don't want to hurt her. She's happy with Jack, and he's the only dad I've ever known. No sense in chasing a past that I don't need, is there?"

"I guess not."

"What about you?" he asks as the previews begin to play out on the screen. "Would you bring back your parents?"

She considers the question. It's been close to eight years without them now and she's learned to cope in their absence.

The places inside her that used to ache and mourn have been filled by other people—her aunt, Evan, *Liddy*.

Liddy, who is trapped in a place between life and death. Liddy, who's been reaching out, linked because of the accident that killed them both. Not only had she let Liddy's hand go beneath the waves as the current tugged and pried at them, but she'd also apparently left her behind in the place that came after, too.

"I'd bring Liddy back," Casey says, leaning her head against the headrest.

"Me too," Evan replies quietly.

Now, she thinks. *I should tell him about Red* now. *About Liddy. About…everything.*

But as she opens her mouth, the words collide in the back of her throat.

Evan turns his head, his hair sweeping to the side as he grins at her. "I'm really glad you came." He pulls out two small bottles of orange soda and hands her one, then tips his to clink it against hers. "To Liddy," he says. "The sassiest, most loyal friend we could ever have. Thanks for always being there. We know you're waiting for us on the other side." He pauses, lifting his arm with a flourish that would make their drama teacher proud. "Want to add anything?"

Casey shakes her head, her throat thick. "To Liddy," she whispers, turning her attention to the darkened screen as the movie begins.

She blinks and the darkness fades to an empty alleyway. *Old brick walk-ups with metal fire escapes zigzagging like a rusted maze along their walls tower on either side of her. There's a dumpster, a tipped-over shopping cart, and a bicycle frame without tires.*

Casey jolts back to reality, hunched over. Evan's looking at her oddly, so she reaches for the radio dial, turning the volume up a couple notches. It was almost as if she could hear the scuff of shoes against pavement. A shiver crawls across the back of her neck and down her spine.

Casey.

The word slithers around inside her head. There's no mistaking that it's Liddy, and it's all too much. Her voice. Knowing she's stuck. Evan's impromptu memorial.

She's going to be sick.

Casey reaches for the dashboard, bracing herself. When she lets her eyes flutter closed, black shapes flash behind her lids, and she clamps her teeth together as her stomach roils, threatening to empty popcorn and chocolate all over the floor.

"Case . . . Casey?" Evan says, dropping his popcorn. It spills over his legs and onto the mat, rolling under the foot pedals.

"I need—" She covers her mouth with her hand. "Just a minute."

"It's okay," he says, his voice laced with the kind of panic that comes from someone who can't handle vomit. "I'll take you home. Just breathe and keep it together."

She shoves her popcorn into his hands. Her mind feels like it's spinning, trying to capture a glimpse of the alleyway again. Is it somewhere she's been before?

"Stick your head out the window. Breathe fresh air." The truck starts to move and Evan nudges her shoulder with one hand. "Tell me if you need me to pull over."

She tucks her knees up to her chest, eyes pinched shut.

Casey.

"What can I do?" Evan asks.

Casey shakes her head. She doesn't even know how to help herself. "I'll be fine," she grits out. "Just drive."

"Drive. Yep, I can do that," he babbles.

They drive through the first patches of real night, the kind that's blanketed in hints of blue. On either side, the trees become a patchwork of navy leaves.

Evan yells suddenly, and Casey jolts forward as the truck brakes hard. She puts her hand out against the dashboard but the seat belt locks first and catches her.

"What is it?" she gasps.

Evan points over the wheel to where the headlights stretch into the shadows. Something shifts in the darkness, gathering itself just outside the light. "I'm seeing things, right?"

"Not unless we're *both* hallucinating," Casey says.

Evan lets go of the brake a bit, crawling toward the shadows.

Casey squeezes his arm. "Stop the truck."

More shadows take form in the darkness, shying away from the light, but hovering close enough to send Casey's heart racing.

"Uh, I think that's a bad decision, the driver's handbook definitely says to run over creepy death shadows—"

"Evan, stop!" she says.

He does, jolting them forward again. "What are those things?"

The shadows pull away from the asphalt into tall, lanky forms. Some kind of humanoid shape.

"Oh, hell no," Evan says, rolling both windows up. He throws the truck into reverse, and a *thump* tells her they've run over something. The tires squeal, as if caught. Casey's stomach clenches as the engine begins to chug. Evan presses his weight onto the gas pedal, but the truck only sputters in answer.

Then, as if sensing a change, the creatures cower at the edge of the headlights' glow, tripping over one another in an attempt to escape.

Another figure appears, outlined by the headlights. As he turns, Casey recognizes Red.

His skin is yellowed by the lights, but his eyes are glazed white again. Her gaze lands on the twin flashes of silver near his palms; Red's holding two small blades, twisting them around his fingers with ease.

He slams his fists into one of the retreating creatures, driving it down toward the asphalt. The road erupts before them, chunks of pavement shooting up and out. Red rises to his feet. Casey blinks, mostly in shock, partly in awe.

She reaches for the door and pops it open.

"Wait, whoa!" Evan flings himself across the cab to grab the door and pull it closed again. "Yeah, I think it's better if we stay in the truck, all things considered."

"I can't just sit here," she insists.

His eyes are wide with fear. "Uh, yes, you can! Be the semi-sensible nerd who stays in the car because that's where it's safe. They're always the ones who survive."

Before she can respond, something dives out of the darkness and lands on the windshield. Casey shouts as Evan flails, knocking the windshield wiper knob with his knee. They swipe left, tossing the creature onto the road.

Casey pushes the door open again, slamming it into a patch of darkness. It collides hard with something that is definitely *not* human.

"Casey!" Evan shouts. "Get back in the truck right now! What are you doing?!"

"Red!" she calls, squinting as she steps into the light.

"I'm very angry at you!" Evan yells. He honks the horn to get her attention. "So mad! Like you don't even know!" He grabs his snow brush from the floor of his truck and kicks his door open, knocking a creature into the ditch by the side of the road.

"Evan, get back in the truck!"

"Oh, so you *can* hear me?" he cries, brandishing his snow brush at the dark. "Well, isn't that convenient now that we're outside where the shadow-monsters are!"

Casey's lost sight of Red in the darkness, so she retreats back toward the truck. Evan does the same, holding the snow brush like a baseball bat, and when she's close enough, he yanks on her sleeve, pulling her toward the open door.

Something hisses in the darkness, and Casey pushes Evan into the truck. She dives in after him, closing the door. A shadow-figure smashes into the truck with enough force to nearly knock it over onto two wheels. When the truck falls back to the ground, the figure clambers up the side and onto the roof.

"What is *happening*?" Evan groans.

Casey turns the keys in the ignition. Is this what Red meant by darker things finding their way out of Limbo?

The roof begins to pop and sag. Casey presses on the gas and the truck lurches forward, blasting through the figures. They scratch and claw and cry out in high-pitched shrieks. Evan wraps his hands over his ears and Casey winces.

She steps on the brakes again when she sees Red crawling out of the ditch, hunched over, a hand pressed to his abdomen.

"Take the wheel," she tells Evan. "Keep the engine running."

"What are you doing?" he cries. "Casey? Casey! Have you lost your mind?"

She's already gone, pushing the door open and racing across the pavement to meet Red. She reaches for him, shoes skidding on the pebbled shoulder of the road, and loops his arm over her shoulders. "Are you okay?"

"Fine," he says through gritted teeth. "I'll be fine."

"C'mon," she says. "Let's get out of here."

She leads him back onto the road. When they're close enough, Casey guides Red into the truck and jumps in behind him.

"Drive!" she yells.

Evan guns the engine. As they speed down the road he glances over at her and Red, jaw slack. "What the hell were those things?"

"Don't say that word!" Red hisses. He drops the pair of daggers onto the floor of the truck. They hit the mats, bouncing on impact. When they flip over, the metallic sheen in gone, and a pair of feathers lie in their place.

"Don't say what?" Evan demands. "'Hell'? Why the *hell* not? I think it's perfectly acceptable given the current circumstances." He gestures to the road. "What the *hell* was that?" He gestures to Red. "Who the *hell* are you?"

Red hisses again. Casey looks down as he pulls his hand from his body. All she can see is a dark spot spreading across his stomach.

"Evan, just drive," she pleads.

"Fine. But someone tell me what the *heck* is going on!"

FIVE

"SO LET ME get this straight," Evan says from behind the wheel. "Casey died and then came back to life with super-powers, which you, angel-boy, have come to teach her how to use. And her mission, if she chooses to accept it, is to rescue our dead best friend from hell."

"Not *hell*."

"Sorry, heck."

Red groans. "That's not what I meant." He leans forward, re-applying the pressure to his wound. Beneath the streetlights, the blood that leaks around his hand looks almost black. "Look," he says, "let me simplify this for you. There's an upstairs. That's where I'm from. There's a downstairs. That's where those *things* came from. And there's an in-between, where souls...among other things...sometimes linger. That's where Liddy is. Limbo."

Each time Evan glances at Red, the truck drifts right toward the woods, and Casey's hand shoots out to correct him.

"Want me to drive?" she asks again.

"No. *No.* I'm fine," Evan answers, waving her question away. He looks at Red again. "So it's Casey's job to secure Liddy safe passage or whatever."

"More or less."

"And those *things* back there were . . . what . . . the welcoming committee?"

"Obsii."

Casey's brows draw together. "Which is what, exactly?"

"Lesser creatures of darkness. A minor nuisance on their own, but dangerous and deadly when they gather," Red says, gesturing to his abdomen. "They bring chaos into your world and in the wake of their movements, leave destruction."

Evan makes a face. "What kind of destruction?"

"Disease. War. Famine. The obsii are the bringers of death. The grim reapers from your human stories."

"Basically bad news," Evan says.

"Very bad news." Red looks at Casey. "Which is why the connection between you and Liddy needs to be closed."

"Riddle me this," Evan says, taking a corner sharply, sending them all crashing against one another. "You're like an all-powerful being or whatnot."

"Or whatnot," Red agrees.

"So why don't one of you just waltz on into Limbo, grab Liddy, and head back to wherever it is you came from?"

"Angels can't hear the whispers of the dead." Casey shudders at his words. "It makes it more difficult to locate them."

"Might want to rethink that 'all-powerful' description, then."

"The best we can offer is guidance and protection. Casey and others like her . . . they're a special kind of being. She gets little glimpses of Liddy. What she sees. What she says."

"What is this," Casey asks as Evan opens his mouth again, "an interrogation?"

"No," Evan says sarcastically, "it's a friendly conversation between two people who aren't friends because one of them is a supernatural creature of mythical origin." He sucks in a breath.

Beside her, Red adjusts in the seat, his face contorting in pain.

"Are you really okay?" she asks. She reaches down to pluck the abandoned feathers from the mat, twisting them between her thumb and forefinger.

"I'll be okay once I heal."

"Yeah, that's usually how things work," Evan mutters.

Red rolls his eyes.

Casey hands Red the twin feathers he'd carried into the truck as daggers and he accepts them with a grimace of pain. "Guess that's why you went chasing feathers around when we first met."

"Yes," he nods. "Angelic feathers are imbued with power. Their wielders are able to manipulate them into weapons."

"Any wielder?"

He hands her back one of the feathers, then folds her hand around it. "If given freely by their owner, angelic feathers may be used by anyone."

As if in response to his words, Casey's hand tightens around the hilt of a dagger. Transformed once more, the feather now shines under the passing streetlights, the metal cold against her palm.

"They obey touch and need."

"Need?" Casey says, lifting the dagger, only to find a feather in its place.

Red chuckles at her look of shock, then winces. "There is no threat presently."

"A feather can sense that?"

He nods. "They are as much a part of me now as they were before I fell."

"Your own feathers?" she says, surprised.

"Yes, from my wings."

They make their way through downtown. Evan slows to the speed limit despite traffic being nonexistent. The last thing they need is to get pulled over.

"Where are we going?" Evan asks.

"My place," Casey says immediately.

"Is Karen home?"

"She should be asleep by now."

Evan nods, taking a left off Main and pulling down the oak-lined street, driving through pools of orange cast down from the streetlights above.

They turn into the driveway and hop out of the truck. Casey watches the agony on his face as Red stretches up to his full height. The bloodstain spreads around his hand.

"Here, let us help," Casey says, slipping beneath his arm. Evan takes his elbow. Casey staggers a bit. "You're heavier than you look."

His arm rests like dead weight on her shoulders. Sweat beads along his brow and neck; Red walks on, grunting and shifting pressure on the wound, but otherwise never once complaining about the pain he must be in.

They guide him up the porch steps, hesitating in front of the door.

"Just," she says, reaching for the doorknob, glancing from Red to Evan, "try to keep it down."

"Yeah, Red, bleed quietly," Evan whispers.

They step inside and she closes the door behind them. She flicks her hand against the wall and the lights blink on in the dining room. "Evan, can you grab the first aid kit?" she whispers, hyperaware of her aunt sleeping upstairs. "Red-and-white bag under the bathroom sink."

"On it," he says, dashing off down the hall.

Red pulls away and staggers on his feet, using a nearby chair to keep from tipping over. His hand drops and the blood oozes freely.

"Keep pressure on that," Casey urges. "If—"

Red whips his shirt over his head before she even has time to finish her thought. He crumples the shirt into a ball and presses it to the middle of his gut, right alongside his navel, hissing through his teeth.

Evan returns, dropping the first aid kit on the dining room table. He unzips it, pulling out some gauze pads and handing them to Red. "Oh man, that's a lot of blood."

Casey nods in agreement. She's learned basic first aid—mostly at Karen's request—but now that she's gotten a look at the wound, she knows this is beyond what she can handle herself. "We should take you to a hospital," she says.

"No." Red's face contorts in pain. "I just need some time."

"You need help! This is bad."

Red doesn't look convinced. "I can't go to a hospital. There are too many people." He grips her hand, pulling her attention from the blood-soaked shirt to his face. "I can't be seen like this."

Like what?

His eyes are intense, focused, and she feels dazed looking at him. Turning her head helps. She shakes it off and remembers that she wants to scream at him. "I can't help you. I don't know what to do!"

"And I can't help *you* if I'm dodging invasive questions at the local emergency room. You think a few people talking about a giant hole in the ground is bad, wait until they try to explain *me*."

"Wait," Evan says, "how did you know people were already talking about that?"

"We're always aware of the marks we leave behind."

Casey still wants to yell, to rage against his stubbornness, but he's right. Red's peculiarity must extend beneath the surface of his skin. The look of dread on his face tells her as much.

She rubs her hand over her eyes, blinking as she pulls away. At first, she thinks it's a trick of the dim dining room light, but it happens again: a glimmer along his shoulder blades. She steps to the side, pushing gently on Red's arm, urging him to turn around. When he does, her breath stills in her chest.

Eventually, her thoughts catch up and her fingers freeze inches from his skin; she's transfixed by the miniscule remnants of feathers that run along his shoulder blades and down his spine before receding into his back, each piece jagged and torn as if his wings had been ripped . . .

She shakes that very unpleasant thought away.

Beneath the skin, they rest like a muted, unfinished tattoo, but when she reaches out, fingers finally connecting, the shape is raised. Red's back arches and the feathered remains cut through his skin again, leaving thin rails of blood beading from the tiny wounds.

He hisses as the feathers recede once more. "I can't control it right now. Everyone would see."

"Can you fly?" she asks.

He scoffs. "You do remember me falling out of the sky and almost colliding with your car, right? Giant crater in the road ringing any bells?"

"Uh . . . right."

"Yeah, that's a big flashing sign that says 'Not from here,'" Evan says.

His words snap Casey from her daze, and she yanks her hand away. "Okay, all right, no hospital. But you have to see *someone*."

Evan pulls out his phone. "Sure, let me just find the closest supernatural walk-in clinic." He shakes his head. "Yeah, nothing popping up for wingless angels."

"I don't need medical intervention," Red growls. "I can't be seen like this."

"Let me guess," Evan says, "rule number one, do not reveal your secret identity?"

"Something like that." Red readjusts his grip on the shirt,

moving it to inspect the damage. Casey tries not to notice how much of it is soaked in blood.

"I think it's stopping," Evan says, face contorted. "The blood."

"It won't," Red says. He presses his hands to either side of the wound, squeezing a black, bile-looking substance from it.

"Stop," Casey cries. "Don't do that."

"I can't heal with that vileness still inside me. Raphael, give me strength." Red's eyes ghost over, white and pale, and he sways a bit.

Evan puts his hand on Red's shoulder, steadying him. "Look, I don't know who this Raphael guy is, but you better sit down before you fall down."

When Red pulls his hand away, a crude line of pink skin has pulled the edges of the wound together again.

"Flamin' heck," Evan whispers.

"What the hell is going on here?" They all turn to see Karen standing frozen in the hallway, dressed in her pajamas.

"Oh no," Evan says. "We say 'heck' now."

"Excuse me?" Karen says.

Red gets to his feet, towering over Casey.

Karen's eyes widen when she notices his wound. "What on earth happened?"

"There was..." Casey glances at Red, then to the drops of blood staining the hardwood by their feet. She doesn't know what to say.

"Gabriel," Red whispers, "with your guidance." His eyes blur misty and white, as if clouds were crawling over the cool blue irises. "There's nothing to worry about," he says with a calm, firm confidence.

There's a passing sweep of something that makes Casey lightheaded. She turns away, her fingers in her ears.

Beside her, Evan shakes his head like he has water trapped in his ear. "Raphael . . . Gabriel," he mutters. "Is anyone else really tired all of a sudden?"

"You should sleep," Red insists, looking at Karen. "It's late."

"I—Yes," Karen mumbles, the words fuzzy. "It's late." She blinks owl-like at Casey. "See you in the morning."

"Night," Casey says, puzzled. Her aunt clears the room, wandering away in a daze.

"So . . . that's not normal," Evan says.

"Will she be okay?" Casey asks Red. He nods once, an almost imperceptible thing. Really just a flinch of his jaw, but it relieves Casey greatly. "That was that veil thing again, wasn't it?"

"Is it dangerous?" Evan adds. "Am I like secondhand hypnotized or something?"

Red shakes his head. "A veil is merely a sort of mental manipulation."

"I *am* hypnotized," Evan says.

"I only guided her toward a certain line of thinking. The more outrageous, the harder it is to sway the will of a person." Red shrugs. "Your aunt was tired. It wasn't much of a stretch. I just made her think that her exhaustion outweighed her curiosity."

"If you could do that this whole time, why didn't you let me take you to the hospital?" Casey demands.

"It takes energy to influence a veil. More people means more energy. And right now, I need to be using it for more important tasks."

"Like that patch job?" Evan says, gesturing to Red's abdomen with his chin.

"Among other things."

Red glances at Casey and she feels the question in his gaze. She could undo it all. With Red's help, she could pull Evan back into a world of ignorant bliss.

"Don't even think about it," Evan murmurs with his fists balled up at his sides. "You keep your twisty-eye nonsense to yourself."

"I wasn't," Casey says, pretending like the thought had never crossed her mind. "I promise." She gestures down the hall. "Wait here, I'll be right back."

She shuffles through the piles of clean clothes on the shelf in the laundry room. Some of them belong to Evan. They've been friends long enough that the laundry room has become a sort of lost-and-found for the things he leaves behind. Casey finds a long-sleeved shirt.

"Here," she says, tossing the shirt to Red when she returns to the room.

"Hey, is that mine?" Evan says.

She gives him a shrug. "I think I have socks in my room. You can't go running around barefoot all the time."

"Are those mine, too?" Evan calls after her.

"We can't stay here," Red says with urgency. He groans, but follows when she doesn't respond, and Evan helps him up the stairs. They hover in the doorway while she looks through her sock drawer. "I'm compromised. Healing from this injury will monopolize my power. We need to be somewhere safer. More secure."

Evan squeezes past him and sits on Casey's bed. "So, after the nice shadow things attacked us on the street, you want to go back out there in the dark and play hide-and-seek with them again?"

"No, I want to be in a place with defenses beyond myself. I can't protect this place right now, so it's best we go somewhere else."

Casey finds a pair of navy socks and tosses them to Red. "Those things . . . the obsii or whatever. Are they in Limbo . . . where Liddy is?"

"It's possible. Yes."

"Are they as dangerous to her as they are to us?"

"Yes."

Evan is still shaking his head. "You're out of your mind if you think we're going back out—"

"Stop arguing," Casey says, interrupting him. She grabs a duffel bag from under her bed and hands it to Evan. "Pack up. We're going."

SIX

"CHURCH?" EVAN SAYS as they pull down a narrow gravel drive. "A rickety, old run-down church. You know, I figured you had some weird, fortified, supernatural bunker in mind, but this is good, too. With all the broken windows, it'll get good air circulation. Probably a few bats if we're lucky. Maybe a raccoon."

"It's not about the building," Red says. "It's about what's inside." He gets out of the truck and walks up the path to the church.

Evan reaches for Casey's hand across the cab. "You know, there's still time. I can back us out of here and pretend like we never met this dude."

Casey laughs a little, savoring the feel of his hand on hers. "Do you think I'm crazy?"

"No more than I am."

"I'm serious, Evan. This is . . ."

"Wild. Insane. Impossible . . . etcetera."

"Yeah, pretty much."

The corner of his mouth flickers, like he isn't sure whether to smile or not. "It is all those things, but it's kind of comforting in a way."

"Yeah, I'm not following."

"I mean . . . I thought the craziest thing that I was ever going to experience was staring at one of my best friends in her casket, dead at seventeen." He lifts his shoulder. "It's kind of nice to know that it's not." His brows draw together tightly. "Does that make sense?"

"In a weird kind of way," she says, "yeah, it does."

"I think we've far surpassed weird tonight."

"And you're not running for the hills yet?"

"Well, I'm not running without you, so I guess that means you're stuck with me."

Casey's caught off guard by how sincere he is.

"I already lost Liddy, and by the sounds of things, I almost lost you, too. So you can't blame a guy for sticking close."

"Guess not," she says quietly.

"Just promise that we'll be careful. We'll look out for each other. Protect each other. And whatever happens, nobody falls for the angel."

He's joking of course, about the angel part—or maybe he's not—but the rest of it is said with an intensity that warms the air between them. Casey leans a bit closer. "I promise," she says.

"Good. Great." He grins and thumps the steering wheel. "We should probably go . . . before we make him wait any longer."

CASEY FOLLOWS EVAN up the path. Streetlights from the road highlight the exterior and she studies the design of the church. The gray stone walls rise up in matching geometric patterns to a tower that houses a bell. Some of the windows are boarded up. Others have been kicked in. There's an entrance on the side of the building where the locks are broken. That's where Red waits.

As they enter the church, Casey takes in their new surroundings. It's much darker than it is outside. Evan holds up his phone, using it as a flashlight; the only other light comes in through the broken windows. Red leads them beneath an arched doorway, decorated with sculpted filigree and spray paint.

Wooden pews sit in three neat sections, rows extending all the way to the back of the building, with aisles between each. An upper balcony houses an old pipe organ. At the front, marble steps lead to a stone altar.

Red crosses the front of the church and stops before a marble statue that rests in a decorated alcove. Its rounded features and sweeping white wings, each feather meticulously chiseled, are covered in a wispy cloak. It's clearly an angel. One that makes Red nervous judging by the way he drums his hand against his thigh.

There are other alcoves with other statues, but they're all

either shattered or scorched with marks that mean someone was playing with matches.

Evan puts his hands on his hips. "Well, this is nice," he says. "Cozy. Safe. Definitely secured against those shadow creatures. Might as well call it a four-star retreat."

"It's the safest place in town," Red says.

"How do you figure?"

Red circles the statue, running his hands along the marble. For a moment his eyes glaze, becoming a ghostly mirror, and a gust of wind slithers through the church. "This is Michael. One of four winged-protectors that reside on earth. They've been here for a long time, the first to come to the aid of humanity in the fight between good and evil."

"Archangels," Casey says, recognizing the name from some old stories they studied in an ancient history class last year.

"Yes," Red says. "They are the strongest of our kind. Every legion of angels since has been trained in their likeness." He drops his hand. "Michael is the warrior and protector. From him, we derive strength and the skill to strike down darkness. We'll be safe here tonight."

Red crosses to the other side of the church. Evan chases after him. "Hey, hold up," he says, gesturing to the statue. "You mean like . . . this guy here . . . he gives you power?"

"The statue is only a placeholder. A way to access an archangel should we need it. But yes." Red leads them toward another door and down a short stairwell. "The archangels are the original wielders of the divine gifts. Michael holds physical power. Raphael is the angel of healing."

"So you summoned an archangel into my dining room?" Casey says, fairly certain that Karen isn't going to be overly happy about it.

"Only the power," Red explains. He stops at the bottom of the stairwell and turns into a basement room. There are half a dozen tables with assorted mismatched chairs. Red lights some candles with a matchbox that sits on an old, wooden podium.

The orange flicker of light gives him an eerie quality. He glances over at Casey as if he can hear the frantic beat of her heart. After a moment, she breaks the spell by looking away.

"Which ones are left?" she asks.

"What?"

"You said there were four. Who are the last two?"

"Gabriel," Red says. "The great messenger."

"What's he good at? Emailing?" Evan's grin falters when neither of them laugh. "Harsh," he whispers.

"From him we learned the ancient languages and tongues of the world. The veil. The old symbols that give us access to doorways."

"What doorways?" Evan says.

"How else do you think we enter Limbo?"

"So, we have Michael, Gabriel, Raphael—who's the last?" Casey asks.

"Uriel. The archangel closely associated with the elemental means of worldly creation: wind, water, fire, and earth. Of all the divine gifts, Uriel's are the most complex and require a great amount of care to learn to control. It is patience that alludes even me at this point."

"Even more difficult than healing?"

"Exceptionally more difficult." Red looks up suddenly, his eyes tracking something above them. Something neither she nor Evan can see.

Casey strains her ears for a noise. "I thought you said we were safe here?"

Red's expression is curious more than anything else. "We are," he insists. "Stay here." He leaves them alone, heading back upstairs.

"Oh, well, that's comforting," Evan says. "Guess we're spending the night." He looks around glumly, but then he smiles. "This is marginally better than the bed-and-breakfast where the volleyball team was booked for our away games last year. The owner charged us extra for killing the spider in our room; apparently it was her pet."

"Well, glass half full and all that." Casey watches him cross the room. "Where are you going? Red told us to stay right here!"

"To poke around. Church basements have all sorts of donations and things. Maybe I'll find an old board game or something."

"Don't go too far," Casey says, hugging her arms to her chest.

"Why? Does it feel like the makings of a horror film yet?" He backs away slowly, whispering in an eerie, low-pitched voice. "A group of teens. Alone in an abandoned church. Middle of the night. No one around for miles!"

"There's a twenty-four-seven convenience store down the street," she deadpans.

"You're no fun," he grumbles, then winks. "In case I don't make it back . . . would you miss me?"

"To be decided," she says. She knows he's only teasing, that they're both only teasing, but in light of everything that's happened, the joke lands flat. Of course she'd miss him. He must hear it in the silence that follows, because he winces and walks away.

He never actually leaves her sight line. Turns out the basement is really just one giant room with a lot of closets.

"Found these." He returns, unfurling a couple raggedy quilts and she watches a cloud of dust engulf him. "They've probably been holed away since we were born. But it beats sleeping on a pew."

He lays the quilts on the ground, doubled up for comfort.

"I don't know how much actual sleeping I'm going to do," Casey says.

"What are you talking about?" Evan flops down, stretching out and resting his arms behind his head like a pillow. "It's just like summer camp. Pretend you're looking up at the stars." He loosens one hand to reach for hers, tugging until she lies down beside him.

Evan tips his head toward her, cheeks twitching. "You know, seeing as there are dark creatures hanging around, we should probably stay close." He shifts next to her, until she can feel the warmth of him against her, despite the layers of clothes. "Probably right next to each other, cuddled up like when we were little. Before we grew up and caught cooties."

"Playing the hero, are you?"

"Heck no, you're the Limbo-walker. I'm coming to *you* for protection. You can be my knight in shining armor." He waggles his brows. "You know, buddy system. Safety in numbers and all that."

The candles flicker around them, flames reaching toward the ceiling. They cast orange shadows that twist and dance and sputter. The light bounces against the walls, highlighting gold-framed paintings of old stories with fiery light and winged angels with soft features. In others they are clad in brilliant armor, wings spread in defiance. And still there are more, angels painted in blues and blacks, with their wings ripped away as they're cast down from great heights.

Casey's heart pounds in her chest and she lays her hand against her skin to contain the beat. Reality settles in her bones the way sleep does: slowly at first, then all at once.

Red is an angel. Liddy's soul is in trouble somewhere. And Casey—the girl she thought she was before—she died that night on the beach.

Evan rolls onto his side. "What are you thinking?"

"A lot of things," she confesses.

"Like what?"

"I just ... I wonder if Liddy's scared? Being alone, wherever she is. I wonder if she knows I'm trying to find her ..."

Evan stares at her for a long moment until Casey realizes that he's looking through her and not at her. "Do you remember that one summer when we were, I don't know, about ten, maybe, and we went hiking in the woods behind my house?"

"And we got lost," Casey says, taking in a breath of memory. It surfaces like a reflection through glass, a little distorted at the edges, but preserved in crystal clarity. "I do remember that."

"But do you remember how I cried for like half an hour straight? Just sat there in the mud, bawling my eyes out. And it was Liddy who eventually dragged me to my feet and figured out how to get us out."

"We weren't actually that lost," Casey points out.

"No, but what did we know at ten? We could have been halfway to the South Pole." His fingertips touch the tops of her knuckles and the entire room starts to buzz. "Anyway, my point is that if anyone can figure out this Limbo place, it's her."

Casey's heart swells a bit, her entire chest tight, like there isn't enough room for the feelings to escape. She rolls onto her back, trying to loosen the tension. She glances between the flickering shadows around them, the winged figures glowing brighter than before.

Suddenly, thunder crashes overhead, rattling the candlesticks.

Casey bolts upright.

Evan rolls onto his stomach, hands braced against the floor, his eyes trained on the stairwell. "What the heck was that?"

"Storm?" Casey offers pathetically, shifting until her back is to the wall.

Evan hums his disagreement. "The sky was clear driving over."

Casey's skin prickles. Her hair begins to float in front of her eyes, the way it does when someone rubs a balloon over their head, creating all sorts of static.

Evan reaches out, tangling his fingers in the strands. "Weird."

Another roll of thunder crashes, and the entire church shudders. Casey's hair falls limp and she scrambles up.

Evan springs to his feet in front of her. "I was kidding about that horror movie thing."

"Let's go find Red," Casey suggests. They race up the stairs side by side, elbows knocking. At the top, Casey's breathless, spinning wildly through the darkness until she spots a figure by the light of Evan's phone.

"Red!" she yells, racing down the center aisle toward him. Behind her, Evan's heavy tread echoes, drowned out only by the pounding of rain against the roof. *Rain?*

"Casey, watch out!" Evan cries, grabbing her elbow and yanking her back.

Glass shatters near the roof, raining down in sparkling sheets. It clatters across the wooden pews as Casey covers her head. Above them a shadow sweeps across the upper level and a rustling wind blows through the organ pipes, sending eerie notes rattling around the church.

"Stay back," Red says, throwing his hand out.

A figure, tall and dark, lands beneath the arched peak that separates the main part of the church from the entrance. It fills the doorway, highlighted by a flash of lightning. Then Casey notices its wings.

"Flamin' heck!" Evan says, staggering backward. He loses his footing and lands hard, shuffling across the carpet like a crab.

Red straightens up between them, the fight uncoiling from his muscles. "Malakhi," he greets. "I wasn't expecting to see you so soon."

Outside, the thunder has disappeared, the rain silent, like the storm has simply vanished or maybe . . . *landed*, Casey thinks.

The angel stalks toward them, his long wings dragging along the ground. His hair is jet-black but his eyes burn even darker, swirling and swirling. It makes her lightheaded to look at him.

"Is this the Limbo-walker?" Malakhi asks. He's young like Red, but his voice is so deep it almost trembles.

"Yes," Red answers. "This is Casey."

Malakhi looks them over, eyes narrowing on Evan, before they settle on Red. "You were supposed to close the soul connection."

"I'm working on it," Red says.

"Actually, *I'm* working on it," Casey interrupts. "Who are you?"

"Malakhi," the angel replies. "The Messenger assigned to this tasking."

Evan climbs to his feet. "What's a Messenger?"

"Exactly what it sounds like," Red says. "My link between this world and—"

"The upstairs," Casey finishes for him. "So, he's *your* babysitter."

"I'm the one who has to answer for what he gets up to down here," Malakhi clarifies. "That attack tonight will be the first of many if you can't get things under control."

Red's shoulders tense. "I'm trying, Malakhi."

"Well, try harder. Or do you not want your wings back?"

Red bristles under Malakhi's appraising stare. "Of course I do," he says hotly.

"And to think," Malakhi begins, "you were almost finished

with these menial tasks. Now you've gone and thrown it all away."

Red's face darkens, his features turning cold. "You don't know what you're talking about."

"I know loyalty. I know family." Malakhi strides toward him until his face is inches from Red's, his chin tilted in disgust. "You gave it all up, Red. You gave *us* up. So if you want to earn your place back, then prove it. Take the girl to Limbo and close the link. How hard is it to grab one little soul from where she died?"

"Where she . . . died?" Casey says slowly.

"Yes," Malakhi answers. "When a soul gets trapped, they occupy a part of Limbo that will reflect some version of where they died."

She thinks about Liddy. About the shadows and shapes. About the dark woods, and the alleyway, and all the other flashes she's gotten since the accident. If these are really moments of Liddy trying to reach out, really glimpses of where she is now, then . . .

"Liddy's not at the harbor anymore," Casey says.

"What?" Red and Malakhi say together.

"It's been six weeks," Evan snorts. "You thought Liddy, of all people, was just going to sit around, waiting to be rescued? That's the most un-Liddy thing ever."

"Hush," Malakhi tells him, throwing up a hand.

"If she's not at the harbor anymore, then where is she?" Red asks.

"I don't know," Casey confesses. "An alleyway near some buildings, last I saw. I didn't recognize it."

"She's moving," Red says. He looks to Malakhi. "Wandering."

"Brilliant," Malakhi grumbles.

"What?" Casey asks.

"She's wandering," Red says again.

"So you said," Evan retorts.

Red rubs his temples. Apparently, they've just given him a headache. "Haven't you ever heard that you're supposed to stay put in one place when you don't know where you are? It makes it easier for help to find you."

"What are you saying?" Casey asks. "That Liddy's lost?"

"I'm saying...yeah, that's more or less it. She's wandering through other parts of Limbo. Through deaths that belong to other souls."

"You'll have to track her," Malakhi says firmly. "Through these other places until one of them leads you to the girl." He turns on his heel, sweeping toward the door. "And, Red?"

"Yes?"

"Don't make me come back down here."

SEVEN

CASEY WAKES UP slowly, reaching for her phone before her eyes have even opened fully. She grapples for it through the fog of sleep, but her fingers grasp pebbled bits of carpet instead. *Carpet?* She cracks one eye open. This is not her bed—her backache attests to that—and certainly not her room.

It takes her a moment to get her bearings—remembering their visitor last night, his warning words, and Evan's decision to make camp at the base of Michael's statue instead of in the basement.

You know I think this protective rock business is a load of crap, he'd said. *But considering there are angels crashing through the ceiling, I figure we need all the help we can get.*

She's stiff as she rolls over onto the flattened jewel-tone carpet, sort of like she's a visitor in her own body, and she has to break it in again.

Beside her, Evan snores lightly, the sound getting caught in the back of his throat. One arm is tossed over his eyes, blocking out the light that peeks in through a hole in the domed part of the church ceiling.

She shifts up, leaning against the base of the marble statue. Michael towers over them, a stony and silent guardian, his marble sword held between his hands

Compared to last night, the church is a completely different place.

Under the daylight that streams in through broken stained-glass portraits, it looks like some secret, fairy-tale hideaway with carved pillars of marble framing the center aisles and tall, arched windows spilling color onto the floor. Moss climbs the walls in shades of lime green, and pools of water from last night's rain reflect the light high along the walls. A bird sings somewhere in the rafters.

Through a tangle of hair, Casey spies Red by the altar. She gets up and pads over to him. He wears a long, silver chain around his neck, the end tied off in a knot around his feathers. They look so soft, it's hard to envision them as the sharp weapons he'd wielded yesterday against the obsii despite having held one herself. Red barely stirs as she approaches, caught up in thoughts of his own.

She clears her throat. "Are you okay?" she asks when he looks over.

"Just thinking."

"About last night?"

He hums.

She tilts her head back to look at the light-dappled dome

overhead. "Kind of nice here, isn't it? In an old, rustic, antique sort of way. Liddy would have appreciated it."

"Did she have a fondness for churches?"

Casey shakes her head. "For pretty things." She remembers being about eight, maybe, buried in the sand up to her waist while Liddy decorated her mermaid tail with sea glass. Washed and rinsed in the sea, each one sparkled under the sun in teal blues and pale pinks, with the occasional iridescent oyster shell in the mix. Liddy grinned at her treasure. She'd always had a knack for finding the pretty things in life.

"What are you thinking about?" Red asks.

Her lips twist into a small, puckered smile. "Just memories. You know, my life was far less complicated before you showed up."

"It won't always be," he says. "This complicated, I mean."

Somehow, it sounds like a promise, though Casey doesn't believe him. "Anyway, that Malakhi guy was really ... intense," she says.

"He has every right to be," Red says. "We were as close as brothers. Family always takes it the hardest when they think you've betrayed them."

"Did you?" she asks quietly.

"It didn't feel like it at the time, but perhaps I did. Things always look different after the fact."

"What did you give it all up for?"

The corner of Red's mouth lifts into a kind of mournful smile. "A girl."

"Oh," Casey says. She looks over at Evan, sleeping beneath the scratchy church quilt. Her heartbeat kicks up. Was keeping him around a mistake? Was she dragging him toward a danger he couldn't understand—one *she* didn't even fully comprehend yet?

"What happened to her?" she asks.

"I made a choice," Red says. "And she chose differently." He swallows. "But that's all in the past now."

She recognizes someone vying for an out when she hears it, so she changes the subject. "How are you feeling? Did you heal okay?"

Red lifts the edge of his shirt. The skin is unmarred. No scar. Not even a raised red bump.

"Whoa," she says. "You were serious about the whole healing thing." She studies his mismatched outfit as he fixes his shirt. "You know, if you're going to hang around for a while, we might need to go shopping. Get you a proper change of clothes."

"A shopping trip, huh?" Evan says, climbing to his feet. "Does that mean we're all friends now?"

He walks over, stretching his arms behind his head, the muscles in his arms bulging against the cuffs of his shirtsleeves. Once upon a time Evan was that lanky, gangly boy who'd trip on air walking down the hallway. Then he found volleyball. "Admiring the guns?" he says to Red. He winks and strikes a pose.

Red snorts but it's Casey who has to look away quickly, feeling warmth touch her cheeks.

"Don't let it go to your head," Red says. "You'll tip over."

"Oh, angel-boy has jokes, does he?" Evan claps his hands together. "And here I thought you lot were supposed to be the best of all of us."

"We are," Red says. "It's not that hard."

Evan yawns and rubs his eyes. "It's too early for this kind of thing. I need sustenance to keep up with your level of sass."

"We need to eat," Casey agrees. "And change." She feels gross and sweaty and exactly the way she imagined she'd feel after sleeping on the floor of an abandoned church, clutching a statue for protection. "I need to shower."

Evan throws his hands up. "I didn't say anything."

She nudges him, smiling at his teasing. "Come on. Let's—"

The low wail of sirens begin outside, drawing closer and closer, the sound reaching a peak, then receding as the sirens scream down the street outside the church. It's followed closely by another.

Evan sticks his finger in his ear, rotating his jaw. "Police chase?" he guesses.

"Because there are so many high-speed car chases here," Casey says sarcastically.

The sirens fade eventually and Evan inclines his head to the door, swinging the keys to his truck around his finger. "Shall we?"

Casey and Red follow Evan out the side entrance and down to his truck. The three of them pile in together and Casey feels bad when she momentarily wishes it was Liddy and not Red on her other side.

They don't get very far before Evan has to pull over to let a fire truck go racing past. It spits dust behind its massive tires as it swerves between the traffic.

"Wonder what that's all about," he says as they start down the road again.

The sound lingers and Casey rubs at her ears, trying to get the ringing to stop.

As they near the beach, the traffic is stopped in both directions, cars wedged bumper to bumper. Red stiffens beside her, his fist drawn up to his mouth, eyes locked on the dashboard so intently Casey knows he's not really seeing it. On her other side, Evan shields his eyes from the sun as he leans out the window to try and see past the traffic ahead of them. "Looks like every emergency responder in town."

Casey rolls her eyes at his enthusiasm, wondering if some boys ever grow out of their love of trucks and sirens. The flashing lights spiral in the distance, red and blue strobes dancing through windshields and windows.

Evan opens his mouth to say something when a group of kids on bikes race along the shoulder of the road toward them from the direction of the sirens. He throws his hand out to flag them down.

A lanky teen skids to a stop, his tires chugging on gravel.

"Hey!" Evan says. "What's going on down there?"

"Accident in the crosswalk." The teen casts a wary look over his shoulder.

"Oh, damn," Evan says. He drums the steering wheel, then glances in Casey's direction.

The lights flash so fast, putting her in a kind of trance, and she has to close her eyes to break it.

A breeze blows through abandoned kiddie swings that border a giant play structure that boasts two yellow plastic towers and glossy blue monkey bars. Dozens of footprints carve up the sand where buckets and toy scoops wait to be played with.

Casey snaps her eyes open, brows drawn together.

"What is it?" Evan asks.

"What did you see?" Red asks.

"I . . . just—" She turns to look at him, blinking once. Behind him the woods dip down, stretching into the beach.

She knows it without even seeing it. The blue water touching the horizon. The reaching sand dunes, spiked with grassy bushes and the bravest of dune-jumping children.

"Casey?" Evan says, but his voice is distant as the entire world around her fades. The divide between her and Evan, mere inches of space, feels like a canyon suddenly. Like he isn't sitting right beside her, but worlds away.

There it is again: *The sprawling green lawn surrounding the park, the empty neighborhood street.*

Red seems to breach the divide, calling her out of it, and suddenly she's back in the truck, pushing against him until they both spill out the passenger door. Casey whirls around. Her stomach lurches as recognition bleeds over her, a shiver racing down her spine, rooting her to the spot.

It's Liddy.

"What are you doing? Get back in the truck," Evan calls, reaching his hand out for her.

She registers his confusion, a question on the tip of his tongue.

"You saw something, didn't you?" Red says.

"Liddy. We have to go. We have to get her. Now!" She tugs on his arm.

"Not here," Red says, looking around at the stalled cars and wandering eyes that find them out of boredom.

"The church," Casey decides. It's the closest. Plus they'll never get through the police blockade right now.

"Hang on a second. Casey, wait!" Evan yells.

"I have to go," she says, already nudging Red in the direction of the church.

"Wait!" he says again, scrambling out of the truck after them. A couple of cars roll down their windows, braving the heat in order to listen to the exchange.

"What is it?" she hisses under her breath. "I have to go."

He gestures from them to the truck. Then something else passes over his features. A kind of realization. "You're going somewhere I can't follow."

"Evan—"

"I already lost Liddy."

"Nothing is going to happen to me," she says.

"But we don't know that." He grabs her hand. "We don't know how any of this works. What if you just don't come back from wherever this Limbo place is?"

"I have to try." She works to untangle their fingers, but Evan holds tighter. "Evan, please," she begs.

He squeezes—once, twice—then lets her go. "I know . . . just be careful, I guess."

"I will." She backs away, in the direction of the church, away from the sirens and lights and the gathering crowd of cars and people. "I'll come find you later."

"No, I'll come. Just let me turn the truck around."

Casey shakes her head and his face falls. She knows she's hurting him, but what if it's dangerous, this Limbo place? What if she unknowingly invites Evan there, into a danger he can't see or control?

She can't risk it.

"Go home," she tells him. "I'll find you when it's finished. I promise."

She knows it doesn't mean much. Promises like that are easy to make, but so much harder to keep. Liddy had promised her an epic pre-senior-year road trip. She'd promised to help her figure out what this thing was between her and Evan. In fifth grade, she'd even promised to always be Casey's best friend even if they had to live far away from each other and could only talk on the phone after their homework was finished. Look where all those promises had gotten them.

Evan stares at her, lost in the commotion of traffic. It's an odd feeling. The sense that she's leaving one friend behind in order to save another.

Casey turns away and sprints down the side of the road with Red. She runs, feet slapping the pavement, kicking gravel up behind her. Red's chain of feathers bounces against his chest. She pushes on, until the bottoms of her lungs burn from exertion. Pushes and pushes before she can lose the wispy figments in her mind.

Before Liddy disappears again.

Red gets there first and he races around the side of the church, his hair spilling around his face, framed in the arched doorway like some sort of ancient deity: the kind painters and sculptors used to covet in their artwork.

She's breathless when she arrives, bent over, hands on her knees.

He reaches for her.

"Just—" She snaps her mouth closed, tasting bile, and holds up her finger instead. "Give me a sec."

He nods and snatches a feather from the chain around his neck. In his hand it turns to the hard, steel dagger she'd watched him wield last night, etched with faint decorative veins. It's as if metal had been smelted from the feather's core and forged into a weapon in the fires.

Inside the church, against the raised stone steps in front of the altar, Red slams the feather turned dagger into the marble floor and carves a circle around himself. The blade leaves a faint white glow in its wake, and Red stops just short of closing the loop. Light streams in from above, painting him in spots of green and gold. Casey hovers on the edge of the circle, her pulse rushing in her ears.

Her hands shake against her thighs.

She can do this. She *can*.

Red holds his hand out to her. "We should go now."

Casey's eyes trace the length of the circle. Big enough for two. "And those things—the obsii—they'll be there, too?"

"It's hard to say. Limbo is vast and distracting, even for creatures like them. But I won't let anything hurt you, Casey. Trust me."

She takes a steadying breath, reaches out, and lays her palm in Red's outstretched hand, allowing him to pull her into the space. Then he closes the circle with the dagger.

Immediately, Casey feels the lurch beneath her feet, tearing her from one world and into another like she's been sucked into some sort of dark vacuum.

When she sees the light on the other side, she's already

moving. Falling, really. She rolls over herself, arms and legs twisting, down the side of a short hill. She tucks her body as she spins, then comes crashing to a stop. Her back takes the brunt of the hit; head spinning, she sits up and brushes grass from her elbows and knees.

At the top of the hill, Red stands, peering down at her. He takes a knee, slams his dagger down, and carves into the ground.

"What are you doing?" she calls.

He slides the blade in an intricate pattern. "Sealing the doorway," he says simply, like it's the most logical thing in the world. *None of this is logical*, she wants to remind him. "We don't want anything leaving that isn't supposed to."

She watches him through squinted eyes, still trying to catch her breath.

Yellowed grass crawls up the side of the hill, weeds bending around Red's feet as he makes his way toward her. He slides to a stop beside her, though he manages to stay on his feet the entire time—a rather more graceful entrance than her own.

Casey frowns at him, throwing her hand up to shield her eyes from the sun heating the ground beneath her. Red lowers his arm, hand held out for hers.

She reaches for it, yanking herself to her feet. "Next time can we choose a less energetic entrance?"

"That's not up to me. We were following your tether to Liddy, to the last place she was."

"And when we leave, is it going to spit us out into the church?"

"If you leave through the same spot you entered; if not, Limbo could spit you out anywhere."

"'Cause I'm not tethered to anything?"

"Exactly."

"So, hypothetically, it could spit me out in Europe or somewhere else just as cool?"

"Like the middle of the ocean," Red suggests drily, and Casey feels herself pale.

"Okay, bad idea noted," she says, scanning their surroundings. It's the park from the vision she had. The yellow towers stand like flagpoles in the distance.

"For you, Limbo really only has two rules," Red says. "Leave where you enter, for already discussed reasons, and *always* seal the doorway. On both sides."

"Both sides?" Casey says.

"Once on the inside. And again when you exit."

Simple enough, she thinks with some uncertainty. Exit where you enter. Seal the door. Keep those dark, shadow things contained.

"This is . . . I think this is the park behind Main Street," Casey says, recognizing the baseball diamond where she used to watch Evan's games. It's been years since she's been here and she doesn't remember the playground ever being this big. Apparently, it's gotten an upgrade. "That means Liddy was here, in this part of Limbo, right?"

"Yes, it seems she wandered through this death. Perhaps even interacted with the soul it belongs to."

"Do you think she's still here?"

"You tell me." He trudges forward, cutting a deep line through the tall grass. "You're the one who can hear the dead."

"Right, yeah," she says, following after him, "but how do I—"

Red waits expectantly for her question but she's distracted by the faint sound of singing. It's pulled to her on the wind, whimsical and soft, like a child humming under their breath.

She follows the sound to the playground where a little boy comes into view. She hesitates upon seeing him.

"What is it?" Red asks. He's standing so close his arm presses against hers, almost in support.

"He's so young," she whispers. "Can't be more than five or six."

"Death knows no age, Casey."

Of course, she thinks. Or else Liddy wouldn't be here either.

The boy, with his tufts of brown hair and cheeks reddened from the sun, sits in the sand, flicking piles of it into a bucket. He works his shovel until the bucket is full, flipping it over with both arms wrapped around. He lifts the bucket to reveal a castle. Slowly, the sand melts from formation, the small castle collapsing into a tiny lump.

She can't help but smile at the frustrated turn of his mouth. Wrinkling his nose, he sets out to try again.

"Hello," she calls, stepping closer. Red hovers a few feet behind her, eyes trained on the street that runs parallel to the park.

The boy turns, staring up at her. "It's not working." He huffs. "That girl made this one really tall," he points to a shaped pile of sand that still carries the designs from the bucket, "but this one won't work at all."

"That girl," Casey says quietly as the boy begins filling the bucket again. "What girl?"

"There was a girl," he says, "big like you." He points down the street with the shovel. "She came from over there."

"And where did she go?"

The boy giggles into his hand. "Not telling."

Casey glances back at Red. He flips the dagger back and forth, eyes scanning. There's nothing that feels inherently dangerous here, barely a shadow except for their own. Red must think the same thing because in the space of a single breath, the dagger quivers and into the air floats a feather—far less threatening.

Casey sinks down beside the boy. "What's your name?"

"Henry."

"Well, Henry, this is very important. I need to know where the girl went."

His lips twist mischievously, but the look melts when his sand castle falls apart again.

"How about we make a deal?" Casey says. "I'll help you make a perfect sandcastle if you tell me where she went."

"Okay!" Henry agrees eagerly, handing her a scoop.

If this is what it takes to get Liddy back, Casey thinks.

"The trick to sandcastles is that they work better if the sand is wet," she says. She looks around until she spies her prize. Picking up his bucket, she carries it to the water fountain at the edge of the playground and fills it. Then she brings it back and pours it down into the sand between them.

Henry reaches into the hole, splashing in the water with a giggle. His eyes are curious as he leans around her shoulder, looking at Red who waits patiently, sitting on a bench, puffs of breath keeping the feather dancing in the air. Henry's lips break around a gap-toothed grin.

She wonders if he can sense what Red is.

"All right, hand me that shovel," she says.

Together they fill the bucket with moist sand, and Casey bounces it on the ground a few times to get the sand to firm up. It's been years since she's made a sandcastle, but she'd spent most of her childhood on the beach with Evan and Liddy. Before teendom had consumed them, they had spent hours by the water together, carving entire cities out of sand. She'd forgotten how much she enjoyed it—the gentle rush of the waves, the warm breeze, the quiet focus required to place the castle exactly right. Evan would certainly be jealous if he could see her now, stealing back some of that unknowing innocence.

"That's a good one!" Henry shrieks, clapping his hands together as Casey lifts the bucket and reveals a much sturdier castle.

"I told you, water does the trick."

Henry starts to fill the bucket again. "You must have built lots of castles."

Casey laughs. "A fair few."

"Is this where you live?"

She pauses halfway through helping him fill the bucket. "No."

"Oh." Henry makes a fish face at her. "Then why do you have so many toys?"

She glances beneath the play structure, noticing for the first time all the abandoned toys covered in sand, some buried like ancient relics, others neatly laid out.

"I—" she starts. "They're not mine."

"You must have lots of friends then, but I'm the only one here right now." He sighs, almost grumpily, looking down the street.

"Now will you tell me what happened to the other girl?" Casey asks him.

He tilts his head to regard her, like he's still considering it, but then he nods. "She said she couldn't stay. She had to get back."

"Get back to where?" Casey asks.

He shrugs. "Home, I guess." He climbs to his feet and dusts the sand from his knees. "I'm ready to go, too."

Go where? she wonders. She looks to Red. "Liddy's not here anymore."

"She's already moved on," Red agrees. "Before we even got here by the sounds of it." He watches Henry.

"We can't just leave him here," Casey says. "I want to help him. I can do that, right?"

"You're a Limbo-walker. You can navigate these paths better than I can."

"Right. Okay," Casey says, turning back to Henry. "Do you want your toys?"

"No," Henry says. "I'll leave them. Maybe someone else will come later and you can play with them."

"That's really nice of you."

"Mommy says I have to share." He skips a little as they walk toward the street. On the way, he fills his pockets with rocks, his shorts making a *click-clack* sound as they walk.

When Red joins them, Henry hands him a smooth white rock that glitters when it catches the sun.

At the crosswalk, Henry hesitates, looking around nervously. "I'm not supposed to cross the street by myself." He wiggles his fingers at her. "You have to hold my hand."

His palm is soft and warm, his small fingers curling around her larger ones. There isn't a car or a person in sight, but Henry looks diligently back and forth, back and forth.

Holding his hand, Casey is struck by something so powerful it almost doubles her over.

Accident in the crosswalk, she hears the teen say on repeat inside her head.

Had Henry been that accident?

With a steadying breath, Casey leads them across the road and through the seemingly deserted neighborhood. Each house stands boxy and colorful, but as silent and still as a picture. She watches the windows for signs of movement. For a sign that they're being watched or pursued. She doesn't know if it's her imagination that moves the window drapes or one of those strange, mindful breezes, so she focuses harder, but all she can hear is the tread of their feet. Until—

"Stop," she says. "Wait a second."

"What is it?" Red asks.

She shivers, and like it's alive, a gust of wind rips toward them, carrying with it the hollow shrieking sound of the obsii.

Red looks around for the source of the sound, feathers melting to daggers in his fists. The sound moves though, twisting and shifting, until it's hard to pinpoint the source.

Henry drops her hand and slams both palms over his ears. "I don't like this house," he cries.

"This is wrong," she agrees, grabbing Henry under the arms and hauling him up on her hip. "We have to keep moving."

They do, hurrying along the sidewalk, the sun beating down in hollow rays between the massive trees that line the road.

"I like this one better," Henry says, wiggling out of Casey's arms suddenly and hopping in place when she slows in front of a gated property. "It's nice."

She draws closer and squeezes his shoulder encouragingly. "Me too."

At the center of the property is a small house, surrounded by the kinds of wildflowers that stretch almost to her elbows. There's a tire swing and potted window plants. Birds chirp, bursting from the grass, and the flutter of honeybees makes the air around them buzz. Casey stops at the low, white iron gate that surrounds the property. From inside, she can hear the swell of voices. Warm, rich timbers and airy sopranos. There are too many voices to break up the conversation, but it's the kind of sound that draws you in. Laughter, mostly. All right behind the door.

Henry stands on the swirling metal loops at the bottom of the gate, studying the house. "Can I go in?"

She looks to Red but says, "Yes. If you'd like."

"Okay!" Henry shouts excitedly. He jumps off the gate and pushes inside, running down the path to the porch. His clumsy hands pull on the doorknob until it opens and he turns back to her once, smiling before heading inside.

His disappearance is sudden, here one second and gone the next. And though he should be just beyond the door, Casey senses he's somewhere much farther, the voices that greeted him gone now.

"He'll be okay, right?" She wraps her hands around the gate, which is warm beneath her palms.

"You don't have to worry about him," Red promises.

She lets go and turns away from the house and the white iron gate, heading back down the sidewalk.

Red catches up with her. "What's wrong?"

"He saw Liddy," Casey says. "Talked to her. We were so close."

"And we'll get close again." They reach the park, crossing the field to the gently peaked hill. "I know we didn't find Liddy, but you did a really good thing here today."

"Yeah," she sighs, looking back over her shoulder. The sun crawls across the playground, casting the castle they built in shadow.

"What is it?" Red asks.

She tips her head back so she can see him. "There are a lot of toys down there."

THEY ARRIVE IN the church in a gust of wind that sucks all the oxygen from her body. Casey collapses in a heap above the marble steps, gasping and clutching her head like she's just been shot through the air dryers in one of those drive-through car washes.

Red bends, carving those strange symbols into the ground, then offers her a hand. "It gets easier."

"Says the angel-boy."

He stands above her, tall and strong against the backdrop of the altar. For a moment, he looks like a warrior, some heavenly being sent down to defend the earth. The image breaks as he pulls her to her feet, and dissolves as he rubs at the back of his head with a look of indecision.

Casey reaches into her pocket for her phone. It flashes at her once, then the screen goes dark—dead battery. She sighs. "I need to find Evan. Let him know I'm okay." She's already heading for the exit, eager to be outside, when Red catches up.

There's a second set of tire tracks outside the church, like Evan had come back despite her telling him to go home, to find that she'd disappeared. Literally into thin air. The truck is gone now, though, only the marks of where the tires spun left behind.

"Guess we're walking," she says to Red, starting onto the shoulder. They walk the same path they'd run earlier, eventually past the place where they'd been stopped in traffic. The fire trucks have cleared out, but a few cruisers remain. Yellow caution tape surrounds the scene of the accident. Casey nudges Red and they cross the road, eerily quiet now.

But when they pass that playground, with its swings and towering yellow spires, Casey averts her eyes, a sick feeling rolling around in her gut. She can still feel the weight of Henry's small hand in her own and it makes her want to fold over onto the sidewalk. Whether she wants to cry or throw up after that is still undecided. The thing that comforts her is knowing Henry is safe on the other side of that gate now. At least he's not wandering like Liddy.

The closer they get to downtown—a stretch of road sandwiched by brightly painted restaurants, decorated glass shop fronts, food stalls, and picnic benches—the busier it gets. Casey figures all the drama this morning has scared most of the tourists away from the park and the beach and into the shops and restaurants.

Red looks left and right. "Are you hungry?"

"Is that a question," she asks, "or a subtle way of telling me *you* are?" She's still disoriented by it all and food seems like the farthest thing from her mind. On one hand, she's shaken by the realization that, like Liddy, Henry is no longer a part of this world. But on the other, she'd held Henry's hand in hers. Talked to him. Sat under the playground and built sandcastles with him.

Casey had helped him find his way across Limbo. She knew he was okay, even if no one else did. Now if she could just get to Liddy as easily. It seemed they were no closer to finding her than they were before Casey knew about Limbo and angels and everything else.

"The business of saving souls works up an appetite," Red says.

Casey glares at him. "Don't put that on the business card."

He's not wrong, though. She should eat something even if it's bound to taste like sandpaper in her mouth. She fishes in her phone case for some cash, then they join the line in front of a food truck parked by one of the art galleries.

"Not very catchy? What about as the slogan on a food truck?" Red says, reading the menu painted on the side of the truck.

"Do angels even cook?"

"It's not a foreign concept," Red says, studying the menu. "We were human once. Though only those who have fallen are required to sustain a corporeal form."

"Why is that?"

"Because without my wings, you and I share more in common than I would like—the need to eat and sleep for starters."

"Think highly of humanity, don't you?" She steps up to the order counter and asks for two hot dogs.

"It's not that," Red says. "It's just harder." He brushes his finger along the side of one of the feathers that hang from his neck. "Everything about what I am is tied to my wings. Without them, I'm weaker. That's not a feeling I like."

Casey studies him while she waits for their food. The woman in the truck hands her two foil-wrapped hot dogs and Casey shoves the cash across the counter.

She hands one to Red and he moves to the condiment bar, drowning his hot dog in ketchup.

"When did you die?"

"Getting personal now, aren't we?"

She takes the ketchup from him. "You know when *I* died. *How* I died."

Red looks up at the back of the art gallery. There's a giant, multicolored fish with bulging eyes painted against the bricks. "Angel-human privilege," he says.

"Did I sign some sort of confidentiality agreement I don't remember?" She takes a bite of her food. She almost burns her tongue, but finishes half of it before they even reach the sidewalk again, starving all of a sudden.

"I know what's necessary to help you. That's all."

"Was it a long time ago?" she says, licking ketchup off her finger.

"Yes."

"A *very* long time ago?"

He avoids her question by taking a bite and chewing.

"Give me a time period," she says. "Twentieth century?"

"Not quite."

"Before then?"

"Give or take fifty years."

"The eighteen hundreds?"

"Memory's a bit foggy, but I figure about then. It *was* a long time ago."

Casey tries not to let the food roll out of her mouth as she stares at him. "Do you remember it?"

"My life?" he asks. "Or my death?"

"Either . . . Both?"

He considers it. "Pieces of it, I suppose, like everyone else. There are memories of my family. Of a time before. And then after."

"When you became an angel?"

"Yes."

"Does everyone who dies become—"

"No," he says. "Not everyone."

"Then how do you—"

"Can't tell you that," he says. Then he laughs. "In case you go blabbing."

"Who am I going to tell?"

"Evan, probably. He already knows far more than he's supposed to."

"It's not my fault those things attacked us while Evan was around."

"So you're telling me that you never would have told him any of this otherwise?"

"I don't know. Probably not."

Red shakes his head, snorting in disbelief.

"What?" Casey demands. "How else would I have explained you or Limbo or even what's going on with Liddy to him?"

"People will believe more than what you think." He lifts his chin. "So, what's the deal with you and Evan, anyway?"

"There's no deal," Casey says, frowning.

"I meant *between* you . . . you know, feelings."

"We're just friends." She balls up the foil wrapper in her hand and throws it at him. "We've always been just friends."

"I may be the oldest person you know," he retorts, "but even I can tell when there's something going on."

"You might also be the most annoying person I know," she deflects as she turns down Evan's street.

Red laughs quietly to himself.

When they reach Evan's house, they climb the porch steps and Casey knocks. And waits. And knocks. And waits.

"Maybe no one's home," Red says.

Casey points to Evan's truck parked on the street. "He's home. Let's go around back."

"Breaking and entering?" Red says.

Casey unlatches the gate and walks up the deck to the back door. It slides easily. "Just entering," she says. "Evan?" she calls as they step into the kitchen.

The kitchen is dark, just like the dining room and living room. She walks down the hall, spying Evan's shoes at the front door.

"He's probably sleeping," she says but when she turns around, Red has his feather-daggers in hand. He twists slowly, following some invisible path across the ceiling.

"There's something here," he whispers.

Casey's stomach lurches and she races up the stairs.

When she skids into Evan's bedroom, clutching the door-frame to keep her balance, the darkness feels different, and Casey hesitates at the edge of the room, waiting for her eyes to adjust. A sinking feeling pools in her gut, climbing up her throat like bile. Something else is in the room.

She finds Evan's pale features, the long limbs and rumpled clothes on the comforter, and then she sees it, black shifting against the black.

Lanky, crooked fingers fall across Evan, stroking his skin. She follows them up to that humanoid face, reflecting something dangerous.

"Get away from him!" she screams.

EIGHT

THE WORDS TEAR from her throat.

Fear and panic and anger explode inside her limbs, flooding them with adrenaline. She grabs in the dark for the first thing she finds. Whatever it is, it's heavy, weighted on the bottom. She throws it as hard as she can, sending it sailing toward the shadow-figure. There's the shrill cry of a wounded animal, that desperate, decaying sound of the obsii, and then Red flicks the lights on behind her.

The obsii, whether destroyed or having fled, is gone. Casey's arm trembles with the force of the throw as Evan, awakened by noise, scrambles off the bed.

"Flamin' hell!" he shouts. He notices Red. "Flamin' *heck*," he amends. He stands there, plastered against the wall, eyes wide with fright. "Casey? What's going on?"

She just dashes across the room and throws herself into

his arms—into the familiar circle of strength and warmth—and squeezes until she thinks her heart might burst.

"You're alive," he says. "Limbo didn't swallow you whole or anything." His eyes widen as he pushes her back to see her face. "Liddy! Did you find her?"

Casey shakes her head.

"She was already gone when we showed up," Red explains. "But we were close."

"Oh . . ." Slowly, Evan bends to pick up the pieces of the Little League trophy that she'd pulled off the shelf and thrown. He holds the little gold figurine in his hand. "Wait, what just happened?"

What feels like hours later, they've worked their way downstairs and the conversation has shot in so many directions Casey is having trouble keeping it all straight.

"But where did it go?" she demands. "That . . . obsii thing. What happened to it?"

"So the soul just poofed?" Evan says from his spot at the dining room table, clearly following a different train of thought.

Casey turns to him. "I mean, it didn't just poof into thin air, but yeah, he just sort of walked through the door and disappeared."

"Wow, that's nuts."

"Just like that thing sneaking in here?" She crosses the room. "I don't even know what it would have done if we didn't come in right then."

"But you did come in," Evan says.

"And threw a Little League trophy at it."

He lifts his shoulder. "It was a participation trophy. I never liked it anyway."

"I shouldn't be around you," she says slowly, the thought dawning on her all at once. Evan had been perfectly fine until she'd gone looking for him again. "These attacks, I'm dragging you into them."

"No, Casey. Don't even go there."

"We shouldn't be here." She gets to her feet, glancing at Red. "Right?"

"That's up to you. I'll go wherever you choose."

"But it's putting him in danger, right? Me being around him?"

"Don't answer that!" Evan says stubbornly to Red as he rises to meet her. He sweeps both of Casey's hands into his.

"I'll let you two talk a moment." Red wanders into the living room. Casey chooses to ignore the look he gives her over his shoulder.

She turns back to reason with Evan. "It's way too dangerous. You didn't see that thing. It was about to turn you into some kind of snack."

"Safety in numbers," he argues. "Isn't that a thing?"

"At, like, summer camp and on field trips and stuff! This is none of those things."

Evan's entire face relaxes into that easy way of his. "No, this is definitely worse than camp, but not as bad as that time we went to the zoo to study biomes for biology class. People were wild. That kid zapped himself trying to climb into the camel exhibit, remember?"

She feels the indecision in her body—in the tense form her

shoulders hold, in the focused way she breathes in and out, but something seems to melt. Perhaps it's the barely there hum that escapes Evan's throat as he pulls her into a hug. Then he gives her a gentle, nudging shake as if saying, *It's okay to laugh. It's okay to find something a bit funny in the middle of all the chaos.*

"I don't know," Casey breathes against his chest.

"Say yes," he pleads. "Say 'Yes, Evan, I'll stay.' C'mon." He tugs on her arms. "Text Karen and tell her you're staying over. We'll make peanut butter sandwiches and camp in the living room like we used to do when we were ten."

"That's your big plan? Liddy is trapped somewhere in the afterlife and dark creatures are sneaking into your bedroom and you want to eat sandwiches in your living room?"

"Uh . . . yeah." He ticks the next words off on his fingers. "Shelter. Sustenance. A defensive position while you wait for Liddy to make contact again."

"This isn't a joke, Evan." She pulls away but his hands tangle around her.

"I know. Hey! *Hey*, I know. Look, I'm just trying to help, okay?" He shrugs. "It's the best I can do seeing as I'm just little old me. No superpowers." He looks into the living room where Red's studiously examining the remote controls. "Angel-boy, you hungry?"

"Yes," Red says.

Casey grumbles. "I just fed you!"

"There," Evan announces. "It's settled. You stay the night here; we can fortify this place like Fort Knox if it makes you feel better."

"Fine," she huffs. Honestly, she doesn't have a better plan. And if it's not Evan who's in danger because of her, it'll be her aunt, unless she resigns herself to spending the foreseeable future living in an abandoned church. At least Evan's already in on her secret.

"Good." He puts his hands on her shoulders and steers her toward the counter. "I need a sous chef in the kitchen."

The kitchen is small, with minimal counter space, so they cram together side by side at the cutting board. Evan pulls a stack of plates from the cupboard and hands them to her. A green vine with blue flowers circles the ceramic.

"Where are your parents, anyway?" Casey says.

"One of those nonrefundable last-minute vacations to some island I can't remember the name of."

"You didn't want to go?" she asks, smoothing jam across a piece of bread.

Evan slaps some peanut butter on another slice. "They booked it for me. Thought it might be good for me to get out of town for a while."

"Then why did you stay?"

He shrugs. "Because you were here. I didn't want you to be alone after . . . you know."

"Bet you're starting to regret that right about now," she retorts. "You could be somewhere with white sandy beaches and tiny umbrella drinks and giant floppy hats."

"Never," he says. "Though I do like a giant floppy hat." He lifts his slice of bread and drops it onto hers with the sandwich-making precision that comes from not knowing how to operate the stove properly. He raises his brows in a *look at that* motion.

She shakes her head. She won't let herself spiral down the fantasy rabbit hole. Projecting *what if*s and *maybe*s and *might be*s. *Keep your head*, she tells herself. Getting emotional right now, when Liddy needs her most . . . it can only end badly.

But then Evan smiles at her, a twisty, half grin with just a bit of teeth and all jawline. It makes her giddy to the very tips of her toes.

"I'm glad you stayed," he says quietly.

"Me too."

When did it get like this between them? When did Evan turn from a friend—a *best* friend—to someone who makes her heart beat to the tune of cheesy pop ballads?

She cuts the last sandwich in half, putting it on a plate, then takes it and heads into the living room before she has to give herself an answer.

Red is still attempting to navigate the contraption that is Evan's entertainment system. She snatches the remote from his hand and puts a plate in it instead. "Let me," she says. "You'll end up in space before you figure out how to change the channel."

Red inhales half the sandwich in two bites.

"Anyone gonna need seconds?" Evan calls, poking his head through the doorway.

Red gives him a thumbs-up, mouth stuck together with peanut butter.

"Bet you never thought you'd be here doing this," Casey says, leaning over the back of the couch.

"The price of my fall," he says. His head turns toward the ground, casting his face in shadow.

Her breath leaves her in a rush as the image of Red hurtling toward the ground plays out in her mind. It had taken on a kind of comical impression before, but now it conjures an image of intense fear. Watching the ground draw closer and closer must have been a terrible sight, even if he hadn't been harmed in the process.

"I'm sorry," she says, not knowing what exactly she's apologizing for, but recognizing how heartbroken he sounds.

His laugh is resigned, drawing up short. "There are worse things to be, I suppose."

"Are there for your kind?"

"Yes. Without a doubt."

"And how do you . . . get back?" She struggles to find the right words. "When are you no longer fallen?"

"When I earn my wings back. Until then I'm grounded." He smirks at his own joke and hands her his empty plate.

Casey clutches it against her chest. Are Red's wings riding on her finding Liddy? Is that the price of his freedom from the ground?

"Hey!" Evan calls from the kitchen. She looks up and he gestures with his head for her to come into the kitchen.

When she meets him, he hands her a plate with a sandwich with the crusts cut off. She trades him for Red's empty plate, which he slides onto the counter.

"You know I outgrew my phobia of crusts on sandwiches, right?"

"Lies," he says.

She looks down at the bread, peanut butter bursting over the edges.

"What's wrong?" Evan asks. "No good?"

"It's not that," she says. "The sandwich is fine."

"Then what is it?"

"What if I can't do this?" she whispers. "What if I can't find Liddy?"

He takes her plate from her and slides it onto the counter beside Red's. Then he folds his hands over her arms, rubbing up and down until her skin is warm from the friction. "Stop thinking like that."

"I'm just being realistic."

"Nothing about this is realistic. It's not even reasonable. We're dealing with something completely out of the ordinary."

"What does that mean?"

"It means you can't screw it up."

"*No*," she says slowly, dragging out the word. "I think you'll be surprised to learn that I can."

"You actually can't. We don't know how any of this works. There's no precedent. There's no rules or guidebook or handy info packets. All you've got is a fallen angel who can't even hear Liddy."

"But—"

"But nothing," he says. "I know you're not a quitter and that you'd run to the ends of the earth to get Liddy back," he says with a shrug. "That's just what you do."

"Thanks, Evan," she whispers.

"Good enough?"

"Good enough."

He pretends to wipe sweat from his brow. "Good, because my uplifting speech reserve is tapped. That's all I had in the tank."

He makes a face and Casey bursts out laughing.

Her heart flutters in an unusual way, only really sticking out in her mind because these days she's functioning in a state of constant fear or anxiety. But this isn't the desperate race of her heart as she faces off against dangerous, nightmare creatures or as she tumbles into some dark, in-between world chasing Liddy. This is lighter . . . like a butterfly has landed upon her chest, brushing its wings over her skin.

The flush in her cheeks is warm, the rush of her blood, hot.

Her pulse hums beneath her skin as Evan's head tilts, tipping closer. She steps onto her tiptoes, places one hand along his cheek. Her hand traces the edge of his jaw before feathering into the hair at the back of his neck, and his arms loop around her waist, pulling them together.

And then his forehead dips, his brows knotting above his nose. His eyes lift, looking over her shoulder and his fingers tighten in the fabric against her hips.

"Evan—?"

"Move!" he shouts, knocking her out of the way.

She catches herself against the counter, taking the hit against her ribs. Casey turns to see the slender stretch of shadow. Behind that she can see Red hurdle over the back of the sofa like a track star.

Evan smacks the obsii hard with a frying pan and the creature soars backward toward Red, who punches his arm out to drive his dagger directly through the creature. It melts around his hand, covering it in wispy black tar.

"Damn, these things are everywhere," Evan groans.

"I wondered where that one had gotten to," Red says.

"It's drawn to me," Casey says, worry beating away inside her. "I can't stay."

"We're not doing this again," Evan says. "You're going to stay."

"And what, stay awake all night?"

"We'll sleep in shifts if we have to," he says. "You're not going anywhere." He drops his hands to his hips. "We're going to *Home Alone* the shit out of this place."

"WELL, IT'S NOT exactly bandit-proof, but I think it might do for some soul-sucking shadow leeches." Evan lines his baseball bat up against the wall in the living room, looking around proudly.

Casey turns on another light switch. "Do you have any more lamps?"

"I think we ran out of outlets." He rubs the back of his neck. "You really think we need another light?"

"It makes me feel better," Casey says, glancing from corner to corner. "The alternative is sleeping in a church every night."

"Yeah, no thanks," Evan says. "Knocked it off the bucket list. Don't think we need to repeat it. Creepy statues. Creepy angels." He glances at Red. "No offense, but your buddy isn't what I would call 'people-friendly.'"

Red stretches out along the length of the couch. "Malakhi isn't bound to the church. There's nothing stopping him from coming here next time."

"Next time?" Casey says. She sits up from her pile of pillows and comforters on the floor.

Evan crawls into the sleeping bag stretched out beside her, poking his head out. "Uh, no. The house has a strict one-angel-per-night policy. My mom would be pissed."

"Malakhi doesn't exactly take orders."

"Well, he hasn't met my mom."

Casey closes her eyes and tries to sleep to the sounds of Red and Evan bickering until one of them starts snoring and then sleep seems to drift further away.

Morning arrives slowly, dawn creeping into the room beneath the frayed drapery that hangs from the window; it dances in the cold air that escapes from the vent below the window frame.

Casey watches for shadows, but none come. The night had been filled with short bouts of sleep, always disturbed by the smallest noises. The dripping of the bathroom tap. The click of the air conditioner. The slide of car tires outside. Each one became a nightmare in her fever-like dreams. The drip of water turned to the steady ooze of blood that had dripped from Red's wound. The *tick-tick-tick* of the air conditioner became the clawing pursuit of some rotting creature. And the tires, their sliding scuff transformed into the pull of dark, shadowed limbs upon the ground.

Each time Casey had bolted out of her sleep, Evan had lain next to her, eyes open, staring at the ceiling. Even now he's awake, the whites of his eyes rimmed red. He's unnerved by it all. He'll never admit it because he so desperately wants to be a part of this with her, but she can tell.

She reaches across the divide between them, searching for Evan's hand in the tangle of blankets. When she finds it, she gives it a gentle tug. "You okay in there?"

"Just lost in thought."

"Didn't think you had any thoughts."

He yawns, then nudges her in the ribs. "Oh, you got jokes, huh?"

She grins, rolling away from him. "If I asked you to run away with me forever, would you?"

"Yes."

She rolls back curiously. "You don't even want to think about it first?"

"Not really." Evan closes his eyes. "Do you want to run away?"

"What I really want is a shower and a change of clothes."

"Then let me take you home." He sits up. "I'll grab something for Red to borrow. Can't be toting around a stinky angel."

The car ride is quick. There's no traffic yet, only the occasional early-morning dog walkers and joggers.

With her first step inside the town house, Casey shivers as the air-conditioning catches her full blast; Karen is oblivious to the cold. Red and Evan pile in behind her as she kicks off her shoes and looks for the telltale signs that her aunt is home. Her stethoscope and keys are missing from the front-door hook, but there's a note from Karen taped to the fridge.

Brownies. Enjoy. It's circled with a heart.

"I'm going to shower," she says.

"I'll help myself." Evan goes straight to the fridge. Red follows him.

"Boys," Casey mumbles under her breath. She grabs a change of clothes, locks herself in the bathroom, and steps under the warm spray, helping herself to copious amounts of strawberry-hibiscus-scented shampoo and some very bubbly body wash. When she's done, she wraps herself in two fluffy towels and brushes her teeth in front of the mirror. This is usually the kind of thing she does with music blasting; now it just feels like a chore that she's rushing through. The dark circles under her eyes only serve to remind her of how little sleep she's gotten these past couple of days. Weeks, really, if she thinks about it. She hasn't slept right since *that* night.

Girl, throw some concealer on that, inner Liddy says.

Casey ignores her.

She dresses in clean clothes, runs a brush through her hair and pulls it into an easy ponytail.

When she gets back to the kitchen, Red and Evan are downing glasses of milk like thirsty men in the desert.

"Aw, Case," Evan mumbles around a mouthful of chocolate fudge. "You gotta have one of these."

She picks up a fork and takes a piece right out of the pan. Her aunt really is a good cook.

"Shower's free," she says to Red. He takes the rolled-up bundle of clothes borrowed from Evan and heads down the hall.

"You smell like a strawberry milk shake," Evan tells her, tugging on the end of her ponytail.

"Hope that's not one of your better pickup lines," Casey says, covering the brownie pan with plastic wrap and putting it back in the fridge.

Suddenly, she realizes that this is the first time she's been alone with Evan since yesterday in the kitchen. Since their almost-kiss was interrupted by some shifty creature. Ugh . . . *wow*. What is she doing trying to kiss him? What is she doing with these feelings? *Feelings are the worst*, Casey decides.

Everything just sucks.

Except the brownies. Those are okay.

"So," Evan begins awkwardly, letting the word hang there between them.

Casey wants to close her eyes, count to ten, and hope this moment disappears into oblivion. *So what?* she wants to ask him. *What does it all mean? Where do we stand now that there are all these tipsy, bubbly, confusing feelings in the way?*

But she doesn't. She doesn't ask him anything. She just smiles a bit, too much lip and not enough teeth.

It's moments like these that hit her the hardest: Liddy would know what to say.

"Shore Fest starts this week," Evan says, cutting straight into her mopey self-chatter.

"What?"

"Down on the boardwalk," he explains like they haven't been going to Shore Fest every year since they were toddlers. "You know . . . food . . . fun . . . fireworks."

"I hadn't realized," she says, resting her head on her hand where she's propped against the island counter.

"Yeah, I wasn't going to say anything considering the current circumstances, but . . . I mean, maybe this will all be over by then. Or maybe it won't . . . but that doesn't mean you stop living in between, right? It's good to get out. To do normal things."

"Normal," Casey repeats.

"Yeah, you know . . . Wait, not that you're not normal anymore. I mean, you did die. And you can talk to dead people . . . Can you talk to dead people? Well, they talk to you at least. But that's fine, you're still you. What I meant was—"

He stops talking.

"You okay?" Casey prods.

"Yeah, I just ran out of breath."

"Well?" Casey asks when he's had time to recover from his bout of babbling; something so uncharacteristically Evan that it's caught her interest. Granted, Evan likes to talk. He's good at it. Communication is one of his better skill sets. But rarely does he babble for no good reason.

"Well, what?" he asks, blinking owlishly at her.

If there were crickets around to chirp, it would happen about now. Casey resists the urge to drop her head into her hands in frustration. Instead, she looks him in the eye.

"What did you mean?"

"Oh! I wanted to know . . . I guess I just wondered if maybe . . . if you wanted to go with me one night. When you're not busy trying to save Liddy's soul or anything like that. I mean, I get it. Priorities, right?"

Casey's lips pucker, fighting a grin at the eager look on Evan's face. At the way he clutches at the counter, doing push-ups against it while he waits for her answer. He's fidgety and it's kind of endearing.

"Shore Fest," she says.

"Yeah."

She nods. "Sure, why not?"

"Okay," he says letting go of the counter and stuffing his hands in his jeans. "Great. I mean, yeah. It'll be great."

Casey moves the dishes to the sink to give her something to do with her hands. Why does this feel different from every other year? From every other weekend or weekday? Why does it feel like he's asking her on a date?

Because he is, dummy! her inner Liddy squeals.

Casey squeezes soap into the sink. The bottle sucks in air as the last of the soap spirals through the water. She puts it on the counter and crosses into the hall closet for a new bottle, quite aware of Evan's gaze on her. It makes her nervous all over, but in a good way.

In a way that makes her heart stutter. She tries to control the smile, to reel it back into something semi-normal.

As she touches the doorknob, the world around her fades. *Harsh fluorescent lights. Whitewashed hallways. Signs promoting hand hygiene and one of those automatic hand sanitizer machines.*

She closes her eyes, trying to capture the already fading images.

"Casey?"

A circular desk filled with patient charts divides a forked hallway. On the corner of the desk sits a stuffed bear wearing a white T-shirt. It reads: ST. MARGARET'S UNIVERSITY HOSPITAL.

That's the same hospital Karen works at.

Casey!

"It's Liddy," she says, letting go of the knob like it's burned her.

"Where?" Evan says. "Now?"

The bathroom door opens and Red steps into the hall, toweling off the dripping ends of his dark hair.

"We have to go back to Limbo," she says to him.

He drops the towel on the counter and strings the chain of feathers around his neck.

"What can I do?" Evan asks. "There must be something. I can help. I can ..."

She takes his hand in hers, fingers laced together. "Go somewhere else. Please. Somewhere busy, with people and light. So I know you're safe."

Evan tries to pull away, to dismiss her worry. "They're not after me, Casey."

"Please," she begs him with all the urgency she can muster. If there was ever anything that frightened her as much as losing Liddy, it was now the thought of putting Evan in danger. Especially when that danger is something he can't hope to fight on his own. "Go somewhere they can't hurt you," she pleads, fingers squeezing his. "That's how you can help me."

"All right, fine," he says, but the look on his face is torn, the struggle between what he wants and what she wants clearly at odds. "I'm going. I'm going."

NINE

RED GRASPS THE edge of the coffee table and pushes it toward the couch, leaving an empty space in the middle of the living room. He kneels on the carpet, carving the circle into the ground, hesitating long enough for her to join him inside. She waits for the uncomfortable, squeezing pressure of Limbo. It strikes Casey as what it must be like to go through the spin cycle in the washing machine.

They arrive in that strange in-between place, pressed against a door, a bright light visible against their shoes. The door opens against Red's shoulder and they spill out beneath harsh, industrial-standard lights.

Aside from that, the white walls, paint-chipped handrails, and poorly waxed floors tell her she's in a hospital. Casey recognizes the tiny stuffed bear from her flash of vision. She takes it off the nursing station, looks it over, then puts it back in exactly the same spot. It's a hospital, all right. Only different. The constant mumble of nurses and patients, the whine of machines, even the dull buzz of the elevator—it's all eerily quiet.

Red looks up and down the hall once, then turns around and carves the protective markings into the utility door that secures their entrance and exit.

Casey wanders down the abandoned hall, brushing her hand along the laminated public service announcements on hand-washing, flu outbreaks, and the signs of stroke. She pushes against the release bar on the stairwell door, but it doesn't budge. Next, she stops at the elevators and presses both buttons multiple times with the incessant impatience of a toddler. Neither lights up no matter how forcefully she jams her thumb against it. She lays her ear to the dinged-up stainless-steel door. Not even a hum from the motor.

"Casey, wait!" Red hisses, finishing his work quickly and running to catch up. He hesitates as they approach the end of the hall, putting his hand out before pulling ahead of her. He peeks around the corner first, then cocks his head, and she falls in step beside him.

"Liddy was here," she says. "The bear at the desk, it's the same as in the vision I saw."

Ahead, there's a howling kind of sound, like air being forced through a small, confined space. It isn't the usual hospital noise, and that's what draws her to it.

Beside her, Red's eyes dart left and right, taking stock of every closed patient room. He pops the doors open, doing a sweeping check of each one before closing them again. When they get to the end of the hall, he reaches for the last knob but Casey catches his hand.

"Not yet," she says, pressing her ear up against it. Soft murmurs echo from inside. Voices press together, then part, not quite in song, but something awfully close. It reminds her of the door Henry had disappeared behind, and she pulls away.

As they round the next corner, where she expects to see another whitewashed hallway, they find the side of the building blown out, wind whipping through shattered panes of glass. *That explains the howling*, Casey thinks. Plant life climbs up the rubble and wreckage, curling around bits of stone and rebar. A kind of dystopian wonderland come to life.

"What happened here?"

"It's a *version* of where the soul died," Red says. "That doesn't always match the physical world."

She leans forward, caught by Red at the last second and yanked back from the edge. "I wasn't going to fall," she insists.

His fingers tighten against her shirtsleeve. "I know."

Casey stares over the edge of the building. Rubble piles up the side like some sort of forgotten staircase. Below sits a grove of trees, limbs spread as if waiting to catch her.

"What do you think?" Red says.

Casey clicks her tongue. Rooms are empty. Elevator's broken. Stairwells locked. "I don't want to, but I think we have to go down there. If Liddy is still here, in this part of Limbo, it's not up here."

"If you say so," Red says. He hooks his dagger in the loop of his pants to free both hands for the climb.

"So, we're just going to freehand this, then?"

"I forgot my climbing gear," Red deadpans. "And last time I checked, still no wings. So unless there's a secret escalator around—"

Casey glares at him, stepping to the edge of the building. "You're not funny."

He takes a step forward, dropping down to a platform that looks like it once belonged in a doorway. Red bends his knees, testing the stability of the platform. It trembles under him.

"Can you not do that!" Casey snaps.

Red flashes a perfect set of teeth at her. "Scared of heights?"

"No."

"Good."

Casey follows Red onto the platform, bracing herself, hands clutching a rusty piece of rebar above her head. It's slow moving. Every step sends bits of rubble shifting and Casey has visions of the debris collapsing beneath them and both of them hurtling toward the ground.

"Are you?" she asks when they've made it to the halfway point. Even halfway is too high.

"Am I what?"

"Afraid of heights." She slips on a piece of glass, arms shooting out as her leg slides off the concrete blocks they're crouched on.

Red nabs her by the collar of the shirt, holding her steady. "Only when I'm falling."

"Well," Casey says, heart hammering. "Let's avoid that."

"Touché. I try to keep the falls to once a century if I can."

Casey focuses more intently on her footing, but she's intrigued by Red's comment and can't help prodding. "You're talking about the actual fall, aren't you?"

"Oh yeah, the big one. Straight down through the clouds. Not as fun as it looks. It's like an ice bath inside those things."

"So you've fallen before," she says. A statement, not a question.

"Don't look at me like that," Red replies hotly.

"I'm just—"

"Shocked? Speechless. Disappointed in my moral character? You'll have to get in line for that one."

"Trying to figure out why," Casey finishes.

"Angels fall for many reasons. It's not exactly a science, the things we do. Even *we* make mistakes."

"They'd have to be pretty big mistakes," she says, doubling back at the look he gives her. "I'm guessing . . . you know, to go through all the work of . . ." She flaps her hands like wings.

"Your charades game needs some work."

"You know what I mean," she says exasperatedly.

"Of course I do."

"So, was it always for the same thing?"

"Sometimes."

"Didn't learn the first time? Or—"

Red stares straight down. "Sometimes there isn't a choice. Protecting humans is a messy job. You wouldn't believe the kinds of things you get involved in."

"Why would you be punished for something like that?"

"Because there's always a better way." Red says it like he's imitating someone. "You know how it goes. Rules. Ancient and unbreakable."

"So you break it—"

"—you buy it," Red says. "A one-way ticket to ground-town." He reaches up to help her off a high ledge.

"Was this time the same as the others?"

Red hesitates. He doesn't look directly at her, but she doesn't miss the way his back tenses, shoulder blades sticking out sharply. "No, this time was different from the others," he says quietly.

His voice is strange, lost to her in a way, and she doesn't know what to say to get him back. It's almost a relief to reach the tangled moss at the bottom of the debris mountain.

Almost.

Above them now the hospital looms, a relic of the human world that doesn't belong here. As if in answer, the plant life is slowly consuming it.

"It doesn't look as bad from down here," Red says.

"Remember that when we're going back up." Casey steps into the grove of trees, noting how the earth softens beneath her feet, a kind of black tar oozing around her shoes with every step.

Red pauses as his feet sink into the sludge and he immediately summons a pair of daggers, twisting them over his palms as if to ready himself. "I don't like this place," he says.

"Welcome to the club." Casey presses her hand to the bark of one of the trees as a warm breeze passes around her. The bark beneath her fingers softens and when she pulls her hand away, that part of the tree is completely black, almost charred. Yep, *bad news*.

The farther they walk, the worse it gets. Fruit and flowers litter the ground, boiled and blackened, rotting flesh about to burst. It smells sweet and sour at once—life and death at odds.

"It's sick," she says as soon as she realizes. "Like an infection."

Red drags the tip of his dagger through the sludge-filled moss. He rubs the sludge between his fingers, inspecting. "That's exactly what this is. You still think Liddy is here?"

Liddy . . . hang out somewhere like this? *Not a chance*, Casey thinks.

"Didn't think so," Red says at the look on her face.

"Wait," Casey says suddenly. "Hear that?" She whips around, following the sound of muffled tears.

"Casey, slow down," Red warns, trudging after her.

She doesn't; she can't. Not until she finds who the voice belongs to. She trips once. Then twice. Hands sinking beneath the moss. She wipes them on her pants as she stands. The voice is closer now. Close enough it ping-pongs between the trees.

Casey twists in a slow circle. Then she stops.

The tears belong to a girl; it's not Liddy. That instant realization makes her entire body sag like a weight, but then something else takes over . . . something like relief.

The girl is about her age, maybe, and gowned in hospital garb. The blue-speckled cloth drapes over her thin knees, and her hair hangs in scraggly strings around her face. Bruises dot the inside of her elbows and the backs of her hands, almost as dark as the circles that shadow her eyes, giving her a haunted kind of look.

Casey offers a small wave as she approaches.

The girl huddles near a tree, glancing past Casey to Red, her eyes trained on the blades in his hands.

"It's okay," Casey calls. "Don't be afraid. We won't hurt you."

"I'm sorry," she whimpers, looking around, terrified. "I don't know what I'm doing here." She sniffs, wiping her arm across her face.

"Don't be," Casey says. "What's your name?"

"Melanie," she answers before looking up at the towering remains of the hospital. "I . . . I don't know what happened," she sobs. "I don't want to be here anymore."

A tightness spreads across Casey's chest. She wonders if Liddy is sitting somewhere like this, head pressed into her hands, overcome with confusion and tears. She kneels down in front of the girl. "Melanie, have you seen anyone else here? It's really important. A girl, maybe? With blond hair?"

Melanie shakes her head. "It's just me. I've been alone since . . . since . . ."

"You don't have to be scared," Casey says again.

"I can't help it," Melanie blubbers, tears clinging to her eyelashes. "It's this place, I can't get out."

Casey's entire body stills as Melanie casts her eyes around, and it only takes a moment for her to realize that there's something trapping her here. Beginning like a trickle of water along her spine, Casey's senses wake, sharpening where they were dull and heightening where they had simply existed. She whips around, watching a pair of shadows crawl across the ground toward them.

"Red!" she cries, pushing to her feet to warn him, but it's too late. One of the shadows rises in a wave, crashing a tsunami of black sludge over him, pushing Red to his knees and choking the air from his lungs.

She watches in horror as the other shadow moves, climbing up the tree bark before shooting out. An obsii reaches with its long stretch of limbs to wrap around Melanie's ankle. Sobs bubble out of her, painful and afraid.

Casey stumbles back as Red lets out a frustrated roar, watching the other obsii crawl over his back, forcing him into the moss turned quicksand. He forces his head above the surface, and for a moment Casey sees only pain. Not fear, just pain.

She lunges for his dagger, a sliver of steel and silver trapped in the sludge. She wraps her hand around the hilt and swings. The strength of her lunge sends her sprawling toward Red, cutting into the obsii.

The blow frees Red, and he pushes up on his hands with a growl, shucking sludge and moss from his shoulders.

Casey turns back toward Melanie and throws her entire body weight at the second obsii, slicing into shadow. Black goop splatters across her face and in her hair.

She lets out a triumphant cry as the shadows scatter, and then Red is there, pulling Melanie to her feet.

"This way," Casey says, heading for the hospital. They have to get out of the trees.

Melanie cowers under the shade of the debris mountain, digging her heels in. "No," she whispers. "I don't want to go back there."

Casey looks from her to the building above. This is where

Melanie spent the last days of her life. Of course she doesn't want to be there.

"Can you trust me?" she says to Melanie. "I know you don't know me, but I can help you. I promise. But we have to go back up there."

Melanie staggers, containing her tears, but nods.

Together, she and Red help Melanie climb the makeshift staircase, holding her steady when stone and brick and metal shift beneath her.

Once inside the narrow white hallway, Casey moves ahead, pressing her ear against the closed doorways, searching for the one with the voices.

Finally, she slows, her hands warm against a door, her heart skipping, not in fear, but in recognition.

"Is this the one?" Red asks.

"Yes," Casey says with certainty as a bubbly laugh spills from beneath the door. She looks over with a smile, realizing too late that she's the only one who has heard it. "This is it," she tells Melanie with confidence.

"I just . . . I just go inside?" Melanie flattens her hand against the door, sliding it down toward the knob. Slowly the bruises begin to fade from her skin, the shadows disappearing from her eyes, the delicate marks of past pains becoming nonexistent.

Casey's words catch in her throat at the sight. She clears it. "Whenever you're ready."

"And you . . . you don't get to come?"

"Not this time," Casey says. She gestures toward the door. "Go on."

Melanie does, pushing inside, and Casey turns away as a light steals her sight, blinding her with an intensity that makes her bones shake. The door closes with a soft *puff*, and she jumps when Red places his hand on her shoulder.

"She's gone," he says. "We can go."

Casey spares one more glance down the hall, wondering how close she was to Liddy this time. With a nod, he leads her back to the door that holds their exit.

She relishes the pressure that pulls her back to the physical plane and the feel of firm ground beneath her for a split second before she tumbles to her knees. Red carves the sealing mark into the floor. On her hands and knees, Casey watches the glow fade and notes the black sludge caked under her fingernails.

She heads to the bathroom, turning on the taps with her elbows. Hot water spills over her hands and she rinses the muck away, furiously scrubbing the dirt from beneath her nails, all while watching the black water rush down the drain

When she looks up from the sink and into the mirror, Red fills the doorway behind her. His hair is loose around his face, his clothes mismatched and too short in places because they're Evan's, black splotches staining his skin. Even now, as he stands there, he looks like some sort of fairy creature; some impossibly beautiful and knowing being that's appeared right when her life is in shambles. The sight of him only makes it harder to process. If there were really beings like Red to offer protection, why did terrible things have to happen?

"You're upset," he says.

Hands now clean, she splashes water on her face. "I'm fine."

"Why are you upset?"

She grips the edge of the sink. Untangling the thoughts in her head seems almost impossible. "I just . . . Every time we miss her, it feels like it's by an inch or a second. Like we've passed each other without knowing, and it reminds me of that night."

Red steps into the bathroom, closer to her, his hand moving but never quite reaching her shoulder.

She spins to face him. "You know, one second we were in the boat and the next the water. And somewhere between then and the next morning she was dead."

Red looks torn, not broken or sympathetic, but like he can't bring himself to tell her otherwise. Like he's stood in her place before, lost it all, and had nothing good to offer. No condolences. No soft promises. Just exacting truths.

Casey hugs herself like it might hold in the emotion. "I helped that girl today because when I saw her, I thought it was Liddy at first. I couldn't shake the thought that it would be me letting her go all over again. It's all I can think about . . . that night . . . leaving her behind."

Red swallows hard. She can see the veins in his neck bulge with the effort. "Casey, I—"

"Why can't I remember what came after?" When Liddy's hand slipped . . . no, not slipped . . . When Casey had let her go because the current was too strong . . . What happened next? Why had she been lost and Casey saved?

"You went through something very traumatic."

"Stop," she says, already annoyed with his words.

If she could have held on longer or tighter, would Liddy still be alive?

"It's true."

"Don't say the same things as every other person, Red. You're not the same as any other person."

"I don't have the answers you want, Casey. Sometimes we lose the people we love." His voice turns soft, his words almost a whisper. "And you can give up *everything* for them. But they are still lost to you. Not even angels hold a monopoly over life and death."

TEN

CASEY'S AWOKEN THE next morning by incessant knocking on her door. She rolls out of bed and narrowly misses putting her foot down on Red's head by toppling into a kind of unbalanced triangle above him with one foot stuck straight up in the air.

He opens his eyes and stares at her. She watches his brows go up, then down, then draw together, creating one long line of confusion.

"Stay very quiet," she whispers—not unlike the first time she'd snuck him into the house. She pads across the room and opens her door just enough to squeeze out. Karen's standing in the hall, so close Casey almost smacks into her before she can utter good morning.

"Oh, you are here!" Karen says. "Good." She's dressed in scrubs, but her feet are bare and her hair is already hanging loose around her shoulders, something that only happens after a shift. "I've been calling you all morning."

"You have?" Casey says, pulling the door closed. "I...I thought you were working this morning?"

"I worked nights so I'd be around today. It's the open house. Remember?"

"Open house?"

"Yes. That thing called high school that I force you to attend. You know, pick up your senior schedule, talk college applications, meet with your guidance counselor."

Casey resists the urge to whack her palm against her forehead. She hasn't exactly been keeping track of the calendar. "Yeah, yes." She snaps her fingers. "Right. I'm just getting dressed now."

"Hey, bestie!" Evan calls, appearing at Karen's shoulder. He wears the widest smile she's ever seen. It stretches his face until she's unsure of whether it's gotten stuck. "It's open house day! That thing we do in the middle of summer because we have nothing better to do."

Casey gives him a look. An *are you okay?* kind of look.

Karen glances between them. "You two get stranger every day."

When she walks away, Casey yanks Evan into the room with her and closes the door. Red's still sitting on the floor, hunched over in some kind of stretch.

Evan breezes by them both. "No call! No text! Even a letter by carrier pigeon would have been acceptable," he proclaims dramatically, his tone completely different now that Karen's gone. He flops down on Liddy's favorite purple beanbag chair in the corner of the room, arms crossed. His entire face puckers into a grumpy wrinkle. "I fell asleep with my eyes open staring at my phone. I swear my home screen is burned into my corneas."

"Good morning," Red says to him, rubbing a hand over his face.

Evan reaches beneath him to free a stuffed heart-shaped pillow they won with Liddy at Shore Fest last year and chucks it hard at Red.

Red tilts his head just an inch and the pillow sails by him.

"Good morning my a—"

"Anyway," Casey says loudly.

"No, not 'anyway,'" Evan says. "You don't get to disappear on me and then not let me know that you got back okay. I spent half the night wondering whether I was going to have to lie to Karen about what happened to you while she plasters your face on milk cartons and billboards and bathroom stalls at the airport."

"We don't have an airport."

"You know what I mean!" Evan shouts as he points a finger at her.

"All right," Casey says waving both hands in a *calm yourself* motion. "I'm sorry. It was a lot yesterday and I fell asleep."

"Obviously," he snaps, then rubs his hands over his knees trying to soothe himself. "So, what's up with the Liddy situation?"

"No developments," Casey says. "She's *still* lost. The link between us is *still* open. And now we have to go spend the afternoon pretending we care about which college we're applying to next year."

"So we're going to school?" Red says.

"I'm going with Karen," Casey says, standing in front of the mirror tacked to the wall beside her closet. She turns to Evan. "I need you to bring Red just in case."

"Why doesn't he just do that"—he waves his hand around—"veily thing and we all ride together?"

"I don't want to lie to Karen any more than I have to," Casey tells the mirror.

"Fine," Evan says, glaring at Red. "But I'm not getting you breakfast, so don't even ask."

Casey pulls her hair to the top of her head and twists a hair tie around it, catching the loose strands with a few bobby pins. Wearing yesterday's now-rumpled T-shirt and shorts is giving her a convincing bohemian summer look. The kind that says *not trying too hard*. Though in her case, she's not trying at all.

Clearly Evan's not quite over his earlier feelings. Annoyance threads through everything he says—and doesn't say—as he pouts at her from the beanbag chair.

She sticks her tongue out, trying to get him to smile. She knows she should cut him some slack; if the roles were reversed, she'd be going out of her mind trying to figure out how to maintain a friendship—a *more than* friendship—that, as far as he's concerned, is quickly becoming a second-rate priority in the face of this angelic mission. That's not what she means to happen.

She sighs when Evan doesn't take the bait. Every part of her wishes she could go back to the day of the accident, to a time before. When Limbo was just a fantasy in books she'd read and Red was just a stained-glass portrait in old church windows. When they still had Liddy.

"I'm going to get Karen," she says before she can dwell on it too much. "Give us five minutes before you leave."

She doesn't wait for a response, just slips through the door, pulling it closed.

It swings open again before she reaches the stairwell.

"We're okay, right?" Evan's head sticks out between the door and the frame, a floating ball of boyish apology.

"Yeah," she says.

Something in his features softens. "You'll get her next time," he says.

Before she can let her emotions run away, she hurries down the stairs, meeting Karen in the front hall.

"Ready?" she asks, impossibly chipper for someone post twelve-hour night shift.

"You bet," Casey says. She throws her hand up halfheartedly and cheers, "School."

Karen chuckles, tossing her arm around Casey's shoulders and giving her a squeeze.

They get black-tea-and-blueberry lemonades on the way there and a breakfast sandwich that drips grease onto her jean shorts. Casey wonders if Evan's earlier threat about no breakfast is actually going to fly with Red. Now that she thinks about it, she wonders what level of awkwardness they'll achieve between them during the ride to school. Part of her is sorry she's going to miss it.

Karen clears her throat suddenly and Casey lifts her head, thumb jammed in her mouth. She licks the last of the cheese and egg and drops her hand to her lap.

"I just wanted to say," Karen begins, "that if you're not ready to see everyone yet, then we can go back home. I realize I didn't really give you the option this morning."

"You didn't exactly wrestle me into the car," Casey points out. "That was an independent decision."

"I've missed you lately. I don't know why it feels like we haven't seen much of each other. I swear I tried to take some more time off this summer."

"We see each other plenty," Casey tries to assure her. She wonders if this is the remnants of Red's veil wearing off, leaving Karen slightly confused.

"What I was getting at before, was that if you're feeling uncomfortable—"

"It's fine."

"I swear I'm a sympathetic person," Karen says. "I'm not trying to overwhelm you."

"I'm okay," Casey says, facing Karen long enough for her look to imbue some sort of false assurance into her aunt.

Satisfied, Karen smiles and Casey relaxes into the seat. *Parental-figure crisis averted.*

She's not okay exactly; everyone within the town line can see that. But she doesn't let Karen press her any further about it. She knows how much it means to her aunt that Casey's seeking out normalcy. That she's playing the part of the functioning teenager again. And after everything Casey put her through, she thinks Karen deserves that much. So she can play the part for a couple hours. *Get in and get out,* Casey mentally chants to herself. *And don't engage. How hard could it be?*

She sees the line of cars waiting to turn into the school. The billboard at the school entrance is decorated with maroon and silver balloons, the school colors. In blocky black font, the billboard reads: WELCOME BACK, CASEY.

She sinks down in the passenger seat, mortified.

Karen hums awkwardly but chooses not to comment, blowing by the sign as fast as she can with speed bumps every ten feet.

Once in the parking lot, Casey debates telling Karen that she's not getting out of the car. Maybe ever again. But then she looks at Karen, with her eyes shadowed after her night shift, hair a bit frazzled, still wearing her white nursing shoes. She's here for her. To support her. Casey can't let her down.

They get out of the car and wait in line at the sign-in table. The secretary, Mrs. Boyce, hands her a name tag and an itinerary for the afternoon. She holds Casey's hand for an extra moment, giving it a firm pat.

Casey walks away as soon as she lets go, then tosses her name tag into the first trash can they pass. They might as well write BACK FROM THE DEAD in flashing neon letters on it.

Footsteps hurry to meet her and Casey braces herself, but it's only Evan.

He nods to Karen, who pulls ahead, and he slows by her side. "I take it you saw the sign?" he mumbles.

"We're not talking about it," she says, hurrying through the front doors of the school.

"Right. Good. I mean, welcome back? Welcome back where? To school. From the dead?"

"Evan!"

"Right, shutting up now."

"Where's Red?" she asks, looking around for him in the familiar but vaguely distant crowds of students that gather in the atrium. It's like there's a bubble around her that says DO NOT APPROACH. Maybe she's put it there herself.

"Off somewhere pretending to be a student," Evan tells her.

"You just let him wander away alone?"

"Have you ever tried making that guy do anything?"

"Are you two fighting?"

"No, he just kind of got swept away in a crowd following the smell of grilled hamburgers and cheap potato salad."

Casey glares at him pointedly.

"I swear. We're cool. Guys don't brood in enclosed spaces," he says, reading her mind and looking offended at the same time. "That's a girl thing."

"That's not what I was thinking," Casey replies defensively.

Karen waves at them, pointing to a bulletin board with a map of all the locations around the school that are hosting college info sessions. Casey shoots her a thumbs-up.

"We stopped for food and I gave him lessons in pop music," Evan says. "Thanks to Radio 103's nineties' music hour, he now thinks the Backstreet Boys and the Spice Girls are competing for musical world domination."

"So you did get him breakfast."

Evan lays his hand against his chest. "I'm not a monster. But raising an angel in the city is expensive."

"This isn't the city."

"He eats a lot is all I'm saying."

"Oooh," Karen says, running over and rubbing her hands together as she shoulders her way between them with a smaller, laminated version of the map on the wall. "Where to first?"

Casey is less than thrilled by the choices. "I should probably go get my schedule since we're here."

"Maybe I'll pop into a few of the college booths," Karen muses. "We can divide and conquer. I'll bring you key chains and brochures."

"Sounds fun," Casey says lamely. Karen pats her cheek and walks away.

"And the barbecue started"—Evan pretends to look at his watch—"fifteen minutes ago on the football field, so that's where I'll be if you need me."

Before he can walk away, Casey snags him. "You just ate."

"I'm a growing child. My cells are still dividing. I *have* to fuel them." He rocks back on his heels.

"Can you please find Red?"

"But *free food*," he whispers.

"Evan, *please*."

"He's an angel with superpowers, how much trouble can he get in?" The look she gives him must change his mind because he touches her shoulder, letting his hand linger. "All right. And I'm sorry about earlier. I wasn't really mad at you. I mean, not *really* mad, you know. Just worried."

"I worry about you, too," she says softly.

"It's just the two of us now. We've gotta look out for each other and that's kind of hard to do when you're in another dimension."

It's the closest anyone's come to putting into words just how she feels about the dwindling pool of people around her. First her parents. Then Liddy. Even the universe must agree that she's not allowed to lose any more. Now she's not just a statistic. By these odds, she's just incredibly unlucky.

"Divide and conquer," Evan decides, echoing her aunt as he backs away. "I'll find angel-boy. You get your schedule. Meet you back here in twenty."

"Shh . . ." she hushes him.

"No one's listening." He laughs. "Didn't you hear me? There's free food."

Alone now, Casey makes a straight path for the front office. If there was one thing that singles you out in high school, it's standing alone in the middle of a crowded room. For some reason, it puts a homing beacon on your head.

"Casey, wait up!" Erica Mendara, the dance team captain for the past two years, jogs across the atrium to catch her. Her hair is tied into a bun at the top of her head, her Westwood track shirt stained with sweat. Casey wonders if they've already started tryouts for the new year or if they've just been performing last year's routines for the parents.

Casey had been on the team for about two and a half seconds back in freshman year. *It'll be fun*, Liddy had said. *It'll be something we can do together!*

Lies.

Casey shakes her head at the memory. Ask her to serve a volleyball? Sure. But ask her to point her toes and twirl in circles to a strong R & B beat? Nope. The coordination just isn't the same.

"Hey, girl. How's it going?" Erica says when she reaches her.

"Fine," Casey says. "You?"

"Awesome. I was just popping over for some advice. We were thinking of doing something at homecoming. Nothing too crazy. Just a little tribute to Liddy."

"Oh," she says.

"A few streamers. Some confetti. You know how Liddy liked to end routines with a bang."

"Uh—"

"What color?"

"Huh?"

"For the confetti cannon? We're going shopping this weekend."

"Purple," Casey says automatically. "Definitely purple."

"Thought so. Just figured I'd check with the expert. Thanks again, girl." She squeezes Casey around the middle and then skips off.

Erica's nonchalance about the whole thing makes Casey feel like she's just participated in some sort of shady deal. It also feels so permanent. Like they've already closed the door and said goodbye. Like Liddy isn't just across the room, still in Casey's head. *She's not gone*, she wants to scream. *She's still here.*

Lost in Limbo.

Casey walks toward the front office where a line is queued up for schedules and parking passes. While in the haze of missing Liddy, she wonders if Evan already got a parking pass for next year, because if he has, then she won't bother.

The line moves quickly, everyone eager to be out on the football field with friends or toting their parents around to make nice with the teachers they're going to schmooze for better grades this year or, in the case of the more academic few, actually engage with the college presenters.

As Casey steps up to the counter, her balding, mustache-wearing, motorcycle-riding guidance counselor, Mr. Depuis, grins at her before realizing it's actually her, and then his smile seems to short circuit.

Finally he settles on: "How's summer been treating you, Casey?"

Does he want her actual answer? Or does he expect her to give him the same *Fine, yeah, good* she's given everyone else? It's such a stupid question to ask someone after a tragedy. The answer is never going to be *good*. She just thinks people should stop asking unless they're prepared to hear that her summer thus far has been crap.

Her next thought is completely derailed into next year. On the paper in Mr. Depuis's hand she sees two words that make her insides shrivel into nothingness.

Lidia Courtland.

Plain as day. Written on the top of Liddy's schedule as Mr. Depuis licks his thumb and flips through the others in search of Casey's. It hasn't even been long enough for the school to take her out of the system yet. There's proof of it all over. And yet everyone is running around, planning little somethings, and asking her how her summer's been, like her best friend isn't buried in a cemetery two states away.

Mr. Depuis seems to catch the mistake on his second time through the pile and he delicately pulls Liddy's schedule from the others, holding it like an infected Band-Aid, and slides it facedown onto the table.

"Here you are, Ms. Everett. Glad to see you reconsidered taking physics."

Casey holds her hands out. Both of them. Cradling her senior schedule like a child as she walks away from the counter half numb, half filled with red-hot rage.

She keeps walking, ignoring the other students who wave her over or the sympathetic parents who try to offer some wise words that she's probably heard before. She wanders down the hall, intent on the solace that comes between the English and foreign language departments, the windowless stretch of lockers that don't stare or wince or wave when they see her.

Casey closes her fists, crumpling the schedule, before she jams it into her pocket. As she turns the corner at the end of the hall, the lockers disappear.

Grim evening rises up around her, crooked wheat fields climbing from the earth.

She stumbles against a bank of lockers. The doors pop open and bang against each other, crashing in response. Casey holds her temple, trying to memorize the vision.

A gate swings open in the distance, wood crashing against a metal frame.

"Casey?" Evan shouts and she looks up to see him and Red racing toward her. "What are you doing down here?"

Red reaches her first, but Evan loops his arm beneath hers, helping to keep her steady.

"Is it Liddy?" Red asks.

A packed-dirt trail weaves through the fields, hiding naked birch trees and robust evergreens among old rusted tractor parts.

"Not again," Evan hisses. "You just got back."

"It doesn't exactly have a schedule," Casey says. "Go keep Karen distracted."

"And what do you want me to do, huh?" He follows her down the hall as she traces the signs on the doors for one labeled CUSTODIAL.

Red throws the door open and steps inside.

"I don't know, Evan. Talk to her about college. Talk to her about anything. Just don't stop talking. You're good at that. It's why you're the distraction guy."

"I'm going to choose to accept all that projected frustration as a compliment and also let you know that this job sucks. FYI. Next time, I don't want to be the babysitter."

"Look, if you don't want to help, then just tell her it was too much and that I had to go." She steps into the closet. The entire room smells like old mopheads, stagnant water, and drain cleaner.

Evan throws his hand against the door, holding it open as she tries to yank it closed. "I'll do it," he insists, looking guilty and properly ashamed, "just hurry up and find her already. And when you do, tell her she's still a pain in the ass."

Casey pulls the door closed.

"And be careful!" Evan yells in the crack between the door and the frame.

ELEVEN

"ARE YOU SURE you're up for this right now?" Red asks.

Casey gathers herself, her arms trembling as she closes the door in Evan's face. She turns around and falls against it, leveling Red with her best glare. "Stop looking at me like that."

"Like what?" he says. "It's dark. You can't even see me."

"Like you expect me to combust or erupt or ignite or whatever other explosive metaphor you can come up with. I'm not going to crumble under the pressure."

"That's not what I meant. It's been a long couple of days, that's all."

"And Liddy's lived those same long nights and long days, alone in a place she doesn't belong. So yeah, I'm up for it."

"Just checking," Red says. He kicks a mop bucket out of the way, judging by the sound of wheels rolling across the floor.

A wooden porch, faded and chipped, comes into view. Footsteps echo. One. Two. Three. Slow and carefully measured. A pale hand lifts to knock on the paint-peeled door, then it coils back in … fear?

"Wait," Casey whispers.

"What?"

"Nothing. Let's just go. Now!"

She imagines the determined and steely look on his face, the quick, darting movements of his arm as he loosens a feather, dagger appearing moments later. There's a flash of heat as he drops to his knee on the cold linoleum floor and drives the dagger into the tile. It splits without effort or mess and Casey closes her eyes before the pressure swallows her whole.

Like a dip on a roller coaster after a climb, Casey's insides jolt. Before she even opens her eyes, she feels nauseous and jumpy. She glances around, eyes darting, taking stock of their situation. Limbo unfolds before them as an old farmstead. She doesn't recognize it, but somehow she senses the darkness that lives here. A darkness she has no intention of chasing.

Behind her, Red seals their entrance and for once she considers simply turning around and walking straight back through it.

The barn is washed with fading copper paint. Shingles and pieces of siding hang loose in places; in others, they're missing altogether. The barn door is jammed shut. One of the hinges is gone, so the door fits crooked. She turns away from the sight, but not before a scream rips from behind the door. Her heart jumps and she looks at Red, but he doesn't flinch. He doesn't even look at the barn.

Instead, his gaze falls to a series of animal pens; each of them abandoned and locked with wire.

Casey takes a few steps away from the barn and turns to study the farmhouse. It's in a similar state of wear, gutters bent and dripping onto the peeling white porch. A swing rests at one end of the wraparound deck, chains in a pile instead of hanging.

"This isn't right," she says, searching the grounds for any sign of Liddy. This feels too . . . *dangerous*. Liddy wouldn't come here, would she?

She sets off at a hurried pace.

Red jogs after her. "What do you mean this isn't right?"

On the house, the screen door bounces in threes each time a breeze whips by: a beat Casey can't shake from her mind. It makes her skin crawl, and she takes a deliberate step back, colliding with Red. To his credit, he barely flinches.

"I don't want to be here," she whispers. It's the same peeling door she saw in her vision and the same porch steps. Is this where Liddy had stood?

"I don't think anything wants to be here," he says. She tips her head up to see him. His eyes are wide, flickering constantly. Assessing. Calculating.

"This isn't like the other ones, Red." A hard breath escapes between her lips, vibrating them together. "It doesn't feel the same."

"Do you think Liddy is here?"

"She was," Casey says, sure of that much. "Maybe she still is." And if she is, Casey owes it to Liddy to find her. "How do you feel about a tour of the house?" She takes a bold step around him.

"I'm right behind you," he says.

It's three steps up the porch. She jumps up them, hand

ghosting over the chipped railing. A cold slither begins at her feet and slips up her back, using her spine like a ladder. It makes her want to crawl out of her skin. "I'm going to be sick."

His hand on her shoulder grounds her, calms her, like he's sent a bolt of his own assurance into her body. "We can stay or we can go. Either way I'd feel better if we weren't lingering out here," Red says. "Too many shadows."

Casey tries the door handle, finding it unlocked. Breaking the quiet feels like a bad idea, so they enter silently.

Inside the house, much of the furniture is covered in white sheets. In the kitchen, dust floats in pockets of gray light like tiny, hanging chandeliers. The rooms look unused for the most part, and she's beginning to think the house is, in fact, empty, until the floorboards creak across the ceiling and her eyes are drawn to a stairwell.

"Liddy?" she whispers, too afraid to call any louder.

Red steps ahead of her, dagger poised as they ascend the stairs.

She looks down more than anywhere else, determined not to make extra noise. Red seems to move with a seamless silence, as if he never quite touches the ground, but she can't hide the tread of her sneakers. She steps in the faded spots along the stairs, each move tentative. Her ears perk at every creak and groan the old house makes.

The upstairs narrows to a single, long hallway with a series of closed doors. There's nothing remarkable about it. Nothing particularly homey. Not a picture. Not even a shade drawn over the windows.

Casey turns to the first door, hand held out for the knob.

"Don't," a voice says, making her jump.

She yanks her hand back, her heartbeat hammering against her throat. The outline of a man takes form at the end of the hallway and Casey's insides give a terrible lurch. He isn't exactly young, but between the scruff on his face and the fact that he won't make eye contact with her, it's hard to tell how old. Thirties, maybe. And yet, it isn't his scruffy appearance that gives her chills, but the blood on his clothes.

He glances up quickly before turning his face back to the floor and Casey's suddenly filled with a lot of questions she doesn't ask.

What happened here?

What's behind the door?

Why is he covered in blood?

The questions rattle around inside her, but she doesn't ask a single one—it feels too dangerous. Even Red is subdued beside her, almost like he wants to blend into the walls. Maybe she's afraid of the answers the man would give if she did ask. Or maybe she's afraid because she already knows the answers to these questions.

Casey glances out the dingy, drapeless window that looks out over the property. The barn looms there as if calling out to them.

She shivers, looking back at the man. He rubs his hands over and over in front of him, but no matter how many times he does, the blood remains, etched into his skin.

"We should go," Red says. "Liddy's not here."

"Please don't leave me," the man says. "Those *things* . . . those creatures . . ."

"Casey," Red calls sharply, already halfway down the stairs.

She should turn around and leave the man. Turn around and forget she ever found him. Liddy had turned before she even reached the front door. This is not a good place.

But there's a tiny, nagging pinch in her mind. One that makes her gut bubble with guilt. If she leaves him here, something terrible might happen to him. And she'll spend days and weeks wondering. Thinking about the man she left behind and whether she did the right thing.

"Come with me," Casey tells him, taking the stairs without looking back to see if he follows.

Red looks at her curiously, but she says nothing as she passes him. Makes no excuses. She just heads straight for the front door.

Outside again, the feeling of unease grows, each step toward the barn making her pulse thunder. The whispers increase, like there's a group of people talking just behind the barn door, but their voices are frantic and harsh. Dread rises up inside her, a tremor of worry coursing through the blood that tingles in her hands.

Two sets of footsteps echo behind her over the wind: one, a shuffling clump of old, worn boots. The other is almost silent except for the rustle of leaves. That's Red. She doesn't turn to talk to the man, she doesn't even turn to look at him.

Something tells her to just keep walking.

They get to the barn and Casey yanks on the hooped door handle. It's caught at the door jamb. "We need to get it open," she tells Red.

He steps up beside her, pulling on the handle, one of his feet propped against the side of the barn for leverage. The door budges with his help, popping open an inch. An icy wind whips from inside.

A dark chuckle reverberates around them, and Casey stops tugging on the door, slipping in the mud. She tips her head, looking into the tree line beside them.

Red does, too. The sound wasn't in her head, then.

"We need to go," he says suddenly. Casey's never seen him so worried.

"No, we need to get this door open," she says, tugging on the handle again.

The man behind them cowers against the barn wall, clutching at his head as that low laughter bleeds through the air again.

Casey whirls around, trying to pinpoint where it's coming from. Something breaks in the trees, a stick or a branch. It's close.

Red tenses up beside her. "Run!" he gasps.

The man makes a dead sprint for the fields.

Casey charges after him, Red right on her heels. Stalks whip by her, slicing at her face as she pushes the wheat out of the way.

She fights it, emerging into a clearing with tall evergreens rising from the ground. Red bursts from the field near her.

"What's going on?" she asks, bent over, her hands on her knees.

A cry, ragged and hoarse, cuts the air and Casey realizes that the man has disappeared, lost somewhere in the fields.

"Casey, wait!" Red calls frantically, but she's already doubling back, trying to find where they lost the soul of the man she was trying to help.

Red catches up to her, cutting a path through the wheat stalks with swift swipes of his dagger.

There's another scream and Red's arm swings out, catching Casey across the chest before his hand snags her collar and pulls her to the ground.

She lands, pain shooting down her arm and a dull ache ringing at the back of her head.

"What the—"

Red hushes her.

Casey rolls onto her knees beside him, spying through the stalks. There he is—the man—bewildered, terrified. Turning in wild circles. And Red—he looks *scared*.

Red catches her eye and presses a finger to his lips. The high-pitched screech of dying animals reaches her ears, and she clamps her hands over them to try to drown it out. The figures emerge from the wheat—the obsii: all bony limbs and slick, shadowed forms.

Red takes a huddled step back, dragging her along.

Then she sees it: wings, glorious and black and feathered, dragging along the ground, displacing stalks with their girth. There's something in the field that even the obsii bow to. Something that reminds her of Red.

Casey's gaze follows the feathers up to a woman. She's barefoot against the ground, clad in robes of inky blue. Long, straight tresses of dark hair tangle with her arms and her wings as she glides through the field. Under her heels, the ground withers and burns, turning to ash.

Beside her, Red's breath becomes ragged.

Casey can't see her face from where they hide, but she knows if she does she'll see only danger. There's something malicious about her presence, something threatening hidden beneath the ethereal glow.

And yet, Casey can't look away, can't stop the feeling that she lies before some creature of immense power. Something that puts everything Red is to shame.

Her jaw drops, a gasp racing up her throat, but Red's hand clamps across her mouth, forcing the sound back into her gut.

"Be still," he whispers, so close she can feel his lips against her skin, the panicked rise and fall of his chest, the crushing force of his hand as it trembles against her jaw.

Casey's eyes widened as the obsii snarl and snap. The man begins to scream again and Red pulls her away, crawling backward across the ground.

He leads them farther, dragging her body, which is still with shock. She can't be certain of the direction, only that it's away from that . . . *creature*.

"Let's go," Red whispers. "While they're distracted."

He climbs to his feet, staying in a low crouch, wrapping his entire hand around her upper arm to help her stand.

"What is that thing?" she mumbles.

Red shakes his head, leading her on. The barn and the farmhouse appear, lonely gray shapes rising up beyond the field. "We need to get out of here."

"Slow down," she says, trying to keep pace. "It's not done. I didn't finish it. We can't leave the soul!"

"Oh yes, we can."

"Stop!" she urges, digging her heels in. He barely stumbles. "What is that thing, Red? Why do you look so terrified?"

"It's Azrael," he says through his teeth, casting anxious glances behind her. "The Fallen."

Casey's brows dip together. "The Fallen?"

"Yes. The angel of death. Now, can we please continue this conversation later? We need to be as far away from her as we can." His words race out in hot shivers, his voice barely under control. "Remember when I said there were worse things in Limbo than the obsii?"

Casey nods.

"She's it. Now, let's go."

Behind them, the man screams, his voice tortured and ragged.

Casey looks back, feeling wretched. This is her fault. If she'd just left him in the house, or maybe if she'd tried harder on the barn door . . . "Red, we have to go back for him."

Red shakes his head vehemently. "That soul is with Azrael now. His fate, one way or another, belongs to her. Your job is done, and this is not up for negotiation."

She rips her arm out of his grasp. "He's my responsibility, Red."

"You saw that house, Casey. You know what fate awaited him."

"It's not my job to know," she says. "It's to help the soul out of Limbo. He's leaving through that door." A shattered cry whips through the trees and without another thought, Casey turns and sprints toward it.

"Casey, stop!" Red cries. "We can't fight them here—we're outnumbered!"

His words have barely caught up with her before his body does. He throws himself at her, catching her around the waist, pulling them both face-first into the earth. Casey feels the rattle of her teeth as her chin makes contact with the ground.

"Let me go!" she growls.

"Hush. They'll hear you!"

She gets to her feet before him, rubbing at her jaw and blinking stars from her eyes as Red scrambles up. His hands find her shoulders, and he twists her to look at him. She drops her gaze to the ground, knowing what she'll see in his eyes. That dizzying, white swirl of a veil.

His hands land on either side of her face as he tilts her head up. She slams her eyes closed.

"Look at me," he pleads. "I can't let you do this."

"Not everything is black and white, Red. It's not all light or dark."

"This is," he says. "You can't fix everything. You can't fix all people!"

She tastes the dirt on her tongue, can smell the pungent odor of earth smeared against her cheeks. Pressure builds behind her eyes, but she refuses to cry.

"This isn't your fault, Casey. It's how it's supposed to be."

She sniffs then, the pressure behind her eyes sinking into her chest. Everything about this world is hard.

Why is death so difficult?

If she opens her eyes, she won't have to deal with it, though, will she? Red could veil her, manipulate her thoughts. Maybe if she asks, he'll help her forget it all. Just for a bit, so she can sleep without nightmares. So she doesn't spend every waking moment trying to hear or see or remember Liddy.

He can do that for her. He *would* do that for her. She just has to let him.

"You're far from home, Red. I didn't think they'd let you back so soon."

The unfamiliar voice brings Casey out of her own head, and her eyes shoot open. Red has grown very still before her. His hands are no longer on her face, but twisted into fists by his side, wrapped around his twin daggers.

Over his shoulder, all she can see are black feathers.

Red lets out a breath. No words follow, but his head turns a fraction, slowly, just enough to lay eyes on Azrael. His next breath is ragged, like he's holding back a sob.

"Turn around," Azrael commands.

Red narrows his eyes and turns, again very slowly.

"Don't look at me like that, little angel of light." She says it with fondness. "I know you missed me."

"Don't believe the stories you hear," Red mutters.

Azrael's face is all high cheekbones and piercing black eyes. It's like there are no eyes there at all, just holes.

"They took your wings," she says with a grim kind of fascination. With the tilt of her head, Casey sees the fine dark lines that thread beneath her skin, like cobwebs instead of veins. It's only in the light, though. They're hidden, like most everything else here, by shadow. "You shouldn't be here," she says, "especially with one so new. You're weaker without your wings."

Azrael looks at her, eyelids blinking over those stony black pools. Casey doesn't know where to look but at her. "Let me see you, child."

Casey steps out from behind Red, compelled by fear, and stands beside him.

"Is this your new charge?" Azrael asks.

Red stiffens. "Leave her alone."

"I like meeting the ones that escaped death. They're always so angry. With a point to prove. It's *fascinating*."

"Leave her alone," Red says again.

"Are you worried?" Azrael laughs. "Do you imagine it went something like this when I made that arrangement with your other little friend? That I threatened her?"

Next to her, Red's entire body stiffens, and Casey can sense the coiling energy that surrounds him, the building momentum contained in his muscles. Ready to spring, ready to fight.

"Red," she whispers, touching the top of his hand with her fingertips in an attempt to call him back from that place of fiery rage. "Don't."

"I know you think it was all me," Azrael continues. "That I tricked her into it somehow, but that would be a lie. She was very eager to work with me. What is it that humans say . . . 'Making a deal with the devil'?" She laughs and the sound is ugly and annoying, full of sharp notes that make Casey want to grind her teeth.

"You're a disgrace," Red spits.

Without warning, Azrael scoops Red up by the throat and slams him against the tree behind them. His daggers fall, lodging themselves into the ground.

Casey dives and scrambles after them, snatching them up before Azrael can make a move.

Azrael merely watches, eyeing the blades almost curiously.

"She won't touch them," Red says, explaining the strange look on Azrael's face. "She can't wield a divine weapon." He struggles for his footing and his breath, but his words are almost a taunt.

Azrael tightens her hold and Red's eyes bulge.

"Red?" Casey says, looking for some sort of direction, the dagger in her hand heavier suddenly.

"You won't hurt me, child," Azrael says, clicking her tongue, like it's all a big game to her. "You can't." She closes her hand tighter around Red's throat.

Casey lowers the dagger, trying to distract her. "Because you're immortal?"

"Because demons don't bleed," Red chokes.

Azrael hisses, striking him hard enough to leave an angry red mark against his cheek. "I am no demon!"

Red slides down the tree as her hold breaks. "You may call yourself an angel," he grunts, "but that doesn't make you one."

Azrael leans toward him, until he's close enough to be swallowed up by the black holes of her eyes. "I made a choice. Choices have consequences. You and I both know that."

"I guess we do."

Anger flashes across Azrael's features like a wave rippling over her, but the emotion disappears as the wave recedes, and she laughs again, that same dark chuckle.

"Oh, Red." Azrael pats his face in a way that makes Casey wince. "No need to be mean. We're only chatting. And let's not forget who has the real power here." Her wings lift, dragging over Red's shoulder, a single black feather rising to brush along his jaw.

Red shrugs it off in disgust.

Azrael plucks a long feather from beneath her wings. From the soft shape grows a long scythe, the metal burnished to an almost black finish. She looks like something out of myth, the kind of creature Casey would not like to meet on a darkened street corner. Not even in broad daylight.

The scythe lowers against him, and Red winces where it touches his arm.

"Burns, doesn't it?"

Red turns suddenly, and Azrael rocks back, moving her arms so the blade of the scythe is now pressed to his sternum. There's a feline grace to her movements, as dangerous as she is delicate.

"Don't test me, Red."

"Or what?" he challenges.

"I may not be as forgiving as your other friends." Her eyes darken to a shade of midnight. Then they drift back to Casey. She tilts her head. "And what is it that I can do for you, child?"

"Nothing."

"We all want something. Me, for example, I'd like to get out of here. To reclaim what belongs to me."

"And what's that?" Red says, only half hiding his sneer.

"My freedom from this wretched prison." She runs a long fingernail against the rounded edge of her scythe and the sound sends an unpleasant tremor through Casey's entire body. "Now, all you have to do is ask, girl," she says. "Go on. What is it you yearn for? What are you hunting? Ask and you shall receive."

"Don't," Red warns her. "Nothing is for free."

Azrael casts her arms out, knocking them both to the ground. Casey rolls over to see Red a few feet away. Azrael glides toward him. "You're even more of a fool without your wings than you were with them."

Casey clutches the daggers still, the metal cold, an idea forming.

She'll never reach Azrael before the angel of death hears her. But maybe . . . Casey holds the weight of the blade in her hand. She's never thrown a knife before. But she has two shots.

She winds up and goes for it.

The first one lands wide, but the second lodges between Azrael's feathers, near a shoulder blade.

Azrael screeches. The scythe falls from her hands as she clutches for the space near her spine.

Red kicks the scythe as far as he can, then runs past Azrael, grabbing Casey as he does.

"I thought you said she couldn't wield a divine weapon," Casey hisses at him.

"That's not a divine weapon. It's cursed. Just like her wings." He urges her forward. "Get to the door!"

Casey was never a track star, but she could be today. Right now, she's keeping pace with Red. Or maybe he's slowed to keep pace with her. Either way, it feels like her arms are about to tear off.

When she turns back, Azrael has reclaimed her weapon, and her wings unfurl, lifting her from the ground. Red takes a few fumbling steps in Casey's direction and bumps against her. She ignores the burn in her lungs and lengthens her stride.

Something explodes from the field behind Red. She barely has time to call a warning.

A shadow lunges at her, nearly bowling her over, and she feels something sharp dig into her skin. A spray of blood, a flash of heat.

She gasps and falls to her knees, clutching her forearm to her chest.

Red finds her in the chaos of high-pitched screeches, his fingers prodding her arm. "Hold it tight," he says.

Casey manages a nod. Steel crashes against steel. There's a groan of effort and a dark chuckle that turns her stomach. And finally, a blinding flash of pain that forces Casey to the ground.

Down, down, down.

Until there's nowhere left to fall.

TWELVE

"LET ME GO, Red!" Casey hisses through her teeth, the burn in her arm spreading.

"Stop squirming. You're making it worse."

Red pushes the front door open as it swings closed again. It crashes into the wall, leaving a dent where the doorknob connects.

"Don't break things!" Casey grits out. She slumps face-first onto the couch, clutching her arm, body twitching from the pain. "And you drive like a maniac," she mutters into the cushion. "Thought I was going to end up as roadkill."

"All of this and that's what you complain about?" he says.

"What do you expect me to tell Karen when she finds the car gone?"

"I veiled her," he says. "How do you think I got the keys? I told her to find Evan for a ride home."

"Oh, perfect," Casey growls.

Casey had spent a good fifteen minutes sitting in the custodial closet while Red went on his mission. Everything had smelled like s'mores. Now she wonders if she was hallucinating from the pain or the lack of blood.

Pain, probably.

Tears burn new tracks down her cheeks and she groans, rolling onto her side. The room spins as Red clutches her by the shoulders and props her up like a rag doll.

"What are we doing?"

"Relax," he orders. His jaw tightens, muscles clenching under his skin. "Let me see."

He fumbles for her arm, but she keeps it seized against her side. "No. Don't touch it."

"Casey, breathe. Let me take a look so I can help you." His eyes are intense as they bore into hers.

When she unfolds her arm, pain shudders beneath her skin, like some sort of poison leaching into her cells.

Afraid to look, she trains her eyes on the ceiling. "What is it?"

"The mark of the obsii."

He stretches her arm out and she jerks back. A weight settles over her entire body. Dread.

"Come," he says, sliding his arm around her waist, pulling her to her feet. "We need to stop the spread."

"Am I dying?" she asks as he half drags, half carries her toward the bathroom. "Again?"

"No," he says. "But I cannot heal you while the infection remains inside."

Casey remembers the night Red was injured and the dark sludge that had spilled from his wound before he could heal it. Ugh . . . she's going to puke.

He stops in the bathroom and helps Casey sit on the counter. "Roll up your sleeve."

He fills the sink with water, then grabs her arm, squeezing the poison from her veins. Her eyes roll back in her head momentarily, reacting to the sharp, stabbing jolt that feeds up her arm to her shoulder. Her entire body cringes. The poison billows and curls like smoke as it drops into the sink, turning into thick, black sludge when it hits the water.

"Raphael, give me strength," Red says, eyes closed, and her skin prickles where he touches her.

She hisses, trying to pull her arm free as pain sears her flesh. Red continues to mutter strange, foreign words. Something in an old and ancient language that no longer belongs to this world. His skin against hers is agony, and she feels tears curl over the contours of her nose.

Red's eyes fade to blank, cold stones.

Cloudy.

Lost.

Slowly, Casey's pain recedes.

Finally, Red slouches against the side of the counter, releasing her. He pulls the plug in the sink, letting the dark water drain away.

Blinking back tears, Casey prods her skin, feeling the place where the gash had been, still in shock. Her arm is numb and cold, but otherwise unmarred.

Red rubs his wet hand over his face before smoothing it through his hair. "What happened back there, anyway?"

"That's what I'd like to know."

"I'm talking about *before*," he says pointedly.

"I was looking for Liddy, okay? I got it wrong. I almost got us caught by the angel of death. My fault, I know." She climbs to her feet.

"That's not what I—"

"No, that *is* what you meant. And you're right. Today's on me. I'm sorry." She stalks into the hall, hoping he has the foresight to clean up before her aunt gets home to find out they've summoned some angel-of-healing mojo into the sink.

She stops inside her room to change her clothes. The image of that man, surrounded by those hideous creatures, screaming . . . it's seared into her brain. If she hadn't been chasing Liddy, maybe they never would have found him.

She bends down to fetch a pair of socks that have rolled under her bed.

"Casey, this isn't your fault."

The yellow light spilling in from the hallway casts a halo around his head, and she rolls her eyes. "Don't tell me you can read minds now, because that's really going to suck. For both of us."

"No," Red says. "Of course not. I just know how you think."

Casey rolls into a sitting position, pulling on her socks. "That's worse. Thinking you know how my mind works."

"I know you're blaming yourself right now." He holds his hand out for her. "Tell me I'm wrong."

"You're wrong." She narrows her eyes, really tired of hearing

183

that things are not her fault. Words are not enough to fix how she feels.

"What was Azrael talking about, anyway?" she asks, shifting the conversation. "She said she made a deal with *her*. Who was Azrael talking about, Red?"

He winces, his entire body seeming to curl inward, and Casey wonders if this is the girl he'd mentioned in the church after Malakhi had visited. If she's the one he supposedly gave it all up for.

Her heart thunders as the moments pass. For a long while, she thinks he might not say anything, that she's pushed too far, but then he clears his throat.

"I loved her," he says quietly.

"Loved?" Casey wants to see if his face matches the turmoil in his voice. "Why do you make it sound like such a terrible thing?"

He laughs, humorless and empty. "It's frowned upon where I'm from. Not impossible, but it goes against what we stand for."

"And they took your wings for *that*?"

He shakes his head. "I gave them up for her. You can't serve the light and be completely devoted to another. It's a sacrifice, one that grounds you for as long as you love."

Casey chews on her lip, processing. It doesn't sound like she's the only one blaming herself for things right now.

Downstairs, the front door opens and Casey's eyes widen.

"Casey! Red?" Evan calls. She can hear him padding through the living room.

"In here," Casey yells back.

"Uh . . . why is there . . . Is this blood on the floor?" Evan swings into the room, eyes wide. "Are you okay? What the heck happened to the bathroom? You know, Karen's in the truck and she's probably going to ask some questions."

"It's nothing," Casey says. "I had a little accident in Limbo. No big deal. Red fixed me up."

"No big deal? Your hallway looks like a scene from a nineties' horror movie!"

"It wasn't nothing," Red agrees.

"What happened?" Evan demands. "And don't say everything is fine. I just had to play twenty questions with myself on the ride over here because your aunt has checked out. It's like talking to a zombie..." He pauses and his eyes land on Red. "You did that thing again. Your weird angel magic."

"I veiled her," Red says. "I didn't have a choice. We ran into Azrael."

"Who the *heck* is Azrael?"

"The angel of death," Casey says.

"The angel of death!" Evan squeaks.

Red crosses his arms. "She's not exactly an angel. Not anymore at least."

"You called her the Fallen," Casey says. "What happened to her?"

"She was an archangel, gifted with the knowledge to traverse the in-between realms, to search out the lost souls. But it wasn't enough for her."

"What does that mean?" she asks warily.

"Understand," Red says, "that this was long before my time. But, as it is told, Azrael raised an army of angels in her pursuit of power."

"Of course she did," Evan mutters.

"She believed that we should hold dominance over mankind."

"Typical," Evan says.

"But she and her followers were struck down and cast out. Never to be allowed to regain their heavenly wings."

"Harsh."

"She was banished to the world below. A world filled with cold fire. For a long time, it was thought that she would never be able to escape. But she did, finding her way back to a place that exists between."

"Limbo," Casey says.

"Yes. And even now she pursues the mortal plane, one step closer to—"

"Upstairs," Evan finishes.

Red nods. "Angels have dedicated their existence to keep her from escaping."

"To keep her from hurting humans?" Casey says.

"And to keep her from finding her way back to the light. She can never be allowed to reach it again. If she does, it is said that she will spread her wings, and it will plunge all worlds into darkness. For now, she is trapped."

"But those shadow creatures . . . the obsii . . . *they've* escaped."

"Because they're lesser creatures. Someone of Azrael's power cannot simply slip through cracks. So that is all she has. A reach through her creatures. Only a divine weapon can break the seal between here and Limbo. Since she can't wield a divine weapon, she's stuck."

"Well, that's comforting," Evan says sarcastically.

Casey crosses her arms. "It wasn't like that, Evan."

"Right, yeah." He looks at her pointedly. "You want to go for a walk?"

Translation: *Can we talk about this? Alone?*

"Sure." The look on his face when she answers is equal parts relief and apprehension. She glances at Red, but he flops down on her bed and closes his eyes. She wonders if healing her arm has exhausted him or if she only imagines the sallow turn of his skin.

Evan waits by her door, letting her take the lead.

She does, tiptoeing downstairs, but Karen's on the couch and she sees them before they can retreat.

"Hi, honey," she says.

"Uh, Evan and I are just going for a walk."

"Sure thing. See you later." Karen reclines against the couch and continues to watch the blank TV screen.

"That was easy," Casey mumbles, hurrying down the steps.

"I told you. Zombie."

"I'm sure it'll wear off soon." Casey wants to protect Karen, but she doesn't exactly like seeing her this way.

They walk down the sidewalk toward downtown. The sun feels good on her skin; the heat of summer is like déjà vu, and she craves giant aviator sunglasses and all-windows-down car rides and Liddy's favorite vanilla bean ice coffees.

For a moment it's like a balm against the weariness she's felt lately. And then Evan stops and slumps into a chair outside the Bean-Eatery, the sign in the window boasting specialty coffees and an open-mic night every Thursday.

"What's wrong?" she asks. She sits across from him in a hard, metal-backed chair, her elbows balanced on the edge of the table between them.

"Besides the fact that you're running around with demons? Um, I'm just living life, you know, spending summer hanging around town while my best friend keeps taking off-world journeys that she may or may not come back from."

"That's not fair."

His frustration is masked by sarcasm, and it's hard to get a read on which part is bothering him most. Is it the whole supernatural-turned-real thing? Because Casey's not exactly having an easy time of it herself. Running around with angels and demons was not on her summer agenda.

Or is it the distance? The space that's growing between them in her pursuit of Liddy? She's felt it, though it's impossible to stop. She can't let Liddy linger in that place. She won't.

"I know," he sighs.

"Then stop making me feel like I'm choosing her over you."

"That's not what I'm trying to do. But—"

"What can I get'cha?" Casey looks up as the barista pops her bright pink bubble gum near her ear.

"We're good," Evan snaps and the barista wanders away, throwing the door to the café open with an annoyed flourish.

"Maybe I wanted something," Casey says.

"Don't deflect. You can't keep doing this. It's dangerous, Casey." He drags his chair closer to the table, the legs scraping across the concrete. "That *place* is dangerous."

"I know that. It's not like I'm the one who has to keep coming and going from Limbo or anything. Thanks for the brief." She laughs, though there's nothing funny about it.

Evan picks at the corner of the table. "Maybe you're not trying hard enough."

"What?" Casey says, dumbfounded.

"Maybe . . . you don't want to let her go." Evan shrugs. "Maybe you like being able to hear her."

"*Excuse* me?"

"You know, if you don't help her cross over . . . then she's never really gone."

Casey squeezes the arms of her chair. "You're being so incredibly ignorant and stupid right now."

"Really?" he says drily.

"I *have* been trying," she insists. "None of this is exactly easy!"

"You say you want to move on. That you want to be able to let her go. Well, then you have to let go, Casey! You have to let her rest."

"Don't tell me about grief, Evan."

"Why? Have I not lost enough in my life to earn it?" Something in his gaze softens. "It's okay that you miss her."

Casey shifts to the very back of the chair, putting the most amount of space between them. "I don't need you to be my therapist."

"I'm not trying to be your therapist," he says, color creeping into his cheeks.

"Then, what?"

"Well, for starters, your friend."

"I don't need my *friends* telling me how to feel."

"'Cause you know all about your feelings, right?"

"Let it go, Evan."

"That's your problem," he says hotly. "Since Liddy, since all this Limbo stuff started, you haven't cared about what happens to you. If you get hurt. If you disappear."

Casey looks away.

"Tell me this isn't all because you feel guilty about what happened with Liddy," Evan says, reaching across the table for her.

Casey pulls farther away. "You weren't there that day, Evan."

"And?"

"You just . . . You don't *know*, okay!"

"I lost her, too, Casey."

"It's not the same!" Her whole body is shaking, and she presses her hands to her knees to keep them from knocking together.

"Casey, we've been over this. You couldn't have stopped it even if you wanted to. It was an *accident*." He sighs. "You have to try to let it go. You have to let *her* go."

"Don't you think I want to?" she says, voice quivering. "Don't you think I've had enough of the whispers and the dark images that fill my mind? Because I have. And I've tried letting her go. I've been trying for weeks, but I can't!"

Casey swallows hard, standing and taking a step away from him. "It's my fault. It will always be *my* fault."

Evan stands up but doesn't follow her. "What does that even mean?"

"I let her go!"

Evan's voice falters a bit. "What?"

"I had her." She holds up her fist. "In my hand. Beneath the water. And I let go."

"Casey—"

"Stop," she whispers. "You don't know because you weren't there. And I can't get over it because she *died*, Evan. In the dark. *Alone*. All because I told her to go faster. And then I let go, because it hurt too much to hold her against the current."

His face is the same chalk gray as the sidewalk. "You never told me that."

"I don't tell you everything."

"Don't you trust me?"

"Some things are meant to belong only to me."

He swallows hard, running his hands along his pants.

She can see him working through it, trying to find something to say. It's the same shame she feels, trying to reason with herself. Trying to place blame on anything other than the moment she let Liddy's fingers slide through hers.

"You know," he whispers, "every time you go there ... I go out of my mind knowing there's nothing I can do to reach you."

"You won't lose me."

"But you can't promise that. And if I do lose you, I'll be devastated." She shakes her head and he clenches his fists. "Stop acting like you don't know. I've had a crush on you since the fourth grade, Casey. And if you don't think you matter that much to me, after all this ..." His voice breaks, "I can't help you."

The world shifts around her. *Not now!*

Daytime. A row of hedges, roses in bloom, heavy and drooping toward the stone path below. Birds sweep down from the trees, dive-bombing into a golden birdbath, shaking water from their feathers.

"Evan—"

Casey!

"Just wait," she begs.

A flash. The sun drops. Smoke curls from a chimney. A door opens, warm light spilling onto the stamped concrete patio.

Casey presses her hands against her temple as Evan's voice cuts through the vision.

"I've *been* waiting," he says. "I won't chase you anymore." He slides his hands into his pockets and whispers, "I have been for years."

Her heart stutters to a stop, winding her instantly.

Evan looks as defeated as she feels, and in the silence that stretches between them, he walks away.

As she watches him, hot tears blur her vision, turning the world around her into shattered glass.

THIRTEEN

CASEY DABS AT her eyes with the thin edges of her shirt, sniffing and crossing her arms as Red appears at the end of the street.

"Were you spying on us?" she demands with the kind of authority that comes only from emotional outbursts. Her voice is pitched and wobbly and she's not sure if the pressure behind her eyes is going to manifest in a bout of uncontrollable tears now or a splitting headache later.

Red's jaw twitches but he admits to nothing. Smart.

"I don't need someone else telling me how I feel," Casey declares. "I *know* how I feel."

"Isn't that the point, though? To talk about it?"

"Think yourself a grief counselor, too?"

"You don't have to do that with me."

"What?" she snaps. She turns back toward the house, hands

balled into fists. She's not sad anymore. Just angry. A flame-coursing-beneath-her-skin kind of angry. All she wants to do is scream into an abyss, or bury her face in a pillow. Maybe both.

Red strides along beside her. "Be combative. I know it hurts, but lashing out does nothing but strengthen the divide between you and the rest of the world. Between you and the people that can help."

"Can you drop it? We need to go to Limbo. Now."

Logically, she knows none of this is Red's fault. But the illogical part of her brain is locked onto him like a target that needs to be destroyed. If he knew what was good for him, Red would abandon this burning pile of wreckage before it erupts.

Casey grinds her feet into the pavement, trying to displace some of the boiling rage into the ground.

"You don't have to do this alone," he says. "Give Evan some time. He'll come around."

"I don't want him to," she snaps. "It's better this way."

"Casey—"

She stops suddenly in the middle of the road, turning to face him. "I've had the stages of grief memorized since I was nine." She ticks them off on her fingers. "Denial. Anger. Bargaining. Depression. Acceptance." She marches ahead, crossing in front of traffic. "You know what's not on the list? Chasing souls through Limbo."

"Is that what you're angry about? Limbo?"

"Angry. Scared. Does it matter? That's where Liddy is."

"It does matter if you're scared," Red says. "That's why I'm here. To help you. To keep you safe."

"I'm not afraid of Limbo!" she says. "I'm terrified of finding her."

"Liddy?"

"Yes! I'm terrified she's going to tell me it was my fault. I'm also terrified that we might *never* find her!"

"And that will feel like your fault, too," Red says as if he's read her mind. As if he's sensed that's what scares her the most. With her parents dead and now Liddy, her world is shrinking, and she's terrified of what that means.

"Why couldn't you tell Evan any of this?"

"Because I was afraid he'd run. That it would be too much for him and I really would lose him. Having him be angry with me seems like nothing compared to that."

"How do you know he would run?"

"Because *I* would," she says quietly, avoiding his eyes now. "If the positions were reversed."

"I don't think you're giving yourself enough credit. You don't seem like the type to run, Casey."

"Well, you just don't know me very well."

"You think Evan's the type," Red prods, "to run?"

"You don't know what people are capable of until they're thrown into a situation," she tells him. She marches up the driveway and into the house. Karen's gone, probably to bed before her shift tonight.

"That's not it." Red closes the door behind them. "I've seen you two together. There's something else bothering you."

"Besides trying to rescue my dead best friend from her shitty afterlife?"

"You're mad at him," Red says.

"I'm not. Why would I be? He didn't do anything wrong."

"And you think you did?"

"I *know* I did."

"I think you'll find a lot of people would tell you otherwise."

"Don't," Casey says, gritting her teeth. "Don't be like Evan telling me what I know. None of you were there that day. You can't possibly know."

"So that's it?" he says.

"Can you leave it alone, Red?"

"You're a survivor, Casey. You don't have to punish yourself for that."

She looks up at him, and the anger deflates into guilt. "Then help me find her so I can stop."

LIMBO OPENS INTO a tangle of grapevines, hanging flower baskets, and crawling ivy that curls across a wooden archway dividing the space between a homely patio and a sprawling garden.

Casey steps from beneath the arch and past a hedge line made of rose bushes. Red carves those same strange symbols into the wooden lattice of the arch, sealing the doorway, and follows after her.

"Where are we?" she asks.

"In someone's back garden by the looks of it."

The sky is an ugly gray color above, clouds churning. The ground gives off the chill of winter without the snow.

Casey steps around a hanging bird feeder to avoid hitting her head. Circular stone paths cut through the yard, along gardens packed with plants and rock figures and funny woodland ceramics. A pair of gnomes at the base of a shed catch her attention, only because they both have white wings.

Odd, she thinks.

A shadow shifts above her, stretching down the side of the shed. The *pop* of metal makes her jump, but when Casey looks to the top of the shed, there's nothing there.

"Liddy?" she whispers.

Red looks up. "I don't think that was Liddy."

"We should get inside," she says.

Red's across the yard in an instant, trampling flower beds.

He's fast, so much faster than she is, but she's agile, slipping between an iron gate and a tall wooden fence that Red has to climb.

Attached to the garden is a house made of red bricks and pale, beige siding. A curl of smoke lifts from the roof.

"In there," Casey says.

Red pulls ahead. When she catches up with him, he's staring at the side door, set between two giant hanging baskets that spill over with purple and yellow petaled flowers. And beyond that is another fence, blocking them off from a street. It's built of black iron that reaches into straight, spiked points. There's no gate, no way through.

Two concrete steps lead the way to the door and Casey steps onto the top one. Next to her head dangles pretty glass windchimes. They make no sound now, though. The air is still.

Hand paused by the doorknob, she curls her fist and knocks instead.

Inside she hears footsteps and Red reaches out, yanking her back. He steps past her, so close she can feel his forearm brush against her skin.

A moment later the door opens, and there stands a woman, wrinkled with age, coils of white hair spiraling around the rectangular-framed glasses perched on her nose. She glances out the door, unconcerned by them, but intrigued by the garden beyond. She waves them in hurriedly, gesturing with the long edge of a curved blade—similar to the dagger in Red's hand.

"Get in, get in," she says, ushering them both into a kitchen. "If you came from the garden, wipe your feet. I don't want you tracking it through the house."

Casey looks down and does her best to leave most of the mud on the mat by the door.

"Limbo-walker," Red whispers. His guard remains up, however, his weapon drawn as he scopes out the kitchen.

"Well, sit down." She points to the table. "Sit. The kettle is still hot. I'll pour you a cup."

Casey looks to Red, but he shakes his head, motioning to a stairwell.

"I'm not blind, just old," the woman barks. "If you have something to say, speak your mind."

Neither of them say anything, and the woman's eyes narrow into slits as she regards Red. "You can explore all you want, boy, but you won't find anything of concern."

"We've had a run-in with Azrael recently, so you'll forgive me for being thorough," he says sharply.

"Oh, you two must have stumbled into a particularly bad

soul. Azrael doesn't usually fuss so much over the good ones. She leaves that to her creatures." The woman toddles away, sporting a heavy limp. "You know, if I've learned anything in these last fifty-seven years it's how to lock up a place from those vile beasts."

"I'll just take a peek anyway."

The woman shakes her head, using her weapon as a sort of cane, muttering, "Angels."

"Stay here," Red tells Casey, moving toward the stairwell.

"But, Red—"

"Stay. Here." He leaves no room for argument before walking away.

"Quite a bossy fellow, isn't he?" the woman calls over her shoulder, knocking a spoon against the edge of a mug.

Casey clenches her teeth. "You have no idea."

The woman returns to the table with the mug and looks from Casey to a chair. Without waiting to be told, Casey slides into it.

"Sugar?"

"Uh, yes, thank you." The mug is set in front of her and a square of sugar is plopped inside.

"What's your name?"

"Casey."

The woman takes a seat opposite her, pushing her glasses up her nose. "I'm Gloria." Somewhere in the house a door rattles, hard, and the familiar shriek has Casey nearly jumping out of her seat.

"Settle down, girl. Honestly." Gloria sips her tea, thin fingers hugging the warmth from the mug. "They come and come, but I never let them in. One day they'll learn."

"Learn what?" Casey wonders, heart still pounding.

"That I made my decision long ago and will not be swayed."

Casey sips at the tea, surprised at the sweetness. "How long have you been here?"

"On and off for many years. I received my calling as a young girl, much younger than you." She gets up again and wanders into the kitchen for a plate of shortbread cookies. Using her weapon, she nudges aside the edge of the curtain covering the window. "Something's got them worked up."

"It's me." Casey sighs. "I think."

"You?"

"I'm looking for someone."

"A particular someone?"

Casey nods.

Gloria shuffles back to her chair. "This wouldn't happen to be a young lady, would it? About your age, long blond hair . . . Bit of an attitude?"

"Liddy!" Casey says excitedly. "You've seen her?"

"She sat in this very chair for a moment with me."

"When?" Casey gets to her feet.

Gloria waves her down. "She's long gone."

Casey frowns.

"I've seen cases like yours before. Soul mates they call them. You know, the voices usually whisper—unintelligible things, mostly—but in cases like yours, you see things, you hear bits of conversation . . . it's remarkable."

"So there are others like me?"

"Of course."

"And you . . . ?"

"Have been walking Limbo since before you were born."

"I don't understand. Liddy's been walking through other Limbos, deaths belonging to other souls. So, are you . . . dead?"

"Oh, this isn't my Limbo. It belongs to my husband." She sips her tea. "That man, I tell you. He's never been ready for anything a day in his life. I should have known he would linger. Barely gone a moment before I heard the whispers, and I just knew it would be him, confused as anything. But I never could rush that man. Not even toward his own afterlife, apparently."

The way she says it all makes Casey want to laugh, but a thought replays in her mind and she stops. *Fifty-seven years.* Has this woman really been walking Limbo for that long? Her face falls.

"What's that look for?"

"Nothing," Casey says. "I just . . . I wondered if I would have to chase Liddy for as long as you've been doing this. Or if I'll ever find her at all."

"You know what my advice would be, child?"

Casey looks up at her.

"To stop chasing her and start pulling."

"What?"

"This thread that links you, this bond . . . it goes both ways, you know."

"What?" she says again, not quite following.

Gloria smiles patiently. "If you can hear her, that means—"

Casey takes a moment to try to understand. "So . . . Liddy can hear me, too?"

"That's why she's running," Gloria says.

"She's looking for me?" Casey frowns. "But Red never said—"

"Angels," she sighs, rolling her eyes. "What do they know of this place? They can't even hear the whispers."

"But she's lost. How do I help guide her back?"

"Go where the link is strongest. The place that connects the two of you."

"The harbor," Casey whispers.

"Call her there, and maybe she'll follow."

She jumps to her feet. "Thank you. Thank you!"

She hears footsteps on the stairs then. An elderly man with wire-frame glasses and a hooked nose comes into view. He stops behind Gloria, placing his hands on her shoulders. "Sorry, dear."

"It's fine, I've had company to keep me occupied while you lollygagged."

"I always did like this house."

"So did the kids." She pats his hand gently before turning her attention back to Casey. "Anyway, we best be off. That pack of mutts outside is getting rowdier by the minute. And you best be getting to wherever it is you're supposed to be. It isn't wise to linger alone in the in-between. It can be hard to keep your wits in a world that never settles." She says it with a wag of her finger, like a grandmother warning to bundle up against the cold. "We're going to pop out through the garden. All the best, child."

Gloria takes her husband's hand, tucks it into hers and guides him through the house and out the door. She looks back once. "Be careful, girl! Your friend might not be the only thing that answers."

Then they wander off into the garden.

"Red!" Casey cries, jumping the stairs two at a time. She

follows the narrow staircase to the second story of the house. Portraits of a happy family decorate every surface and Casey lingers in the warmth that's been left behind.

Down the hall, there's movement, and Red appears in a doorway. "Have they gone?" he asks.

She nods. "Just now."

"Any sign of her?"

"No, but Gloria said Liddy was here. And she told me—"

Help!

A voice startles her and she stops next to the bay window. It has a perfect view of the darkened street below. Oily spots from the streetlamps leave glowing impressions every few feet. Between them, shadows race, never stopping long enough for her to trace their true shape, but something else captures her attention.

Red comes to stand by her. "What is it?"

"Him," she says, touching the window, shivering at how cold it feels.

A slim figure appears in one of the streetlights, his face turned up as if to study the houses that line the street. She can tell he's lost. Perhaps he doesn't even realize he's dead yet.

"Is he calling you?" Red asks.

Before she can turn away to answer, the figure screams. The cry is pure terror, ragged and hot, echoing down the street. He cuts back and forth across the road, skidding on the gravel, tripping on his own feet as he throws his weight away from the black mist. It slithers across the ground, filling every streetlight until there's nowhere for him to run.

It all happens so fast. In the space of a blink. From the shadows the obsii emerge, clawing and shrieking. They surround him, swarm him, and then he's gone, dissolved in their shadow, scorch marks left upon the ground.

"No," she whispers, hand still pressed against the glass.

Was that it? The creatures had claimed him that fast?

Red draws the curtain across the window, like pulling a sheet over the eyes of a body that's just died. "They don't always play by the same rules, Casey. The darkness hunts all souls, regardless of whether they belong in the shadows or not."

"How is that fair?"

"It's not," he admits.

"So the light has to abide by all these silly rules and the darkness gets to do as they please?"

"It can seem like that."

"It *is* like that, Red." She's angry now. Angry that in his last moments, the boy had known only fear. Angry that he's been stolen away. What if it had been Liddy? What would Red say to her then?

Mostly she's angry at Red's resigned acceptance of it all.

For a flicker of a moment, she can see how tempting the darkness is, how easily one could bend toward it. If always doing the right thing means she's destined to lose, is it even the right thing anymore?

"There's a lot about Limbo that is out of your control," Red says quietly.

Casey's lips twitch. "Let's go. There's something I have to do."

FOURTEEN

THE FRAGRANT SMELL of Gloria's gardens chase Casey from Limbo and back into the real world where she promptly grabs her car keys and races out the door. Red is steps behind her.

"Slow down, Casey!" Red jostles in his seat and slams into the car door as she pulls out of the driveway too quickly. "Tell me again what she said?"

"Gloria said I should stop chasing Liddy and use the connection between us to call Liddy to *me* instead." She slows at a four-way stop and glances down at the gas gauge. The red needle points precariously near empty; she'll have to fill up before they get on the highway.

The impromptu road trip sparked by the information Gloria shared is exactly the kind of distraction she needs right now. A distraction that will hopefully overshadow the tangled thoughts she has about Evan and, as a bonus, ease her frustration over her role as this navigator of the in-between, where darkness seems to always be one step ahead.

She doesn't know how to fix things with Evan right now and she certainly isn't going to be able to fix the disaster that is the eternal battle between good and evil. But finding Liddy and helping her move on is something she *can* do.

"And you'll call Liddy at the harbor?"

"Well, I suppose I can call her anywhere," Casey explains. "It makes sense for it to be there, though. It's the place we both died. Gloria said something about the connection being stronger." She takes the next turn too wide, narrowly missing the median.

"Slow down," Red pleads again.

"I am slowing down," she insists, flicking the turn signal.

She pulls into the Stop-n-Shop gas station. Ads for milk and chocolate bars and giant purple Slurpees adorn the window, and red numbers light up to display the lottery winnings and the price of gas. She swings the car around, lining it up with the gas pump.

"So, what's the plan?" Red says, getting out of the car after her.

"This is the plan," she says. "Harbor. Liddy. Home."

She heads inside to pay. A cool blast of air-conditioning greets her at the door and goose bumps bubble up over her arms. Everything smells like flat pop and stale gummy candies. The same bags of sour worms and red gummies shaped like feet have probably been here since Casey was twelve.

The bell above the door rings as it falls closed behind her, but the girl at the counter barely looks up from her magazine.

There was a time a few weeks ago when she drew every eye in the room. When everyone had something to say about the accident.

Now, she's just any other kid coming in for gas and junk food.

Red, though . . . Red draws her eye as he enters. The girl lets the magazine flip closed. Her eyes lift to take him in, head to toe, and Casey sees the moment she jerks back just a slight bob of her chin, registering something unexplainable about him, and yet curiously alluring. Someone else enters behind them to pay for gas and Casey tugs Red down an aisle filled with beef jerky and various types of cheese-flavored chips.

She picks up a bag and checks the expiration date, realizing that she's lost track of the days, of whether it's a weekend or weekday, if it's been three days since Red fell or three weeks. Summer is dwindling to a close and real life is rushing toward her faster than she's prepared for.

Casey stuffs the chip bag into Red's arms. The bag crackles as he turns it around to read the front.

"What's this for?"

"I'm hungry," she says. *And anxious and tired and a little afraid*, but she doesn't say those things out loud. He can probably see them in the scrunched look on her face anyway.

"That's it? Did Gloria say anything else?" Red asks.

Casey pauses in front of the drink cooler. "No."

Red studies her reflection in the glass. His frosted outline is set on the offense, knuckles on his hips, head bent toward her. Questioning.

Casey tries not to look directly at him as she turns. She also tries not to think about what Gloria had said: that other *things* could answer the call. Casey's met those things and she doesn't care. She's definitely not telling Red about it and risking him trying to stop her. Nothing is going to stop her from reaching out to Liddy.

Nothing.

"You know, I let someone lose themselves to the darkness once before. I won't make that mistake again." He studies her in a way that makes her want to shrink down against the cooler. As it is, she bumps into it, jumping as the cold glass meets her shoulders. "There's something you're not telling me."

"No, there isn't. I just want to get this stuff and go already." She walks past him, heading for the counter. She snags a couple chocolate bars and a pack of fruity gum from the bins at the front. She dumps it all on the counter. Red tosses up the bag of chips.

"Just this?" the girl asks. She moves to the register, stuffing everything into a plastic bag.

"And gas for pump six," Casey says. She reaches into her pocket and slides cash across the counter.

The girl spends most of the exchange staring at Red. Casey has half a mind to introduce them, if only to get him off her back. It feels like his eyes are starting to bore a hole into her head.

Casey leans against the plastic lottery ticket cover, waiting for her change.

Suddenly the girl says, "You're Casey Everett, right?"

"Huh," she stutters in surprise, straightening up against the counter. "Yeah. Do I know you?"

She shakes her head. "I go to Dal Tech."

The fine arts college, Casey remembers.

"My younger brother goes to Westwood, though. He's in your grade." She pushes her glasses up her nose as they slide down, adjusting the boxy rims. "Kevin McQuin."

"Oh, right." Casey tries to pull the image of some lanky-haired, glasses-wearing kid from her Spanish class.

"Anyway, I was sorry to hear about the accident. And Lidia. My brother said she was always nice to him."

"She was nice to everyone," Casey says.

"Two dollars and fifty-five cents is your change," the girl says, sliding the money back across the counter.

"Thanks."

Red grabs the plastic bag and beats her to the car, but only by a second. Casey pumps the gas quickly and then takes the first road out of town as she links up with the highway.

"Does that happen a lot?" he asks.

"What, the whole being-recognized-because-I-almost-died thing?" Casey says. "It used to. Not so much anymore. Which I honestly thought would comfort me. But now that it's happening, all I can think about is the fact that Liddy's old news. Most people have already forgotten. When school starts again, summer will just be a nightmare in the past."

"But not everyone's forgotten," Red says.

She thinks about what he said to her in the store: *I let someone lose themselves to the darkness once before.*

He's talking about that girl again. The one he said he once loved.

When she glances at him, he's bobbing his head along to the hum of the radio and drumming on the door handle. "Can I ask you something?"

"Is it the kind of question that I'll want to answer?" he asks.

"I don't know. Maybe not." She thinks on it longer. "Probably not."

He throws his head back against the seat, his hair spiraling out. "What is it?"

"The girl," she begins. Casey flicks the turn signal to change lanes. "You said you *loved* her. That's the past tense. If it's over, why haven't you gotten your wings back?"

She doesn't spare him more than a glance, her eyes trained on the road ahead of them. It's the equivalent of giving him space. Space to think about and process what she's just asked.

"It's complicated."

"Try me. I might understand complicated."

Red turns toward her and she divides her attention between him and the road. "I didn't fall out of love, Casey. Our love was forbidden."

"Why?"

"Because she took Azrael's deal and became a servant of darkness. And where love between a human and the angelic is frowned upon, love between an angel and darkness . . . well, it's forbidden. To pursue that love would mean renouncing my place in the light. It would mean joining that side and I just couldn't do that."

"You still care about her."

"It doesn't matter. That path is forbidden to me."

"So you let her go?"

"I had to. And now I must fix my mistakes by earning my place back. Prove that my devotion to the light and humanity outweighs my choice to fall."

"I don't think falling in love was a mistake, Red."

"Wasn't it?"

"Is it ever?"

He laughs, the sound hollow and hurt. "You have not lived long enough to challenge me with such philosophical questions."

Casey chuckles softly, sadly. "Why would she choose the darkness, knowing what you stood for?"

He sighs. "To save someone she loved." At Casey's look he explains. "The darkness is alluring and deceitful, but most of all, powerful. It makes costly promises that can be intoxicating, something worth fighting for. Living and dying and loving for." It obviously hurts him to talk about her. To know that maybe she's still out there, that perhaps she still loves him, but neither can belong to each other. What a terrible fate.

"Have angels crossed over for love before?" she wonders aloud.

"Some. Our history is long and bloody. Our stories are many, full of betrayal and forgiveness and remorse. But at the heart of it all is that one thing." He taps his chest above his heart. "Love truly makes all manner of creatures blind, both mortal and the divine."

The corner of Casey's mouth turns up. "What was her name?"

"Elise," Red says quietly.

They drive beneath an overpass. There are very few things to look at along the highway. Mostly forest and rocky ledges and the occasional wooden farmhouse set back against the trees. The sign for the next town rises up on a green backboard. The clouds above them turn from white to gray as she takes the exit ramp along the beach. A storm is rolling in from the ocean; she can feel the energy shift in the car.

The drive to the harbor usually takes about forty minutes. Most of the traffic is heading into town, thankfully, so they make it in thirty. Casey pulls into the familiar parking lot full of potholes and cracks where long grass has cut through and grown like some sort of exotic flora. It's been yellowed by the heat and lack of rain. A gray swell of clouds line up overhead and Casey cuts the engine, staring out into the distance.

"How exactly do you earn your wings again?"

"Are you asking for a detailed list? Because that I can't give you. Most of the time your guess is as good as mine."

"I'm asking—" She blows out a breath. "If this fails . . . if it doesn't work—"

"It's not riding on you, Casey. Me earning my wings back, it's not synonymous with you finding Liddy. The light has to be satisfied with my sacrifice. Assured of where my loyalties lie. You might be the first of many taskings for me down here."

"I hope not," she tells him and means it.

"Me too."

Casey opens the door and Red follows her down to the water. Her entire being radiates nervous energy.

She hasn't stepped foot on this shore since the night she died. It's rocky for a few feet, then turns into the kind of white sand that people take home in little bottles as keepsakes. She walks down the beach and toward the ocean. If she doesn't make herself, she never will. The waves crash over the shore and she inches away from the water as it rushes up the sand to meet them.

Everything about this place feels tainted. Her heart begins

to race and she struggles to catch her breath. This is the closest she's been to the water since it happened. Since . . . since . . .

She collapses onto the sand.

"Are you okay?" Red asks, kneeling beside her.

"Do I look okay?"

". . . No?"

She pushes away the hand he lays on her shoulder. "She was right here, Red. The last time I saw her alive. She stood right"— her voice breaks—"here."

Everything is the same. The island with the rocks. The boat rental shack. The lineup of docks. Nothing changed but her life.

A tear curls over her cheek, slipping beneath her chin. It's chased by another. Letting the tears escape eases the crippling pressure in her chest. She takes a few gasping breaths before rubbing her face on her shirtsleeve.

Maybe Evan was right. Maybe she's been reckless in her pursuit of Liddy. Rushing into dangerous situations on a whim, trying to fix something unfixable.

The dead don't come back.

So, yeah, maybe there was a part of her that took comfort in the fact that as long as she had to keep chasing Liddy, she wasn't really gone. It means she hasn't lost her for good. It's funny how easily other people could see the things you so desperately tried to hide from yourself. How simple it was for them to peer into the corners, past the cobwebs, and point out the exact truths you thought you boxed up.

She shouldn't be surprised that Evan can see her best. And maybe that's why his words unnerved her so quickly.

Why his truths hurt the most.

Casey gets to her feet. No, the dead don't come back. But she could at least help Liddy rest.

She kicks off both her shoes, letting them fall into the sand. Then she pulls off her socks and rolls up the bottoms of her pants.

"What are you doing?" Red asks.

"I'm having a moment, okay? Just ... stay here."

She walks down to the water, stopping just short of where the tide reaches. Then, taking a breath for courage, she wades into the water up to her ankles. It's familiar and cool and refreshing and only makes her a little weepy.

"Liddy." Casey swallows as the tide goes in and out. "This has been our craziest summer yet. And we've spent most of it apart." The emotion inside her bubbles up and lodges in her throat. "So, if you can hear me ... come back to the harbor. I've been trying to find you, to help you, but you have to stop running." She swallows again. "Right now you're lost, but I'm going to find you, I promise. Just come back. Please. Come home."

There are no tears this time, but the salty air stings her dry eyes. She doesn't know if it's enough. If it worked or not.

Red comes to stand beside her, socks in one hand, his shoes in the other. He lets the water rush over his feet, wiggling his toes. A soft *hmm* escapes his lips and he gives her a tiny half smile.

It's not a lot, but it's something.

FIFTEEN

"WHAT'S GOING ON?" Red asks.

A police officer in a reflective orange vest holds his hand out to them in a *stop right there* motion; Casey cuts the high beams to save the officer's eyes. He blows a whistle between his heavily mustached lips; the short, shrill blasts linger in the air for an obscene amount of time before the officer pops the whistle from his mouth to yell at some kid who tries to squeeze his convertible out of traffic far enough to make a U-turn.

Groups of swimsuit-clad children and their beach-chair-toting parents meander between the cars as they work their way down to the boardwalk, their path highlighted by neon orange glow sticks and volunteers with glow-in-the-dark headbands.

"Welcome to summer in a tourist town," Casey tells Red. "They're probably doing fireworks or something tonight for Shore Fest."

She rolls down the window and the faint sound of live music filters up from the beach. The notes are light and airy before it cuts out, replaced by the voice of some smooth-talking radio host who introduces the next band as a grunge-garage group called Something to Look At.

A plucky, electric guitar chord echoes across the water. Casey cranks the wheel and slides out of traffic onto the gravel shoulder.

"What are you doing?"

"We're going to be stuck here for a while." She parks and turns off the engine. "Trust me." She opens the door and steps out, leaning her back against it. Turning her face up to the sky, she breathes in the tang of salt and seawater.

Red climbs out, looking at her over the roof of the car.

"We can walk or we can wait," Casey says, "but there's no point wasting gas idling."

BANG!

Red snaps his head around as a blue burst of light fills the sky. Silver sparks zoom across the falling blue stars, landing somewhere in the ocean. He looks back at her with wide eyes.

"Told you," Casey says. "Fireworks."

They follow the line of neon glow sticks down the boardwalk. They fade from orange to pink to yellow. Along the edge of the parking lot, food trucks have sprung up selling giant corn dogs and apples coated in red candy or caramel. Boards of order specials drawn in bright colors are tacked to the sides of the trucks.

The air smells like sweet waffle cones and ketchup; it's the interior of a bakery and a hockey arena all wrapped up into one.

Another burst of color explodes into the sky. Red stops to stare.

"Liddy loved fireworks," Casey says. "Loud. Colorful."

"Sounds like they fit her personality perfectly."

"I think she just liked the way they bring people together. You can't be here and not smile."

On the beach, children spin in circles until they're dizzy, brandishing long sparkler sticks that turn their limbs into neon yellow blurs. They carve their names into the air only to watch them disappear a moment later. They whoop as the sparks jump, tumbling down between their dancing feet.

"Do you think it worked?" Casey wonders, following another firework with her eyes. "Do you think she heard me?"

"I think you did your best."

"So you don't know."

"No," Red admits. "I don't."

The smell of cinnamon and oil strikes a familiar nerve and Casey turns on her heel. A small deep-fried donut cart is jammed among the big food trucks and stalls.

Casey stops in front of the grease splattered window, fingers pressed against the glass. "Liddy loved these," she says. "I couldn't stand the smell. But it's weird the kinds of things you miss when someone is gone."

"Want some?" Red asks. He fishes in his pocket and pulls out a crumpled five-dollar bill.

She looks down at his pocket curiously. "Are those Evan's shorts?"

Red shrugs. "I'm sure he won't miss a few bucks."

Casey chuckles at his boyishly excited grin. "Go on. Order some," she says.

While she waits, she dials Evan's number. Honestly, she's not completely surprised when she gets his voicemail. "Hey," she says after his greeting. "It's me."

Leaving a painful and awkward apology over voicemail isn't how she wants this to go, but she also doesn't want the argument to fester between them. She doesn't want it to turn into the kind of gap that feels impossible to bridge simply because they've left it too long.

Besides, this was supposed to be their night, walking the boardwalk together, honoring Liddy's love of deep-fried dough. He should be here.

"I just wanted to check in and tell you—" Goose bumps prickle down her arms, and she glances over her shoulder, her words becoming unintelligible syllables. "And I...I gotta...I gotta go."

She hangs up and slides her phone into her pocket. A chill climbs up her arm and settles at the top of her spine, dripping like a faucet with a bad leak. *Drip. Drip. Drip.*

"Red." He stands at the counter attached to the donut stand, sprinkling powdered sugar into the bag of donuts. She puts her hand on his arm and he twists.

The look on her face must reveal it all because his eyes lift, scanning the crowd, his head snapping from side to side fast enough to make her neck sore. "Obsii," he growls.

"There's too many people here," she says. "Someone will get hurt."

Red drops the donuts. They spill onto the boardwalk, knocking white powdered dust against her shoes.

He snaps the feathers from the chain around his neck, handing her one.

The quill, soft at first, hardens into sharp metal against her palm. She wiggles the blade, adjusting her grip on the handle. "Point and stab," she says to herself.

"More or less."

"Stop listening to my internal panic."

"It was external," Red says. "Don't panic. You've got this."

"Sure, says the angel-boy."

"To the Limbo-walker, who has already cut down these things before. I've watched you do it."

"That's true; I saved your life." She frowns. Did he even have a life anymore? "Or maybe your existence."

Red looks like he might laugh, but he just whispers, "Stay close." Then he dives into the crowd.

"I wasn't planning on anything but," Casey mumbles as a whistling blast of bright white fireworks explode overhead. Masked by the sound, she swears she hears that shrieking animal scream.

"This way," Red says. She follows him behind a tent selling knockoff sunglasses. He slows to a creep, eyes scanning in the red and blue and purple blasts that pop overhead, but just as they get a good view of the area, the light fades again. "We should—"

"Don't say split up," Casey interrupts. "That never works. In fact, it's usually a bad idea."

"I wasn't going to say that," Red says. "I was just going to say—"

An obsii lunges out from beneath a row of supply vans as they walk past.

"Holy—!" Casey yells, ducking out of the way as a second obsii emerges from the shadows behind the tent without warning, clawing at them both.

Red twists and turns, fighting with unearthly precision. Beside him, Casey just feels clunky.

All the lights on the boardwalk dim as the firework finale begins and she loses sight of Red. The darkness is supercharged, like it's full of energy; she feels powerful and also like she's being crushed at the same time. Maybe it's just the pressure of her heart trying to beat out of her chest. Or maybe adrenaline and fear were battling for dominance, fighting for control of her limbs.

Casey ducks between a popcorn stand and a bouncy castle, jumping over the trailing power cords. She raises her arm to wipe the sweat from her forehead and accidentally slices through a bag of prepackaged popcorn that hangs from an old tarp awning jutting off the side of the snack stand. It rains down on her head as she flails forward over another power cord.

She hits the dirt; her phone flies out of her pocket and tumbles to a stop a few feet away. The screen lights up with Evan's face, the phone buzzing as it vibrates against the ground.

Oh, just perfect.

She army-crawls across the matted grass, digging her elbows in to give her leverage. As she lifts her phone, something tall and dark reflects in the screen and Casey rolls onto her back.

She has no voice left to scream as the shadow lunges at her with the finesse of a great cat. Without thinking, she throws her arm straight up, her entire hand and wrist and forearm disappearing inside the center of the creature before it explodes around her.

She coughs, getting her breath back. Ash-like black tar rains down around her, giving the yellowed popcorn a distinct burned look. She rolls away from the cloud, but something else catches her attention.

Casey, are you there?

She spins on her knees before she realizes the voice is echoing inside her head.

Casey, where are you?

Casey climbs to her feet but the sights and sounds of the boardwalk fade.

The world flashes inside her head: *a raging surf crashes up against jagged rocks. The vision scans down the gloomy beach, storm clouds swelling in the distance. A lighthouse climbs between the clouds, a solitary figure among the storm, the twisting light in its peak flashing against the coming darkness.*

Rain starts in tiny drops. It picks up and the vision rushes up the beach, away from the water and toward the thick woods that run along the border.

"Liddy."

SIXTEEN

"C'MON, RED," CASEY whispers, holding on to the open door and standing on the bottom ledge of the car for a better view. She taps impatiently on the roof. He's nowhere to be seen, still lost in the crowd of Shore Fest goers. Every streetlight on this road feels like the gaze of a thousand people, urging her to hurry, and her heartbeat drives a steady, painful rhythm against her ribs.

She can't wait any longer. She needs to get somewhere safe, somewhere she can enter Limbo. She clutches the feather in her hand tighter. Somewhere Red will be able to find her.

She gets into the car, lets the police officer still directing traffic wave her through the intersection, and then speeds across town, attempting to beat the onslaught of people leaving after the fireworks die down.

She heads home. It's the closest. Her tether to Liddy will pull her to the harbor from wherever she is, but opening up a doorway to Limbo doesn't feel like the kind of thing you do on the side of the road.

Karen's car is gone, meaning she's out or at work, and Casey praises her luck. She races inside and stands in the dull light of the living room.

The clock in the hall ticks and the singular sound of her breathing fills the space between the walls. Outside the odd car passes, someone's garage opens, but nothing distracts her from the feel of the blade curving in her hand, feather melting to metal, obeying her touch as easily as it does Red's.

She hovers in the living room for a moment and watches for movement. For any sign that she's been followed.

Nothing stirs in the shadows and her plan—the frantic and dizzy mess currently rattling around her head—comes to life.

If I wait, it might be too late, she tells herself.

It might already be too late.

She can't take that chance.

She gathers herself, steeling her nerves, hardening like the blade in her hand. Then she's dashing to her bedroom. The door closes behind her with a soft puff.

She's watched Red do this half a dozen times now. Doing it without him is daunting, but doing nothing isn't an option.

Choosing a spot, Casey kneels down on her floor and lifts the dagger. She expects more resistance when she slams it down, but the metal glides as easily as it moves through the air.

It emboldens her. She can do this. Squeezing the hilt, she drags the blade around, closing the circle and that familiar pressure gathers—just pressure, pressure, pressure.

She keeps her eyes open this time, watching for the moment the darkness fades, only to find that it never really does. Instead, the darkness becomes a stormy blue landscape of withered trees. She studies them through the window of a small office, arriving in Limbo behind a counter with an old boxed computer, a desk calendar, and assorted pencils. On the wall beside her are a series of keys. She runs her hands along the blue plywood, familiarity settling in her gut.

She knows this place. It's the inside of the boat rental shack.

Casey grips the dagger tighter, battling down the guilt, replacing it with thoughts of Liddy, opening herself up to the sounds of Limbo.

If Liddy really is here, she's going to find her.

This time, she's going to *save* her.

She rushes to the next window and this one is filled not with trees, but with crashing waves. The center island rises up from the water, the lighthouse standing steady among dark clouds.

The harbor.

Casey slips beneath the counter and rushes to the door and looks up. A wooden board is tacked near the roof. BOAT RENTALS. The world outside the building is chilled, the sand soggy beneath her feet. She stands by the door, waiting for some sort of sign.

It arrives, as she expects, like a whisper. It's not words this time, but a broken sob. Sad and lonely cries, full of trembling fear.

She bumps against the building, hand pressed to her lips.

She waits for the sound to pull her in, to give her direction. Like the needle on a compass, her body bends, automatically tuned to the voices of the dead and she sets off at a run. It leads her toward the trees, to a hill with a sharp incline that overlooks the harbor. The ground is slick, forcing her to lean forward, digging her hands into the earth. Using small tree trunks as footholds makes it easier.

As she nears the top, the sobs string closer together. Louder.

"C'mon, Liddy," she whispers. "Where are you?"

She rolls herself over the top edge of the embankment using her leg as leverage and flops onto her back. The sky is empty, scarred by the limbs of trees that spring outward, reaching their arthritic branches above her.

Propped up on her elbows, she takes in her surroundings. The sobs rattle in her ears, but then she sees her, sitting between the weeds and tall grasses and moss-covered logs that rise up around them, and the world falls silent.

Liddy.

She's filthy, hair stringy around her face, eyes smudged. Her legs are tucked up against her chest, head resting on her knees.

"Liddy?" Casey calls, desperation filling her voice as she rolls over, leaping to her feet. "Liddy!"

Liddy looks up, eyes bright and blue but strained with wiry red lines. Dirty hands smudge the tears from her face.

Casey stumbles toward her, her mind rushing faster than her feet can. She collapses to her knees; it's a jolt of pain she barely registers as she throws herself at Liddy.

The hug feels like enough to shatter her, but Liddy only clings tighter and Casey lets her, overwhelmed by the smell of earth and salty tears. It seems to last forever, but when she pulls away, Casey knows it's too soon and she tugs her back.

"Where have you been?" Liddy whispers through her tears.

"I'm so, *so* sorry," Casey says against her shoulder, over and over, until the words sound unfamiliar.

"It's really you, then?"

Casey wonders how many times Liddy has imagined this moment, wished it, prayed for it.

"I've been searching for you," Liddy whispers, pulling away. She studies Casey. Liddy is still dressed in the clothes she died in—a pink and white summer dress over her bathing suit. Casey watches the realization on Liddy's face as she takes in their appearances. Her jaw tightens. "I wasn't ever going to find you, was I?"

Casey winces and her next words taste like vomit. "You're dead, Liddy."

It takes her a moment, but Liddy nods. "I thought so." Her cheeks twitch. "I thought it was a nightmare for a while. But it never ends; I never wake up."

"It'll end now," Casey promises.

"I heard you," Liddy says. "Before I thought I was chasing a ghost, but this time I heard you, calling me back to this place, like some kind of sick joke. But I came back, just in case you were here."

"I could hear you, too," Casey says, her eyes watering. She takes Liddy's hand. "I have to get you out of here."

"You know how to get out?" Liddy says, so desperately, so broken, that Casey pulls her into another crushing hug.

"I'm sorry you've been lost for so long."

"I don't care anymore," Liddy says. "I just want to go."

"That makes two of us."

A familiar, creeping unease fills her and Casey looks around, searching for shadows among the trees.

"C'mon," she says.

"Where?"

"Anywhere that's not here." Casey takes her by the hand, part of her afraid that Liddy will disappear on the wind, blowing away like smoke, if she lets her go.

"This way," Casey says. She tries to figure out a bearing, but it's hard to sort through the noise in her head suddenly—too much emotion filling up the space.

She tries to find another doorway, somewhere the voices call from, but all she can hear is the creak of the wind between the trees. There's also too much elation in her chest, having Liddy so close again. All these things make it very difficult to concentrate, to put her mind in order.

From the top of the embankment, Casey can see the rental shack. It's like a doll's house, a tiny thing set against the water, storm-beaten and faded.

"Now where?" Liddy asks.

"Give me a second." Casey scans the grim horizon, eyes going wide when she feels an ominous tingle at the back of her neck.

She whips around to look, eyes darting between wiry tree

trunks. Shadows slowly begin to peel themselves away from the bark, hunched figures taking form. Faceless heads turn skyward and that hideous shriek fills the air around them.

Liddy cowers against her, palms pressed to her ears.

"We need to go," Casey cries, eyes trained on the obsii as she pushes Liddy toward the edge of the embankment. "Down, Liddy. Go!"

"Wait!" Liddy staggers against the edge.

Red's voice fills her head. *Run.*

"No time." Casey pushes the spot between Liddy's shoulder blades. "Go!"

Liddy screams as she slides over the edge. Casey throws herself down after her, weight tilted back to avoid pitching down the slope headfirst.

The earth splits under her feet, sweeping and tumbling and dragging her down faster. Behind her, the obsii gather, their cries haunting. Casey drives the dagger into the dirt to slow her skid.

Liddy slides past her, reaching the bottom first. She stands, disoriented, pitching to her knees before she can get her balance.

Run!

Casey's feet hit even ground. The shrill chatter picks up behind them, closer and closer, until her entire body feels charged with frantic energy. Beside her, Liddy cries, tears leaving pale tracks through the dirt against her cheeks.

Shadows tumble down the hill in pursuit and Casey's heart ricochets off her rib cage.

RUN!

She squeezes the dagger. Fighting isn't an option. It isn't

even a last resort. They have to get out of here. She remembers the boy beneath the streetlight, dragged from this in-between world by shadow.

She can't lose Liddy again. Not in this place. And definitely not to those things.

Reaching out, she snags Liddy's hand and drags her forward, pulling her when she trips, refusing to let her stop, refusing to let her go.

But then Liddy is tugging on her. A shadow takes hold of her, dragging Liddy across the sand and out toward the water.

"Liddy!" Casey screams.

"*Casey!*" The obsii begins towing her into the surf.

Casey's feet sink into the sand. She can't. She can't. She can't. *I can't lose her again.*

Liddy bobs on the surface, spitting out water. "C-Casey!" she chokes.

Casey races into the waves.

Sprays of water fly up around her as she picks up her feet, wading deeper and deeper until the swell of the surf is too much and she dives in.

She holds her breath as she kicks beneath the waves, surfacing not far from Liddy. The first thing she sees is the pale shape of Liddy's arm above the swell of another wave. She throws her arms over her head, pulling against the water, propelling her closer to Liddy as she fights against something.

Casey grabs her hand just as Liddy is pulled beneath the water. Their hands tug and slide and Casey locks every muscle in her arm, but the current is strong.

She takes a deep breath and dives beneath the surf, kicking toward Liddy. There's darkness under her; it swirls in shadowy shapes that drag her down. Down. Down.

Casey lets go of Liddy's hand.

She kicks even harder, swimming down past Liddy, and swipes the dagger through the water. The shadows twist and pull, releasing Liddy and shooting off through the murky underworld of the harbor.

Liddy kicks upward and Casey pushes at her feet.

When she finally breaks the surface, she finds Liddy hacking up water. They both drag themselves onto the sand. Casey's arms shake from exhaustion. The surf runs over her fingers in blue-foamed ripples. But then they turn black, the water thick like sludge.

"Get out of the water," Casey gasps. She crawls forward through the sand. "Get out!" she screams at Liddy.

The two of them scramble up as dark shadows climb from the water, their humanoid faces breaking free, their long, clawing limbs driving deep into the sand. They scream that terrible scream and Casey covers her ears.

She whips around. Darkness descends from the trees.

"The rental shack," she says to Liddy. That's it. That's their only option.

They sprint across the sand. Liddy gets there first.

Casey stops, turning to face the wall of shadow that creeps from the ground. Something at the top of the embankment catches her attention. Not the black swarm, but the lone figure that stands among them, dark wings fluttering in the breeze.

Azrael.

The shrieks of the obsii draw her back and she brandishes the dagger.

Every bit of common sense seems to trickle from her mind, and she swings it like a baseball bat, based on muscle memory alone. The first shadow lunges. She catches it midair, turning the creature to mist that settles like dust around her ankles.

"Get inside," she says, pushing Liddy toward the door.

Liddy swings it open and Casey rushes in after her, sparing one more glance in Azrael's direction before slamming it closed. The shadows collide with it, the impact sending her sprawling back. From the floor, she wonders about the stability of the building and how long it will be before the obsii get inside.

Liddy helps her up, but Casey stays on her knees and drives the dagger into the floor, carving around them both.

"What's going on?" Liddy cries as the space around them begins to pulse.

"Keep breathing," she says as the crushing pressure closes around her. It's different this time though, less focused, and for a moment Casey swears she's being pulled in all directions.

When she opens her eyes, she's on her knees on her bedroom floor. Casey rubs her face and rolls over to catch her breath. "That was . . . a little more intense than I planned."

Liddy winces, dragging herself upright.

"Are you all right?" Casey scrambles to her side, prodding and poking at Liddy. "They didn't hurt you, did they?"

"No," Liddy says, an edge of tension in her voice, like she can't quite breathe deep enough. "I'm fine."

"I'm so glad." Casey pulls her into another hug, her throat tight. "It's so good to see you."

"It's good to see you, too," Liddy whispers, her arms making a weak loop around Casey's neck. She shudders against her and Casey pulls away, eyeing her warily.

"Is something wrong?"

"I don't know," Liddy mumbles, pressing a hand to her stomach. "I feel weird."

"Weird like how?"

"Like . . . something's missing."

Casey grabs her hand and squeezes. "It's okay, we'll figure it out. All that matters is you're back. And you're okay."

"I'm back." Liddy's eyes fill with tears and her head drops against Casey's shoulder. "I don't ever want to go back there again," she whispers.

Casey brushes her hands through Liddy's damp, matted hair. "I won't let you go," she promises. "Not again."

Liddy sobs against her as Casey rubs her hand up and down her back, then her door bursts open and Red's outline fills the space.

She looks at him, an explanation dying in her throat.

Red's eyes are fixed on Liddy, but his words are for Casey. "*What did you do?*"

"I—" Casey takes one look at Liddy, shivering on her bed and they both know there's no need to say it.

He runs his fingers through his hair, yanking at the strands. There's an explosive intensity about him that she's never seen, and though it should scare her, she's too shocked to be anything

232

but awed. Fiery energy radiates from him, and not for the first time, Casey recognizes some of that unearthly power.

"I know what you're going to say," she begins, shifting in place as if to shield Liddy from view.

"This isn't how it works, Casey! You don't get to bring people back!"

"Well, there isn't exactly a rule book written out—"

"Do *not* give me that! I said you could help people cross over to the light or the dark. Coming back here with souls was *never* an option!"

She huffs. Some part of her had known it was wrong, had sensed it, but then things spun out of control. And with the obsii in pursuit, how could she let Liddy go again? For her, there wasn't any other option.

"You weren't ready to be there on your own yet." His voice is hard and unyielding.

"Because you say so?"

"Yes! Exactly that! You don't know everything you need to know." He bites his lip, pacing before her, his frantic glances landing on Liddy every few seconds. He stops walking and looks right at her, straight through her. "You knew how dangerous it could be."

"I couldn't wait any longer," she protests. "I couldn't risk losing her again!"

"What if you'd encountered something you couldn't outrun?" His entire body shakes as he works to keep control of his words. "What if it had been Azrael?"

Casey goes quiet, remembering the image of Azrael on the

hill, looking down as Limbo erupted into chaos. "I didn't think that far ahead."

"Of course you didn't. You raced into it all without thinking. Without considering what you would have done had she caught up with you. Had she offered you what every being has sought before you. Unlimited and unyielding power."

"I never wanted those things."

"But you must have felt it. Must have been tempted. I know you thought it in that house, when you said it was unfair, the way darkness bent around the rules."

"That doesn't mean I wanted it."

"Did she offer you an exchange?"

"What?"

"Was Liddy the deal?" he demands.

"No!" Casey says, shock pitching her voice. "Of course not! How could you think I would side with them after everything I've seen?"

"Because I couldn't protect you. Because it's easier."

"I'm not *her*, Red!" she yells, partly in anger and partly because she needs him to really hear her. To actually understand what she's saying. "I'm not Elise."

"You don't know what you're talking about."

"I know I'm the first person you've helped since her. I know that you're scared of losing me to the darkness."

His eyes close.

"And *you* didn't lose her, Red. It wasn't your fault. You can't blame yourself for choices other people make. You told me that."

"Stop," he whispers.

"I'm not going to side with the darkness. I won't stand against you." She can't tell if he's broken or relieved.

"Please tell me you at least sealed the doorway."

She opens her mouth. Closes it. Crosses her arms and looks away. That's why the doorway felt so strange. She'd forgotten to seal it.

To protect it from those creatures.

"I didn't think to," she says quietly. "I went in with Liddy on my mind and by the time I realized the mess we were in, there wasn't time. We just ran."

"I told you there were two rules." His voice is like ice. "Only two." Red kneels down and picks up the dagger from the floor where she dropped it. "This is very, very bad."

"You don't need to tell me that," Casey snaps.

"I do." For once the look on Red's face truly scares her. "Because you have no idea *how* bad."

SEVENTEEN

HER PULSE JUMPS beneath her skin. Casey can see it beat against the curve of her wrist as she lays a towel, a change of clothes, and a new toothbrush on the counter. She tucks her arms against her chest, keeping the panicked flutter contained.

She'd changed out of her damp clothes, but she can still feel the chill of the ocean against her skin.

Red hovers in the hallway. She catches his scowl in the bathroom mirror.

"I think that should do it," she says, faux calm, her voice just the tiniest bit too high.

Liddy sits on the closed top of the toilet lid, staring at her, something about her expression vacant. There's a sad uncertainty drawn into her features. "So, this guy just showed up in your bedroom . . ."

"It's not like that," Casey hurries to say.

"You sure?"

"Absolutely. If you need anything else," Casey says, "just call. I'll be right outside."

"Okay," Liddy says, standing to run her hand over the soft plum towel Casey has picked out for her.

"I know it's not up to your usual standards. I'm sure my loofahs and body butter are sorely lacking, but there is coconut oil in the shampoo, so I haven't failed you completely."

A part of Liddy seems to connect then and she giggles. "I tried so hard to mold you. Where did I go wrong?"

"Nowhere, it's in my DNA. I like flip-flops and baggy jeans."

"And you don't like to brush your hair or make your bed."

"Hey, I brush my hair! It's supposed to be this way." Granted, it's sporting a bit more foliage than usual. Casey picks a dead leaf from her ponytail. "That's the style I'm going for."

"Whatever you say." Liddy crosses the room and fiddles with the taps in the shower, sighing as the warm water rushes over her hands.

"All right, then, I'll leave you to it."

Casey slips out of the bathroom and closes the door behind her. In the hallway, Red leans against the wall. He's shrouded in darkness, so she can't make out the look on his face, but she doesn't need to. She can feel the furious energy coming off him.

They wait, stubbornly squared off in the hallway, until they hear the sputter of the shower.

"She isn't supposed to be here," he hisses. "You *know* that."

"I didn't have a choice," Casey whispers.

"You should have waited for me."

"I couldn't. You were gone, fighting the obsii, and I couldn't wait." Casey takes a step toward Red. "Besides, isn't it better this way?"

"What are you talking about?"

"You had nothing to do with this. It's all me. So you didn't break any rules."

"What?"

"Your wings, earning them back."

"Is that what you think of me? After everything, you assumed I wanted my wings more than I wanted to help you?"

"Admit it. If you want to get your wings back, you're bound by the rules!"

"And you think *you're* not?" Red gives his head a hard shake before stalking away.

"I never said I wasn't."

"This isn't a game, Casey."

She follows him down the hall with her arms crossed, face set in a look of defiant rage. "What are you doing?" she snaps.

"Trying to fix this irreparable mess."

"Don't be so dramatic."

"I'm not. You should know me better than that."

The look on his face shifts from anger to disappointment. Red hasn't been in her life long, but he's wormed his way into the darkest and hardest part of it. Into the place her fears live. And, in a way, she's come to know him, too—his fears, the trials he's faced, the sacrifices he's made. She understands parts of who Red is, of who he's worked to be, and so she does, in fact, know that he isn't just being petty. She doesn't think he's capable of petty.

Her initial anger at him makes her feel ashamed, more potent than anything she'd felt moments ago.

"I'll fix this, okay?"

Fighting with Red isn't going to help either of them. Regardless of her good intentions, she hadn't exactly been oblivious to the consequences of Limbo. Did she know all of these specifically terrible things could happen? No. But did she know that bad things could happen by messing with a world she didn't completely understand? Of course. Saying anything to the contrary is a lie.

"I'll do whatever I have to do in order to keep Liddy safe. I promised her."

Red steps close, his voice a resigned whisper. "And what exactly was that promise, Casey? She's been dead for weeks. Her parents buried her. How does this end well?"

"I don't know yet."

"Of course you don't, because this is not how it's done." He glances once down the hall, checking to see that Liddy is still in the bathroom. "You don't get to bring people back to life."

"Well—"

"Not 'well,' Casey. You can't. Bring people. Back. To life." He smacks his hands together, punctuating the words. "Part of them will be missing."

She frowns.

"Her body, Casey. Her physical vessel is a corpse. Decaying in the ground. Without it, you can't stay here in the physical world. You can't exist!"

Casey swallows hard. Liddy had said that much already, that she felt like something was missing.

"All you've done is bring her soul back. And that is infinitely worse."

"Why is that worse?"

"Because souls move easily through the barriers between worlds. And a soul without a vessel to contain it makes room for other things to follow in their place. You left the doorway open and now you've created an entrance into the physical world through Liddy. So, yes, this is worse. This is about as bad as it can be. If Azrael really is looking for a way to bridge the gap between Limbo and the physical plane, you've given her a way to send herself here."

Casey's breath catches up in her throat. "I didn't . . . I didn't know."

That makes Red pause, the expression on his face saddened, but not exactly that. It's almost like he feels sorry for her.

"I know," he says quietly. "How could you know?"

And that's it. They've both just accepted their own role in this mess. Their own faults.

They're both guilty of things: her not trusting Red with Liddy, and him not trusting her enough to share these parts of Limbo with her.

The tentative apology is there on the tip of her tongue, but she doesn't have to say it. Red looks at her and she looks at him, both of them sorry.

Now they have to fix it.

"Where exactly did you enter and exit Limbo?" he asks.

"My bedroom."

"Then we need to try and seal the doorway from our end, at least."

Liddy steps into the hall, wearing borrowed clothes from Casey's closet. Her wet hair is twisted into a braid that hangs over her shoulder.

"You," Red says, pointing at her. "Come with us."

"Okay, bossy," Liddy huffs. "And who *are* you, by the way?"

Red guides Liddy to Casey's bed and sits her down. "Red."

"Like . . . just Red?"

"Just Red," he says.

Liddy crosses her legs, holding her bare feet with her hands. "What's happening?"

Casey blinks at her, once, twice. She's never been so happy to see Liddy and yet . . . it's all completely wrong. "I did something I wasn't supposed to do," she says.

Liddy's lips pucker in understanding. They're together again after all this time but one of them doesn't belong. "I thought so."

"I'm sorry," Casey whispers.

Liddy shakes her head and flips her braid over her shoulder. The edge of her mouth curls from a line to a smile. "I don't think I made it easy for you."

A bubble of laughter nearly escapes her. It's nice to see that some things never change, no matter how many times they both died. "No, you didn't," Casey agrees.

Liddy leans back on her hands and flicks her chin at Red. "So, you've been helping Casey with this new hobby of hers?"

"This is his area of expertise," Casey says.

"Chasing souls through Limbo?"

"Cleaning up messes."

Red looks over at her for a second, then away as he pulls the feathers from the chain at his neck.

Liddy looks at Casey pointedly and Casey gives her head a shake.

"Glad to know I haven't missed that much," Liddy says.

"You haven't," Casey promises. "Now, I know it's utterly impossible for you, but try not to move."

Liddy closes her eyes. "Fine, I'll sit here and meditate while you two carve up the walls."

Red clears some of her furniture away from the walls, moving it to the center of the room. He pulls down photos and tack boards and anything else in the way.

When he's done, he closes her bedroom door and on the back carves the same symbol he uses to seal the doorways inside Limbo. "Copy this exactly onto each of the four walls." He passes Casey one of the daggers. "I'm going to do the other side of the door."

"What the heck am I going to tell my aunt when she sees this?"

"I think you have bigger things to worry about. Namely her," he mutters, pointing at Liddy. "I am so going to hell for this."

"Don't say that!"

"I'm serious. It'll be the only place that will take me when they find out." Red closes the door on himself.

"Well, he's dramatic," Liddy says.

Casey climbs onto her bed and carves into the wall. "Maybe he's right."

"He's going to hell?"

"No, just that . . . this is a much bigger problem than I thought it would be."

"Did you know what would happen?"

"Honestly, I wasn't even thinking about it. I just knew what would happen if I let the obsii get ahold of you."

"The what?"

"Those black, shadow creatures."

"Oh." Liddy shivers in response. "Maybe you shouldn't be so hard on yourself," she says. "Doing the right thing means there's always someone who gets hurt."

"Does it, though?"

"Yeah. Or it wouldn't be such a hard decision to make."

Casey drops her arm, halfway through carving.

The door swings open a moment later.

"We can't keep her here," Red says, caught up in his thoughts. He paces through the room. "Not when she's supposed to be dead. I can veil a lot from your aunt, but this . . . this is too much. We have to find somewhere to hide her," he continues. "Somewhere close, where we can regroup. And we need more people." He looks at Liddy in a way that makes Casey really nervous.

She climbs down off the bed. "Why?"

"Just . . . trust me. We need the help."

THEY SNEAK LIDDY into Casey's car under the cover of darkness and drive across town to Evan's place.

Every glance in the rearview mirror washes Liddy out, a paler reflection than the moment before. Under the glow of the street-lights, Casey swears Liddy has turned a chalky shade of gray, the blotches under her eyes becoming more pronounced.

When she pulls into Evan's driveway, she parks right beside his truck. She hopes his parents aren't supposed to be return-ing home anytime soon, or else this is about to become very complicated.

"Wait here," she tells Red. Liddy seems to be out of it, sway-ing in her seat and shielding her eyes from the streetlights. "Let me tell him first?"

"We don't have time for gentle, Casey."

She shoots him a look in the mirror before she gets out of the car and sprints up the steps, hammering on Evan's door. Before she even gives him a chance to answer, she rings the doorbell over and over again. She keeps ringing it even as the porch light comes on and he swings the door open.

"What the heck is going on? Are you ... is everything okay?" He makes a grumpy face at her. "Casey?"

She wants to launch herself into his arms, to bask in his warmth and humor and the soft way he says her name even after she's hurt him.

But she fights it.

There isn't time for that now.

"I need a favor," she says in one frantic breath. "A really *big* favor."

"Casey, what is it? You're freaking me out."

"I, uh—" She runs her hand through her hair, pushing it away from her face as she looks back at the car.

Evan follows her line of sight. "Who is that?"

Casey feels a miserable ache in her stomach as she prepares to tell him. "Evan, let's go inside for a minute."

"What's going on?"

He leans around her as Red gets out of the car. He nods when he notices him, but pales when he sees who Red helps climb out of the back seat. Evan looks at Casey, eyes widened to the point of pain.

"Is that . . ." Evan grips the door for support, swearing under his breath. "Oh, you didn't."

"Yeah, I sort of did." Casey watches as the color continues to drain from his face. "Can we come in?"

EIGHTEEN

EVAN REFUSES TO sit still.

Casey, Liddy, and Red sit knee to knee on his fabric couch, watching him pace back and forth.

Sometimes he scratches at the back of his head, tipping his neck and wincing, like he's thinking really hard. Other times he stops and stares at Liddy, blinking like she might disappear if he squeezes his eyes tight enough.

Casey studies the house while Evan works through his internal crisis. It hasn't changed much over the years. His mom and stepdad have always kept a neat place. She knows from experience that all of the mess is contained to Evan's room—textbooks and sports equipment and probably last night's dishes. The only thing that changes with any regularity are the photos of Evan on the wall. Each year, his new school picture is framed and replaces the old one.

Finally, he stops pacing and makes direct eye contact.

"Tell me if I have this right. On your first solo trip, you brought our dead best friend back to life, which is against the rules, and now I'm harboring a cross-dimensional fugitive in my living room." He claps his hands together. "No offense, Lids."

"None taken."

"Of course it's against the rules," Red mumbles. "And she's not alive. Not really."

Casey folds her hands in her lap, trying her best not to grimace. "But you're more or less right."

"Well, okay ... *wow*. I mean, it's good to see you, Liddy, but ... it's weird. Impossible, really. I'm dreaming, right?"

Red opens his mouth, preparing to say something, but decides against it.

"We need somewhere for her to stay," Casey explains, "where other people won't see her."

"Like her family?" Evan rubs his chin. "And kids we know? And pretty much the entire population of the town?"

"Yeah, not the best idea right now. And I thought, since your parents are still away—"

"That I might put up our best friend in my spare bedroom so no one finds out you brought her back to life?" He nods. "All right, I'm in."

"Just like that?" Casey asks.

"I was never really out." The smile he gives her is warm and forgiving and immediately she wants to melt into him.

"You two haven't changed," Liddy mumbles. "Still staring at each other with big goo-goo heart eyes."

"Ah, I missed you, Lids," Evan says. "Things haven't been the same without you."

Casey wrinkles her nose. "And we do not stare at each other with goo-goo eyes."

"Please. It's so"—Liddy shudders, like a chill has zipped down her spine—"obvious."

"Liddy, are you okay?"

"Tired," she says. "And sore. Everything hurts."

"Here," Evan says. He pulls a pillow from one of the stuffed armchairs and takes his mother's favorite throw blanket off the back of the couch. "Lie down and rest. We'll figure out what's going on."

Red stands, wandering into the den, where the bay windows reveal an inky, black sky. Flickers of lightning spark across it, seeming to crash into one another.

"That's intense," Evan says when they join Red at the window. "I bet they close the beaches today."

Red stares out the glass, a grim look on his face. "That's no storm."

"Oh, you mean your friend from the church is coming over?"

Red unlocks the screen door and steps onto the back porch. A harsh wind picks up, whipping through the house, bringing with it large drops of rain. Thunder crashes above them, shaking the ground.

Evan's yard isn't fenced, opening into a field. Red walks out to where the sudden storm seems to be gathering. Lightning splinters across the sky, colliding over Evan's house.

"Red!" Casey shouts.

She tears off into the rain after him, with Evan yelling her name from inside.

Red stops below the thundering mass, throwing his hand out before she catches up. "Stay back," he warns. Rain streams down his face, dripping from his chin.

The ground shakes again as a bolt of lightning strikes near them, sending Casey tumbling. It erupts in a golden flame that shoots upward before disappearing. Then the sky is quiet and the rain stops.

Light from inside spills across Evan's backyard, and from the scorched earth steps Malakhi, his arched wings the color of white beach sand. They disappear, receding into his back, as he steps away from the smoldering ground.

"Malakhi," Red greets, his tone not exactly friendly.

"I told you I didn't want to do this again, Redmond."

Somehow—perhaps because she knows Liddy is inside fighting for her existence, or the fact that the figure before her terrifies her more than Red ever has—Casey has the good sense not to comment on *Redmond*.

Red hangs his head. "I know."

Casey scrambles to her feet as Malakhi circles Red, looking him up and down. There are gaping holes in his shirt where his wings have retreated. Through the scraps of material, Casey expects she would see the fine feathered outline tattooed against his skin.

"Only you could somehow make this situation worse. All you had to do was help her track down one measly little soul."

"It's not his fault," Casey interjects.

Malakhi examines her with a kind of scrutiny that makes her want to shrink in on herself. She doesn't know what he's looking for exactly, or if he ever finds it. His expression gives nothing away. Eventually, he just stops looking. "Where is the girl? Take me to her."

"Inside." Red turns on his heel and the two of them stride across the field to Evan's porch.

Casey jogs to catch up.

"You know the entire purpose of this assignment was for you to earn your wings back, right?" Malakhi says coldly.

"I didn't intend for this to happen," Red says, glaring at him.

"Perhaps you weren't as focused as you should have been."

Evan opens the screen door again and watches as the two angels breeze by him.

Casey shrugs at the look he shoots her, following the others back to the living room. "Where's Liddy?" she asks, staring at the abandoned spot on the couch.

Evan gestures over his shoulder. "Bathroom."

From down the hall, she hears Liddy's voice: "What do you want?"

Casey frowns, turning in the direction of the bathroom. "Who's she talking to?"

Casey eyes Evan before they both sprint down the hall. She gets there first and staggers to a stop, grabbing the door frame.

Liddy clutches the edge of the sink, hair falling over her face, speaking to her reflection. Except the image is a dark reflection, pale and trembling, with black veins spreading beneath the skin.

Her voice is low, the whispers too fast for Casey to make out.

Then from her lips spills a sound that makes the lights flicker and the mirror tremble, just like the high-pitched squeal of the obsii creatures.

"Oh, flamin' heck," Evan says. He grabs Liddy by the arm and yanks her from the bathroom as the mirror shatters, exploding into hundreds of pieces that scatter across the floor. "Hey, angel-boys, there's a talking demon in the mirror!"

The three of them cower together on the floor, shock rooting them to the spot.

"Liddy," Casey whispers, nudging her with a foot.

"I don't feel so good," she mumbles.

Evan gestures to the mess. "My mom is probably gonna ask about this."

In his arms, Liddy turns a pale green color, almost like the algae that grows across the surfaces of ponds in the dank heat of summer. Then the green recedes to gray, like dead flesh.

She rolls from his arms, slumping onto the carpet on all fours and heaves, throwing up black tar.

"Liddy!" Casey screams.

Malakhi stalks down the hall and bends over Liddy. He rests a palm against her forehead.

Finally he straightens, turning to face them, his eyes swirling. "She's without a vessel," Malakhi says.

Red nods. "I know. We sealed the access point from Limbo, but—"

"That won't hold against what's coming." Malakhi's dark eyes narrow. "The obsii already grow inside her."

"It wasn't his fault," Casey insists, getting to her feet.

She doesn't know why, but her desire to defend Red is overwhelming. Maybe it's the dismissive way Malakhi looks at him, or the fact that the first thing he did was taunt Red with his wings, the one thing Casey knew he wanted more than anything. Or maybe it's simply because this whole mess really is her fault. Red has done nothing but try to protect her since he got here.

"It was me," she says. "I brought her back. I left Limbo unsealed."

"You were in his charge," Malakhi says dismissively, nodding toward Red. "There is no excuse for this."

"It wasn't his fault," she says again. She rests her hand in the middle of Liddy's back. "I did this. He had no idea I was even there."

"He was supposed to be watching you. Guiding you. So things like this didn't happen."

Casey lets out a small sob as Liddy shudders, spewing thick black bile onto the carpet. Evan slides out of the way as another shudder seizes Liddy's entire body. Evan wraps his hand around her waist when her body begins to jerk, and Casey pulls her hair away from her face.

In Evan's arms, Liddy goes limp and he lowers her to the ground on her back. They watch her eyes roll into her head.

"What's wrong with her?" Casey demands.

"She can't remain here like this," Malakhi says. "The obsii are coming."

"Here? How?" Evan demands.

"Liddy has created a hole, and it calls to them. They will come en masse," Malakhi answers. "Lift her head."

Malakhi turns his gaze on Liddy and Casey feels the dizziness creep in.

Evan rolls away clutching his head.

"A veil," Red says. "You think that will work?"

"It won't hold them off for long," Malakhi admits. "She's too far gone for that, but it might buy us some time."

"Time for what?" Evan demands.

"To relocate somewhere safer. Somewhere we can contain this mess. And we don't need to give them a front-row view of where that is. The less those things are privy to, the better." He crouches in front of Liddy, trailing his finger across her forehead. "Sleep, child. Put the voices in your head to rest."

Liddy's eyelids flutter.

"She's fighting it," Red says.

Casey watches the glaze in Malakhi's eyes swirl faster. It's equal parts mesmerizing and nauseating. He mumbles hushed words, too fast and too foreign for her to understand. A sudden gust of wind spirals through the room, ruffling her hair.

"No," Liddy mutters, squirming against them. "No more. Casey don't let them do this to me!" Her eyes are white as they roll back in her head, her lids fluttering over them.

Crouching behind her, Casey lays her hands against Liddy's head, her hair still damp from earlier. "I'm sorry," she whispers, holding her tighter. After everything, she's only made things worse. Now Liddy isn't just dead, but undead in a way—a soul without a vessel, marked as a path by the darkness.

"You promised," Liddy mutters, her head lolling to the side, trying to see her. "You were supposed to protect me."

Casey's fingers slip, her breath caught in her throat, but Evan's there suddenly, catching Liddy.

"Sleep," Malakhi continues to mumble and all Casey can do is try not to cry.

"She doesn't mean it," Red whispers. "It's not her talking."

Whether it is or not, the words ring true, and Casey bends under their weight. When it's done, Liddy's eyelids close and she slumps against Evan.

"It won't hold them off for long," Malakhi says.

Casey frowns. "Will the veil wear off?"

"Veils are only as strong as the angel who casts them." Red's eyes flicker to Malakhi. "When he grows too weak to suppress the darkness, it will shatter."

"It's true," Malakhi says. "I am only a Messenger. And the darkness that follows Liddy from Limbo is strong and persistent. They know they are close to reaching the physical world again."

"I'll take her back," Casey says. "I'll find the light."

"It's too late for that. What's coming is already coming. The only thing we can do now is fight it." He looks at Red. "Are you ready?"

Red nods.

Malakhi turns to them. "Help her up. We need to move."

NINETEEN

"IT'S ALWAYS THIS place," Evan says, resigned as they pull up in front of the abandoned church.

They're all crammed into Casey's car: two angels. A Limbo-walker. One decaying soul. And Evan.

Red's barely spoken since they arrived, and it makes Casey anxious as she studies the outline of the church in the reds and yellows of sunrise. It looms above them, broken but steady. This is where she first escaped this world for Limbo. It seems somewhat fitting that it should end here, too. Whatever the plan is.

"A great war between the light and dark has already been fought here," Malakhi says. "It will be the safest place to contain what's coming."

Casey tries to sense what Malakhi describes, but all she can feel right now are nerves. They boil in her gut and shoot down each of her limbs.

Beside her, Liddy thrashes, growling as she yanks on the seat belt. She's become more and more uncooperative as the veil has started to wear off. It requires both Casey and Evan to keep her from pulling on the door handle and making a break for it. Casey keeps her hand over the seat belt clip as a precaution.

"What are we *actually* doing here?" she says.

Red turns to her, lips thin and drawn across his face. "Waking Michael." He pulls the keys from the ignition.

"Like the archangel?" Evan says. "The big stone guy?"

Malakhi nods as he scans the church with what Casey can describe only as trepidation. He doesn't shudder or pale at the sight, but something about him bows in a reverent kind of fear.

Casey's stomach leaps at the thought.

Malakhi pushes his door open. "Keep hold of her or she'll resist."

Evan grunts. "Oh, I hadn't noticed."

"Let me go!" Liddy hisses as Casey steps out of the car and grabs her wrist.

"Liddy, stop," Casey urges. "We're trying to help you."

"And you're making it impossible," Evan adds. "Like this is a whole new level of stubborn, Lids, even for you." His grip falters as he climbs out after them, and he has to duck a swinging blow from Liddy's fist.

"It's the darkness," Malakhi explains. "It gives her strength." He takes hold of Liddy's elbow, and Red takes her other side, their combined power enough to combat Liddy's growing strength.

They march her up to the church like some kind of prisoner. She grows stiff between them, digging her feet into the ground.

Before they reach the side entrance, Casey catches Evan's hand, pulling him to a stop until the others have walked out of earshot.

"You okay?" he asks her.

"Yeah. I mean, no?" She blinks. "But that's not why I stopped you."

"Oh?"

She sighs. "You know I'm sorry, right? For everything I said. For making you feel like I didn't care about you or us or—"

"I know," he says. "I'm sorry for doubting you. And for putting extra pressure on you."

"Doesn't matter now," Casey says. "I just wanted to tell you that you don't have to do this."

"I sort of do."

"There's still time for you to go home."

"Can you let me say this?" Evan's lips tighten in an almost-grin. "Besides the fact that Liddy's our friend, I can't let you go it alone. I don't know if you remember, because it was a long time ago, but it pretty much went like this. Boy plays with girl on beach. Girl throws sand in his eyes. Boy falls madly in love."

"Madly?" she repeats quietly.

"The stupid, crazy kind. The kind that makes you do stupid, crazy things." Evan reaches for her hand, tracing the lines on her palm with his thumb. "So if you're waging war for Liddy's soul, then count me in."

"Really?"

He tugs on the edge of her shirt, bringing them together. His voice rumbles low against her cheek, in a way that makes her shiver. "Count me in for it all."

Casey turns her head and lifts her chin, meeting his lips. They taste like mint gum and her berry lip balm. The kiss isn't long or soul-shattering or even particularly romantic, but Casey feels the easy way his lips give against hers, fitting with a simplicity that is incredibly nice when everything else feels like it's spiraling out of control. When they break apart, it isn't because of some desperate need for air, but because the rush of the moment has finally caught up with them.

With a glance at his somewhat stunned face, Casey brushes her fingers over her lips and grins. "We should go," she whispers.

"Yeah, sure," Evan mumbles, his cool blue eyes blank and glassy. "Whatever you say, boss."

She tugs on his hand, smiling despite herself. They hurry to catch up with the others. Red has Liddy pinned to a pew when they enter the church and Casey jumps in to help while Malakhi circles the statue of Michael.

Liddy hisses, her fingers digging into the skin on Casey's forearm, leaving red crescent-shaped marks.

"Stop it!" Casey grunts at her. Liddy narrows her eyes and she squirms, her teeth bared in struggle.

Malakhi runs his hand over the marble armor that adorns Michael's shoulders. He stands back and lets his wings unfurl.

"So, how does this work?" Evan says. "Is there like a magic word or a secret button somewhere? Or do we just go ahead and bust open this giant rock man?"

"In a manner of speaking." Malakhi rips a long feather from beneath his wings, watches it transform to steel in his hand, then drives it into the center of the statue. Tiny fissures spread across the stone.

Liddy cries out, the sound echoing off the walls.

"She won't last much longer," Red says.

"What does that mean?" Casey says, keeping her voice low.

"It means that the darkness is almost here. We need help *now*." Red loosens the pair of feathers from the chain at his neck, turning them into twin daggers, making a slow sweep of the church with his eyes.

Liddy screams, her head twisting like a swivel on the point of her neck.

"She's possessed," Evan says, holding Liddy back against the pew when she tries to bolt.

"It's not a possession," Red says. "You need a body for that. A host. Souls just act as a doorway."

Liddy screams again, the sound settling in Casey's bones. Evan holds his hands over his ears, and Liddy throws herself from the pew, eager for escape.

"Stand back," Malakhi orders as he slams his palm against the handle of the weapon wedged into the statue. The impact reverberates throughout the entire church like the crashing of a gong. Malakhi strikes the statue three times, splattering bits of alabaster stone across the alcove. With each strike, Casey takes another step back, almost tripping over Liddy who's sprawled out, heaving against the ground.

After the third strike, Malakhi stops abruptly. He groans, clutching his stomach as he takes a few stumbling steps away from the alcove.

"What's happening?" Evan asks.

Casey dodges Liddy's clawing fingers, then wraps her hands around both of her wrists, trying desperately to hold her still.

"Someone must stand in his place," Red explains, catching Malakhi as he takes another robotic step, steadying him. "There must always be enough guardians."

Malakhi's jawline locks first, then the twist of his neck. The change happens fast, seizing him in place within a few terrifying seconds and Red guides his stone body gently to the ground.

"So," Evan says, "is that gonna happen to all of us? Or—"

Liddy knees him in the gut when he gets too close and escapes Casey's grip, scrambling away.

Red rushes after her, vaulting himself over the back of a pew with ease.

The statue of Michael begins to tremble, then bursts as something springs from the shattered rubble. It's a towering figure of an angel, cloaked in battle garb, a massive sword clutched in his hand. Michael's skin is like poured wax, pure and unblemished, coating thick muscle. Casey's accustomed to that unearthly beauty and grace and energy, but the most startling feature is his wings.

They're nothing like what she imagines Red's once were, or even like Malakhi's. These are thick and white, brighter than new snow, extending out from his back in a glorious kind of display. Even the air around them seems to crackle, bending in reverence. Casey has the overwhelming urge to drop to her knees.

From his place, Red falls into a deep bow, his right hand pressed over his heart. "Michael," he greets.

"Children," he says, his voice deep, shaking the ground beneath her.

Liddy jerks to attention, scrambling across the floor and away from Michael, who follows her with curious, but deliberate steps. "Oh, child, you have fallen far from the light."

He points his sword in her direction and Casey's heartbeat gallops so fast she thinks she might be sick right there on the floor. But Michael doesn't move to strike.

Liddy, on the other hand, stops backing away, her pale, sunken features turning into something malicious. She rests on her elbows, smiling at Michael with a cruel, twisted grin. A grin that doesn't belong to her face. Then she collapses onto her back, her body twitching.

"What's happening?" Evan demands.

"I know you are not who you pretend to be," Michael declares and Liddy laughs, loud and dark and deep. "Using a child is beneath you, is it not, Azrael?"

"We do what we must," a slithery voice answers, coming from Liddy. Her eyes become wide saucers, blank and black. Then they roll back and her entire body stills.

"Liddy!" Casey shouts, sprinting for her.

Red catches her around the waist, holding her back. "Don't," he warns. He wrestles her behind him, shoving her closer to Evan. "They're coming."

Casey doesn't even have a chance to utter the word *who* before Liddy's entire body begins to seize. Her jaw falls open and from her spills the same inky darkness that haunts Limbo. It erupts from her in a rush.

Like something out of a movie, the creatures peel themselves from the shadows, becoming tangible and dangerous. They move with purpose, dividing into defined shapes, somehow both human and animal-like. Casey's never seen so many of them in one place.

Evan shakes beside her, eyes closed to fight off the sound.

Red wields both his daggers, trained on the place where Liddy lies. Her skin flickers with an iridescent sheen, unsettled as something lurks beneath the surface. Her dark eyes are vacant now, but when she stands, it's with an ethereal grace.

Michael's wings flutter, almost in anticipation, but Liddy—or Azrael—only smiles.

Red squares off against an obsii that crawls over a pew, long black limbs turning to hooked claws.

"So, this looks bad," Evan says.

Red backs into him. "Find something to protect yourself with."

"Yeah, right," he mutters. "I'll go find one of those big chorus books that I used for a booster seat as a kid and start hitting things with it."

"Better than with your fists," Red says.

Casey edges away from the obsii that gather around them. A circle of shadow grows in her peripheral.

"Show yourself, Azrael," Michael demands, his voice booming. Some of the obsii cower before him, slinking away from his reach. "Stop lingering in the doorway. Let's settle this without any human carnage."

"Won't risk the child's soul, will you?" Azrael taunts, running Liddy's hand over her face. "They're so delicate, aren't they? So perfectly malleable, so easily swayed." She laughs, from somewhere deep in Liddy's chest. "That's the thing with you angels, so caught up in the cost of human life, the need to protect it. To *save* them. Sometimes a little sacrifice is necessary."

"We've been through this before," Michael says, sounding almost bored.

Azrael rolls her eyes. "Maybe you thick-skulled light worshipers will get it right one of these days. But I'm doubtful it will be today."

"Afraid you won't hold up after all this time?" Michael asks, amused. Casey doesn't know what exactly is so funny.

"I'm not the one who's spent the last however many years as a rock," Azrael sneers. "And your ranks have been somewhat depleted, I see. What do we have here? A couple of mortals and Red, my poor, wingless angel. How cute." She studies them all closely, before focusing on Red. "You know, we have an army made up of your brothers and sisters—some fallen, like you. But they have their wings now. That's the secret, Red. You can't fall from the darkness."

Red narrows his eyes.

"Not incentive enough?" Azrael taunts. "I thought wings were what all you fallen spent your days working toward." She clicks her tongue, clearly enjoying the game. "Well, keep it in mind. You don't have to do all the pathetic grunt work to get your wings back if you join us; consider them your 'welcome home' gift."

"She's really trying to sell you on this darkness stuff," Evan mutters.

"This is what they do," Red says. "They twist and taunt and turn you against everything you believe in."

"Oh, yes. We spin you around and around until you can't see straight. That's us, deceitful little liars." Azrael plays with the end of Liddy's braid. "Don't you ever get sick of this, Red? Of being told what to do?" She pouts. "Who you can love?"

Red tenses beside them.

"I'm not exactly the relationship expert, but it looks like you got the short end of the stick on that one. All because some high-and-mighty wing-flappers said no. Is that really how you want to spend the rest of existence, wishing for something that's been forbidden?"

The first of the shadows lunge suddenly, and Michael brings it down with a flick of his wrist, driving the tip of his sword deep into the center of the beast. Black mist fills the air around him.

Azrael chuckles. "Pretty, isn't it?"

"It's a distraction," Red says. "She's playing with us."

"Oh, he is a smart boy," Azrael giggles, grinning at him. "Let's play another one." She waves her fingers and the obsii scatter.

One of them rushes at Casey and she steps between Red and Michael. Evan isn't as lucky and ends up on the ground, shadow claws swinging above his face before Red manages to destroy it.

Evan scrambles to his feet, swearing under his breath.

Somewhere, Azrael cackles wildly.

"She can't stay trapped in Liddy's soul forever, right?" Casey says.

"Not if she wants to escape," Red answers. He kicks out hard, knocking a creature over a pew. "She's limited by Liddy's soul. She can't access any of her real strength. We just have to make sure that when she does abandon Liddy's soul, we get to it before the obsii."

Evan picks up what looks to be an old wooden chair leg and swings at something that creeps up behind him.

"And what happens when we get Liddy's soul back?" Casey asks. She keeps a careful position between Red and Michael. So far, the obsii haven't dared cross it.

"We keep it safe until we can get her back to Limbo."

"Easy," Evan says, but Casey can already hear the exhaustion in his voice.

"You okay?" she asks, ducking a shadow that comes flying at her from over the altar.

"Sure, it's just like Little League." He swings again and the chair leg buckles, small splinters appearing in the wood.

"You hated Little League."

"Yeah, but I was good at it!"

"Here, child," Michael says. He lands beside them with a sweep of his wings and hands a slim, golden blade to Evan, who nearly buckles under the weight of it. Michael flies off again, shadows pelting him from above. He cuts through them easily, his muscles rippling with every stroke. The walls shudder with the power behind his swings.

Evan holds the sword like a baseball bat. Then he pivots toward Casey and screams, "Duck!"

She does at the very last second, feeling the air part above her head and the slick mist glaze her skin. It smells like the charred end of a candlewick.

From across the church, Azrael shrieks. A twisted, angel-shaped thing separates from Liddy's body, leathery wings spilling out as Liddy collapses to the floor. Azrael moves with terrifying speed, crawling along the wall.

"That's definitely gonna give me nightmares," Evan says. He cuts the head off another obsii, kicking the body away as it turns to mist.

"Get to Liddy!" Red says to Casey. He gives her one of his daggers, then drives a pack of obsii out of her way. "They've separated!"

Azrael launches herself toward Michael with a shriek, dispersing the obsii. Casey scrambles away while they're distracted, using the pews as cover as she makes her way toward the back of the church where Liddy's soul has been abandoned.

When Casey reaches her, she presses her hands against Liddy's skin, flinching; she's ice-cold. Casey gives her a good, hard shake. "Liddy," she whispers. "Come on."

She's too heavy to carry, but grabbing her under the arms, Casey manages to drag her between the pews, sheltering them both from the battle.

She's pleased to see that Liddy's no longer that eerie gray shade. Her skin's still desperately cold and pale, for the most part, but a fine red tint brushes her cheeks.

"You can come back, Liddy," she says. "Anytime now." From the corner of her eye, she can see the shapes of the obsii creeping closer. They move in and retreat, taunting her, trying to draw her away from Liddy, but she stays close.

"Casey?" Liddy mumbles, coming around.

"Oh, finally," she mutters. "I thought I was going to be stuck dragging you around this church."

Liddy presses her hand to her forehead. "I feel like I was hit by a bus."

"Not quite a bus," Casey says, keeping her head low. "A demon and her shadow army."

Liddy frowns. "Oh."

Casey's skin prickles; she looks over her shoulder to see a dark shadow hovering above them.

Liddy's jaw drops, but before she can utter a sound, Casey thrusts her arm up and plunges the dagger deep into the obsii. It dissolves over them in a black cloud.

"Gross," Liddy mutters, clutching the side of her head as bits of dust settle on her skin. Her eyes go wide as another shadow creature takes its place.

Casey lunges toward it to prevent it from getting near enough to harm Liddy. "I'm getting really sick of you!" She drives the dagger down, splitting the shadow.

Suddenly there's a great roar, and Casey turns to see Michael lifting into the air, swarmed by obsii, and soaring straight for the roof. They crash through it, sending shards of glass and wood raining down on them. Casey crouches, throwing her arms over her head to shelter herself and Liddy.

Debris falls from above whenever Michael moves, battling

the seemingly never-ending swarm of obsii. Shadows crawl up the pillars in droves, keeping Michael on the roof, away from Azrael.

She's keeping us divided, Casey thinks. *Separating us so she can pick us off one by one.*

They're no match for her like this. Liddy's weak. Evan's human. And Red's wingless.

As if realizing the same thing, Azrael turns on Evan first, the closest to her. He blanches, stumbling backward up the steps toward the altar, swinging the golden sword wildly. Azrael cackles, lifting her scythe for a deadly blow.

"Evan!" Casey screams, racing toward him.

She knows it's already too late.

But the blow never reaches him.

Red jumps in front of Evan, and the scythe cuts him across the chest instead, a deep gash spanning his ribs.

"Red!" Casey yells as he wobbles, then falls to his knees, hands pressed against the blood spreading across his shirt.

Evan catches him as he pitches backward.

"I got you, buddy," Evan says. His hand presses against Red's, trying to help contain the blood. He lifts the sword with his other hand, brandishing it at Azrael.

She laughs and advances against them.

Red looks up at that moment, and where Casey expects fear, she sees a strange calm. Red's eyes begin to swirl an endless turn of white cloud.

Azrael hesitates as the air around them begins to crackle and spark, popping like fireworks. The ends of Casey's hair lift from her shoulders. Then a fork of lightning strikes through the battered roof, raining more glass down on them. The flash blinds her for a moment, but then the light is swallowed up as it makes contact with Red.

He seizes against Evan, absorbing the strike. Then, as if pulled by strings, he stands.

Feathers unfurl from his back, beautiful wings sprouting like white spikes around him.

"Oh, heck yes!" Evan shouts, fist-pumping the air.

Red leaps off the stairs and into the air, using his newly regained wings to twist toward Azrael, catching her off guard. They both go soaring across the church and Casey ducks out of the way as they ricochet off the back wall, stone crumbling from the impact. They spiral up to the mezzanine level, crashing into the old pipe organ.

Azrael swipes her scythe through the air and a few white feathers flutter to the ground.

"You're still no match!" she shouts at Red before she kicks him away. He skids across the stone steps in front of the altar. Azrael lands delicately and approaches slowly with self-assured feline grace. The hunter closing in on her prey.

Red struggles at first, staggering like a boxer post knock-out. He winces, his shirt torn and blood-stained, but manages to straighten up. Then he throws his head back, his eyes ghostly and white.

Azrael laughs cruelly. "Yes, summon Michael down here. Go on. Wings or not, you could use the help."

Red stretches his arms out, mirroring the length of his wings. His hands turn up, beckoning to the sky. Casey shivers as the church fills with energy and the air begins to crackle around Red again.

"Uriel!" he shouts over the swell of howling wind that sweeps down through the rafters. A glowing energy begins at his fingertips, swirling around the daggers. His gaze drops suddenly, eyes reflective pools of cloud, and a grin stretches his face into something terrifying. Both his hands ignite, the silver edges of his daggers alight with orange flame.

He strikes toward Azrael, and the fire lashes out like a serpent.

"He's making fire. He's making *fire*!" Evan cries, leaping the altar steps in a single jump and dashing down the center aisle. He grabs Casey and Liddy as he skids to a stop, knocking them both below a pew. "He's gonna burn the whole place down!"

Bits of fiery ash swirl around them like snow.

"We have to help him," Casey says.

"I think he's got it covered," Evan shouts, covering his ears as the obsii screech. "Did you not see the *fire*?"

Casey crawls along the pew, watching Red and Azrael spiral above. They twist so fast, they leave rings of smoke behind them.

Red crashes into the wall, shattering a stained-glass window. He pushes off, colliding with Azrael and sending her crashing into the altar, snapping it in half.

Before Azrael can recover, Red slams into her, using the force of his beating wings to keep her pinned.

"Send her back, Casey!" he cries.

Casey bounds to her feet and she dives forward with the dagger, carving a circle around the entire altar.

"Red!" she calls as she gets closer to the end of the circle.

"Don't forget to seal it!"

"But—"

"Close it!"

But . . . he'll go, too. He'll disappear with Azrael, alone in Limbo. Alone with who knows how many of those terrible shadow creatures.

"Casey, *close it*!" he cries.

She does, just as Evan comes running, knocking her out of Azrael's reach.

Both Red and Azrael vanish. Around them the church grows still. Even the roof stops trembling.

Casey falls to the floor. "Red?" she cries. "Red!"

"Seal it," Evan tells her urgently, lifting her hand until she gathers the strength to carve the symbol. When she's done, he crouches beside her. "Is that it?" he asks. "Does he . . . Can he . . . ?"

"He can," she rasps. "If he's okay . . . I think. If Azrael didn't—" She can't bear to finish the thought.

Evan sucks in a breath. "Aw hell, angel-boy."

A shadow suddenly explodes from the floor and Evan surges forward, roaring as he slashes Michael's sword.

It catches in the crux of twin daggers.

Red stands there, looking windswept, but grins at Evan and they start to laugh.

"Red!" Casey cries, throwing herself at him. She squeezes until her arms ache. Then she steps back to look at him. He's roughed up, his clothes torn, with red, raised welts across his arms. And his wings are gone, hidden beneath his skin again.

"It's over," he says.

"About time." Evan drops his sword. "This was no fun," he huffs, taking slow, deep breaths. "Too much cardio." He reaches for the floor and sits, collapsing onto his back. "No more of those things. Nope. I'm done."

"I am quite impressed with you." Red sits beside him, a curious look on his face. He blinks like he's seeing Evan again for the very first time. "Your skill is good . . . for a human."

"I played a lot of Little League as a kid. But, dude, you were on fire. Like literal fire. It was sort of badass."

"We make a good team," Red agrees.

Casey moves to help Liddy out from under the pew. She's shaky and unsteady, weakened by Azrael crossing through her soul.

"Just let me sit a second," Liddy says.

Casey squeezes her hands. "I'll be right back."

Liddy nods, closes her eyes and rests her head on the seat in front of her.

Evan and Red lay in front of the crushed remains of the altar, sprawled out like starfish, mumbling to each other and snickering. Still high off the adrenaline from the battle.

Red sits up when she returns. "Is Liddy okay?"

"Totally herself again." Casey gestures to the pew where she sits.

Evan gives her a thumbs-up from the floor. "I'm never moving again. Just drag me to the car." He props his head up. "You're a hot mess!"

Casey laughs. "You should see yourself."

Evan wipes his hand over his face, which only serves to rub the shadow sludge into his skin. "Better?"

She catches Red's eye and they all share a smile—one of giddy relief.

They startle when the statue of Malakhi starts to shift, rock falling from his features as quickly as it had appeared. Casey had almost forgotten that he was still here, immortalized in stone. Evan jumps to his feet, picking up the golden sword once more, and even Red keeps his distance as Malakhi springs from the rubble, landing on all fours.

He shudders in the dust that floats around him, sucking in a sharp, noisy breath. Then he stands, shaking out his hair and brushing the dust from his shoulders. Malakhi casts an appraising look around at the scene of their battle before landing on the three of them, standing shoulder to shoulder, flushed with exhaustion. "I see Michael took care of things."

"Look, buddy," Evan says. "You missed it while you were playing the freeze game over there, but all this badass destruction right here..." He gestures around the church at random with Michael's sword. "Yeah, that was all me."

"You were gifted a divine weapon?" Malakhi says, his tone curious and awed. "By an archangel, nonetheless."

"Yeah, next time a heads-up would be nice. And maybe a bring-your-own-battle-garb note. I definitely would have preferred something lighter." Evan sizes up the sword. "Maybe more compact."

"Speaking of battle gear," Casey says. She tries to give the dagger back to Red, but he waves her hand away.

"You're not finished with that yet."

The four of them grow quiet, their attention settling on Liddy who sits patiently in the pew—waiting in a world she no longer belongs to.

Time to set that right.

"The way is clear," Malakhi says to her as if reading her mind. "Michael will have made sure."

"I know," Casey says, sensing as much in the calm that follows the battle.

"Let me say goodbye?" Evan asks quickly, already backing away from them.

"This is the right thing to do," Red whispers to her as she watches Evan and Liddy hug. He's almost a foot taller than she is, and he pulls her completely out of the pew and off her feet. "She won't ever be truly happy here. Not anymore."

Casey nods once before leaving Red and Malakhi alone by the altar. She already knows it's right. That doesn't mean it's easy.

She doesn't want to say goodbye to Liddy again.

But she has to.

Casey walks over to Liddy as Evan is pulling away. "Safe trip," he tells her.

Casey reaches for Liddy's hand. "Are you ready?"

Liddy glances between her and Evan, longing passing over her features, but she huffs, resigned. "Do I have a choice?" she says with a small smile.

"Not really."

"Then let's go."

TWENTY

WHEN THEY STEP through the door to Limbo and onto warm sand, Casey recognizes the place instantly—the curved stretch of beach, the sun-bleached docks, the awnings that wrap around the boat rental shack. Even the blow-up floaties scattered across the sand are the same as that day.

The harbor. The last place they'd been alive together and the one place that connects them more than anywhere else. Only now it looks less like a scene from a nightmare and more like they're expecting a party.

"It looks bigger without all the people, doesn't it?" Liddy says.

Casey swallows. "It's . . . yeah, it's bigger."

She doesn't know what else to say, so instead, she turns around and seals the rock that marks the doorway into Limbo. The one she'll return through alone.

She turns and follows Liddy down to the edge of the water.

Liddy inhales deeply, taking it all in. "I always loved it here. The parties were fun, but I liked it the most when we snuck away on school nights and watched the sunset. When we would build a little bonfire to keep the chill away."

Casey chuckles. "Evan would show off his astronomy skills. And we would freeze while he attempted to find the Big Dipper."

"Eventually we would nod like he had actually found it so we could sneak back before morning." Liddy eyes her playfully. "I think he was always trying to impress you. And you were oblivious."

"I wasn't oblivious," she says.

"Well, you sure took your sweet time catching on. Though, I guess the fact that you put up with all that was very telling."

Casey breathes in her own lungful of salt and sea breeze. "Do you still?" she asks.

"Still what?"

"Love it here?" She tries but fails to keep the pained expression from her face.

Liddy might have caught it, but it does little to affect her brilliant smile. "I think so. We have a lot of good memories in this place." She toes the sand, drawing swirls before the waves come to wash them away, running up over her feet.

"And a couple bad ones," Casey adds. The wind whips through her hair, brushing over her shoulders, but it's infused with warmth. Any sign of the darkness is far away from here.

"But are those really enough to erase all the good?"

"I don't know, Liddy." Casey hugs herself, tucking her arms against her front. She looks across the water, to the island with the lighthouse where a hum of voices echo. "It's a pretty bad memory."

Liddy picks up a stone and skips it into the water.

"Come on," Casey says. She gestures to the dock, where a single boat rests on the waves. The same one Liddy drove that night. "We have to take a ride."

Despite knowing it's the right way, Casey hesitates on the dock, which makes Liddy giggle.

"I'm already dead," she says, forgoing her life jacket as she starts the boat. "It's not like it can happen again."

"I know. That doesn't mean I have to like it."

"Live a little," Liddy says, echoing that day. She lifts the throttle as Casey settles into a seat, and the boat glides out into the harbor on gentle water.

"Well." Liddy claps her hands together. "Second time's the charm I guess."

"That's not funny."

With a cheeky grin, Liddy lifts her shoulder. She plops down on the padded blue leather seat next to Casey, letting the boat drift slowly, and together they watch the dock shrink. "You've got quite the gig going here, huh?"

"Oh, yeah. Exactly the kind of summer employment I was after."

They break into a chorus of gentle laughter.

Liddy tips her face up to the sun, seemingly enjoying the warmth. "It really makes sense when you think about it, this whole Limbo-walker thing."

Casey snorts. "Oh really? How so?"

"You've always been good at helping people. You were the best kind of friend—good at listening, even for the things I didn't know I was saying." The corner of Liddy's mouth turns up. "And . . . you understand loss."

Casey lets that settle for a moment. She's never considered that before: the fact that she might actually be good at this sort of thing. But maybe Liddy is right, as she so often is. Maybe there's an element of fate to this design. *Still . . .*

"I'd rather not understand loss and get to stay with you."

"I am rather fabulous." Liddy flips her hair over her shoulder and winks at her.

"I'm serious."

"For the record, so was I, but I guess we don't always get what we want. At least, not this time. I have a feeling there's a greater plan at work."

"Oh, gosh, don't feed me that fortune cookie garbage."

Liddy laughs, nudging Casey with her foot. "I'm serious about this, too. A few months ago we were hanging around school, worried about exams and what we were wearing to the harbor party."

"If I recall, it was mainly you worrying about clothing choices."

Liddy rolls her eyes. "My point is . . . well, doesn't this feel bigger than all of that? Like all of a sudden, those things feel very small. Not exactly unimportant, but now there are other things that suddenly mean an awful lot to you."

Casey watches the water as it laps against the boat. They aren't going very fast, and she reaches over the edge to run her hands along the waves. "Maybe."

"Maybe?" Liddy repeats.

"Maybe I don't want it to mean an awful lot." She grimaces. "Maybe I want things back to the way they were."

She's finally found Liddy—and made a mess of it, sure—but she knows she'd gladly suffer it all again if she could only go back to that day. Go back and never let them leave the beach. She knows moving backward is impossible, but the thought is still there.

If only she could have one do-over. One chance to keep the surf from ripping them apart.

"Don't get stuck," Liddy warns, bringing Casey out of her reverie. "The past isn't a good place to dwell in."

"And why not?"

"Because you'll never go anywhere else. You'll wait around in a place destined to always remain the same. If you get tangled up in all the *maybe*s, you'll miss out on all the things happening now. I'm going to be okay, wherever I end up. And so are you."

The boat makes a gentle arc around the harbor, heading toward the little island in the center. "How do you know?"

"Because you crossed an entire plane of dead things to find me. And you fought a bunch of weird shadow-monsters to make sure I didn't become one of them. If you haven't built up some good karma by now—"

They both laugh.

"I am sorry, Liddy. That I lost you in Limbo. That I let you go that night."

"Stop," Liddy says, biting her lip. She sighs heavily. "I have to tell you something."

Casey clutches her knees.

"That night, in the water, you didn't let me go."

"What?"

"You didn't let go, Casey. I . . . I pulled."

The truth in her eyes steals Casey's breath.

Liddy gives a little shrug. "I was caught by the current. It was dragging us both down and you had me so tight. So tight it hurt. That's when I pulled away, so you wouldn't be dragged down with me."

"But . . . I thought—"

"You thought wrong, Casey. Always overthinking things, aren't you?" She huffs teasingly. "I guess I wasn't really ready to let you go in the end. Got myself lost, still looking for you. Dragging you into this awful place over and over again."

"I'm glad you did," Casey says.

"Well, recent events aside, I'm glad you came back for me."

The knot in Casey's chest loosens and for the first time in months, it feels like there's room to breathe.

"So," Liddy says, perking up, "stop thinking you didn't save me. Because you did." She catches her hand. "You found me."

Casey clenches her jaw to stop it from trembling.

"And I may not be around as often now, but if I'm gonna be checking up on you all the time, I want something worth watching. So live your life. Go to college. Meet people. Fall in love . . . with Evan preferably. He's good and kind and funny. And he's got good hair, so he probably won't go bald in his old age."

Casey sniffs but manages to roll her eyes.

The boat bounces over some waves on the water and Liddy

gets up to steer them to the little dock jutting out from the island. A symphony of voices swell around them.

They both look up as the shadow of the old, abandoned lighthouse eclipses them.

"This my stop?" Liddy asks quietly.

"Yeah," Casey sighs.

Liddy throws herself at Casey, wrapping her in a hug that squeezes all the air from her lungs, but Casey doesn't care, just hugs her back, just as tight, for just as long.

"Be safe," Liddy whispers.

"You too. Be careful wherever you end up and don't forget me."

"As if I ever could." Liddy pulls away, turning to grin at the lighthouse that rises up between the rolling sand dunes. She pauses at the edge of the boat, one step away from forever. "And don't forget. If you're not living—"

"You're dying," Casey finishes for her.

"Right," Liddy says. "Make sure you do enough living for us both."

Casey nods, her throat thick. "I will."

Liddy climbs over the side of the boat onto the large, flat rocks that surround the island and Casey watches her dash up the sand dunes barefoot. Liddy stops at the top to wave once before following the path toward the door.

And when she finally pushes inside the lighthouse, the last of her long blond hair disappearing behind the door, there's peace.

TWENTY-ONE

THE CHURCH IS quiet when she returns, and for once Casey manages to land on her feet instead of sprawling all over the floor. Carving the sealing mark into the ground feels like the last goodbye she can handle today.

Gentle pillars of sunlight spill in, gathering in warm pools on the jewel-patterned carpet. The air is still around her, almost too still, like they haven't just waged a war for Liddy's soul.

Afraid to disturb that lingering peace, Casey steps silently as she makes her way down the aisle toward Red, running her hands over the pews.

Great claw marks are carved into the wood, and black smears splash across the walls where they battled the obsii. It settles like mold, or maybe even graffiti, each dent and crack passable as weather damage or rot. Definitely not some supernatural anomaly, nope.

The town would probably condemn this place soon, tearing the whole building down on account of safety, oblivious to the war between good and evil, between angels and demons, that had been waged on this very spot. Oblivious to the fact that this spot still belongs to the light.

A funny feeling fills her chest—sadness or acceptance, she can't tell. Maybe that's the crux of their burden: to forever be fighting a war that most people would never even know about.

Casey wanders up to the front of the church. Red stands next to the crushed altar, still and silent. Deep in thought, perhaps. She hesitates to interrupt, but Red, as always, senses her presence and turns around, offering her a smile that turns up only one corner of his mouth.

Casey glances around, taking stock of the bits of stone she now steps over. The crater left behind where Michael had launched himself onto the roof is perhaps the most difficult of all the damage to explain away.

"We really did a number on this place," she says, passing Red the dagger that had delivered her and Liddy safely to Limbo.

A shift of his hand and the dagger disappears, a feather now held between his thumb and forefinger. She marvels at how something so small and delicate could be imbued with so much power.

"You're not going to keep it?" he asks.

"I think I've spent enough time in Limbo, don't you?"

"Not even to remember me by?"

"Like I'm going to forget you." She blows out a breath that puffs her cheeks.

He laughs. "Fair enough."

"Did Malakhi give you the third degree?"

Red holds back a laugh. "He warned me about my failings. Again. As I deserved. And suggested that the worst is yet to come. I have a lot to answer for when I return."

"He's probably jealous. Missing out on all of this, I mean."

"Doubtful," Red says. "Messengers rarely bear arms against the darkness."

"So is he ... gone then?"

"Yes. He has returned, already called back." Red glances skyward. "Michael has taken his place as protector and Limbo is once again secure, so Malakhi must answer his next call. The work of a Messenger is never done. There is always news to be delivered."

"I guess someone's always messing up somewhere, huh?"

"Malakhi delivers good news as well. It just so happens that he's always around to watch me screw up. I think he enjoys that part of his work a little too much."

Casey kicks at the rubble by her feet. "Is Azrael gone for good?"

"No, just weakened. She'll go into hiding until her powers recover, then she'll attempt to reach into the mortal world again."

"Do you think it was her plan all along to use Liddy? Do you think she knew I would try to pull Liddy out of Limbo?"

"Why do you ask?"

"I saw her," she says, biting the inside of her cheek. "In Limbo, when I was escaping with Liddy. She watched from afar. I wondered if maybe she had something to do with it."

"Perhaps," Red says. "At any rate, her forces have been beaten back. Limbo will be a safer place for now, until she gathers strength again."

"This isn't the end, is it?"

Red shakes his head. "The fight between light and dark, good and evil . . . it is not a fight that is ever truly won."

"Seriously?"

"One cannot exist without the other, but balance must always be maintained. There will always be a threat we must rise up against. This is simply the latest chapter." He offers her a reassuring smile. "But you have won your battle, Casey. So enjoy the life you get to live now."

"I will," she says. "I'll try, anyway. And you go enjoy . . . whatever it is you do when you have your wings back. I mean, I guess you won't be falling out of the sky anymore, right?"

Red grins, ducking his head. "Definitely a highlight," he says. "Did Liddy find her way okay?"

"I think so. Maybe you should have come, just to be sure."

"I don't think I was ever meant to help Liddy cross. That's always been your job. It's why she called to you. I think I was sent here to do more than help you learn to traverse Limbo."

"What else was there to learn?"

He places a gentle hand on her shoulder. "To forgive yourself."

She realizes he's right. She's finally stopped blaming herself for waking up in the hospital without Liddy. She's finally forgiven herself for not being able to control the outcome of that terrible accident.

Red's come to know her so well in such a short time, and

suddenly she's overwhelmed by the thought of losing him. "You're leaving, too, aren't you? That's why this conversation sounds so final."

"For now," he says. "I've been called home and I have to answer. Wouldn't be right to start off on the wrong foot."

"Don't you mean the wrong wing?" Casey jokes, though her heart's not quite in it.

"I left that one wide open for you," Red retorts. "And I didn't mean for this to sound so final. You never know, I've fallen before. I might again."

"Hopefully not," Casey says without really meaning it. "I'll miss you. A lot more than I thought."

"Going to deny that for eternity, aren't you?"

"Maybe."

"Don't look at me like that," he says, nudging her arm, trying to coax a smile out of her. "We'll see each other again. After all, you know the way now. So even if I never fall again in your life-time, it's only a matter of time before you come to us."

Casey rushes forward and hugs him, squeezing until he hugs her back. "Say hi to Liddy for me," she whispers against his chest.

"I will."

She sniffs, blinking quickly as she steps away. "Okay, I'm ready."

"I know you are." Red glances down the aisle behind her, giving Evan one last wave.

"Wait, one more thing," she says.

Red cocks his head as a grin splits her face. "*Redmond?* This whole time?"

He laughs, loud and clear, filling the church with music. "You've been sitting on that one, haven't you?" Dimples dip beneath his cheeks. "You have to understand that I lived and died in a time much different than yours. Redmond was chosen by my mother. It means 'wise protector.' I was the oldest of four boys and she thought I'd carry the title well."

"You do," she promises, knowing she'd never have survived this last week without his help. His firm guidance and protection and friendship. "It's almost as if she knew what you were destined for."

His grin is boyish at her words and his eyes pinch at the corners in memory.

"Maybe one day you'll be able to tell me about it."

"Maybe I will. Now, you better stand back," he says, his words clipped with excitement. He crouches, grimacing as the feathers feed through his skin, no longer wispy, fallen remains, but healthy and whole. His pain lasts only a moment before he beams triumphantly.

The feathers are a pale white, sprouting from his shoulder blades and curving in two gentle arcs that brush the carpeting. Even at a full stand, the tips of his wings touch the ground.

He's beautiful in an inhuman sort of way, and Casey knows no part of her memory will ever do him justice like this—Red, at the height of his strength and power.

A redeemed angel.

"I have to say," she confesses, "this is much more impressive than digging you out of a crater in the middle of the road."

"Saved the best for last, didn't I?" Red looks up, positioning himself beneath the hole left by Michael. "You should probably back up a little more. I've got to get some height here."

"What do you—"

Air swirls around her, starting at her feet, then rising up, making her hair whip wildly across her face. Casey lifts her arms to block some of the wind, but through the slits in her fingers, she watches Red burst from the ground in a show of supernatural athleticism. His wings pull close to his body as he twists upward, before spreading wide, sending a final gust of wind blowing across her. He slips between the slats, blocking the light for a brief moment.

And then he's gone.

The air is still.

Everything around her is quiet.

She turns around.

Evan sits in a pew at the back of the church, waiting for her. His little wave is enough to keep her from bursting into a fit of emotion now that Red's gone. Until now she's never spared a second to consider what his absence would mean. It leaves a dent in her heart. Perhaps not the kind of hole left by Liddy's departure, but nonetheless a space that won't ever be filled.

When she reaches Evan, he greets her by lifting the golden sword in the air. Out of context, he looks kind of ridiculous.

"So, I don't know about you, but that Michael guy never asked for his giant letter opener back, so I think I'm gonna keep it. Maybe hang it on my wall or something."

Casey slumps down beside him and presses a fleeting kiss to his cheek. "I think your mom might ask questions."

"I'll tell her I'm going through an ancient artifacts phase."

"Let's just see if we can get it back to your house without either of us being arrested for having a giant sword in the trunk."

Evan laughs hard, clutching his stomach. "Challenge accepted."

He's surprisingly buoyant for a guy who's just faced off against an army of darkness, but she supposes victory does that to a person. After everything, he deserves to bask in the glory for a little while longer, playing out the boyhood dreams of knighthood.

"You handled this all surprisingly well, you know."

"I still think I might have sunstroke and be hallucinating—"

Casey nudges him with her foot. "As if; we know better than the tourists."

"Yeah, that was my only logical explanation and even it was a reach."

"And the illogical ones?"

"You picked up an angel on the side of the road and I cut the heads off some scaly shadow-monsters." He wrinkles his nose. "And none of this counts as extra credit for our college applications, so that sucks."

Casey bursts out laughing.

Evan lets her laughter fade away before tilting his head and giving her a look that makes her slide down the pew and tuck herself against him. He catches her hand, laying the sword down, and covers it with both of his. "You know you can trust me with this, right? All of it. I can handle it."

"I know."

"How is Liddy, anyway? Did everything go okay?"

"She's somewhere better now. Happier, for sure, and I imagine at peace, especially after everything that she's been through."

"That's good. Before you guys left she told me not to let you mope about without her."

"She told me something similar."

"Covering her bases, I guess. So," Evan starts, "I imagine you'll have some free time now that your angel-buddies have flown away and Liddy's tucked safely in her puff of heavenly cloud."

"I'm not sure that's how it works." Casey grins. "Clouds? Really?"

"Hey, let me have this. If Liddy's not up there trampolining between the clouds, my entire life has been a lie."

Casey leans against his shoulder, gazing skyward. "That does totally sound like her."

She presses against the back of the pew, staring up through the chipped stained-glass windows.

"Now what d'you want to do?" Evan asks, looping his arm over her shoulders.

"Well . . ." Casey says, pretending to give it some thought. "I kinda sorta promised you a date to Shore Fest."

"Is that what that was?" Evan says coolly, playing it off.

"It definitely was." She stands and starts back down the aisle toward the side door.

"Oh, you mean now?" Evan calls, hurrying out of the pew after her. "Like *right* now?"

"Why not?" She leads him out of the church and to her car as he fumbles with Michael's sword. "Summer's almost over. Why waste any more time?"

"I mean, you totally deserve the mother of all dates after this, and I am so there," Evan says as he gets in the car. "But first we have to stop at my place so I can renovate the bathroom Liddy blew up. And maybe shower."

Casey climbs in beside him, rolls down the windows, and cranks the radio. She leans forward, arms against the dashboard, and smiles at the statue that now stands on the peak of the church roof: Michael, with his sword pointed to the sky.

Evan glances at it, a grin spreading across his face. "He looks good up there."

"Yeah," she agrees, inhaling the scent of sea salt and pine as the sun winks over the church.

As she does, a single white feather curls in on the breeze, landing in her lap.

ACKNOWLEDGMENTS

THERE WAS A time when seeing my book on a shelf was a *maybe someday* dream. And sometimes I still can't believe that the team at Swoon Reads and Macmillan made that someday a reality. For that, I will be forever grateful. So, starting this off, a big thank-you to Jean Feiwel and Lauren Scobell for fostering this awesome community where readers and writers can come together to champion one another and great YA reads. I don't think I've ever been part of a more devoted writing community.

A huge thanks goes out to my amazing editor, Emily Settle, who has championed this book from the beginning. You have seen Casey and her journey from the earliest stages and helped transform it into what it is today. Thank you for all your comments that kept me laughing, your savvy editing skills, and the title suggestion. Most of all, thanks for believing in powerful girl friendships and adorable love interests.

To the Swoon Squad for their endless support, laughs, and retweets. Your guidance through this process has been invaluable.

To my family, who gave me the strength and support to pursue writing. I am forever grateful to know you are on my team, cheering me on from the sidelines. To Ashley especially, for enduring hours upon hours of phone calls. You heard the very first version of this story and every subsequent one. Thanks for putting up with all my writing-talk and being the best sister a girl could ask for. And to Mikey, for being my brainstorming partner, weapons expert, and my connection to the world of teenagers.

To all the friends who have believed in this book and shouted about it from rooftops, you guys are the absolute best of the best. To Gillian, penpal extraordinaire, for being the most excited about this! Thanks for believing in it and for shouting about it in all of our letters. To Hanako for all the corner meetups, author photos, and coffee-shop sessions. Thanks for keeping me sane through it all! And to Kelly, who spent hours of nursing lectures by my side. Thanks for sharing your notes, goals, and strength with me. You were one of the first people who believed I could do it; I definitely wouldn't be here without your encouragement.

And finally, to the readers. This book would be nothing without you guys.

With all the love and thanks,

Liz

Check out more books
chosen for publication
by readers like you.

DID YOU KNOW...

readers like you
helped to get this
book published?

Join our book-obsessed community and help us
discover awesome new writing talent.

1

Write it.

Share your original YA manuscript.

2

Read it.

Discover bright new bookish talent.

3

Share it.

Discuss, rate, and share your faves.

4

Love it.

Help us publish the books you love.

Share your own manuscript or dive between the pages
at **swoonreads.com** or by downloading the **Swoon Reads app.**